SHIOKARI PASS

SHIOKARI PASS

AYAKO MIURA

Translated by
BILL AND SHEILA FEARNEHOUGH

Fleming H. Revell Company
Old Tappan, New Jersey

Library of Congress Cataloging in Publication Data

Miura, Ayako, 1922–
  Shiokari Pass.

  Translation of Shiokaritòge.
  I. Title.
PZ4.M6935S53 [PL856.I8]   895.6′3′5   76-6868
ISBN 0-8007-0796-6

'. . . unless a grain of wheat falls into the earth and dies, it remains alone; but if it dies, it bears much fruit.'

John 12.24 RSV

Contents

Foreword

AYAKO MIURA is a well-known author in Japan. Her books and serial stories captivate an increasingly appreciative public. No wonder. There is in her writing a sensitivity, a texture which to the Western reader is characteristically Japanese – that quality we recognize in their art, their flower arrangements, their dress, in fact, their scenery, for they are the product of their beautiful environment.

Ayako Miura's heart is in her pen. Reading of Nobuo Nagano and Fujiko you wonder how much is autobiographical. Much is, she admits. But the story is a revealing picture of Japan and the Japanese, valuable to those of us who cannot go there and see for ourselves. Now that it has been filmed, we shall be able all the better to see what we can already imagine so vividly from her writing.

Shiokari Pass, however, is Ayako Miura's own creation, based on the true story of a certain Masao Nagano who, more than sixty years after his untimely death, is still revered in Asahikawa, Hokkaido, where he was a high-ranking railway employee. He was an unpretentious person, choosing to live simply and to dress even shabbily, in order to support his mother and to give his earnings to people in need and to deserving causes. Awarded a princely Imperial Grant for his services to the State during the Russo-Japanese war, he gave it all to found a Young Railwaymen's Christian Association.

Nagano was, in fact, a highly respected public servant, renowned for his integrity and popular with his men. He worked late in his office day after day to lighten the load on his staff, and this did not go unnoticed. Problem

9

personnel tended to be sent to him because of his ability to handle them and win their confidence. Intractably lazy and troublesome characters began to work well. When he was stationed in Sapporo he took pity on a compulsive alcoholic who had been given up as hopeless by his own family and sacked by the railway board. Aggressive when drunk, and beyond caring for himself, this man was unwelcome in anybody's house, yet Masao Nagano shared his home with him, enduring many indignities, until after many months he was fully cured and rehabilitated. Then Nagano prevailed upon the board to re-employ him.

Masao Nagano was a brave man too. A missionary in Hokkaido came under suspicion of being a wartime spy and suffered a great deal of hostility. Disregarding the repercussions upon himself, Nagano wrote to the newspapers and tackled the security authorities on the foreigner's behalf. A quiet and peaceful person by nature, he was nevertheless a powerful and even a fiery public speaker. And he was a fearless Christian in a currently intolerant Buddhist-Shinto society. In his ceaseless efforts to share his faith with his employees throughout the wide area under his control, he travelled widely visiting Railwaymen's Christian Association groups. It was on the way back from an outlying station, one freezing day, that the incident occurred which inspired the writing of Ayako Miura's book. As a result of what happened, many of his employees and townspeople became Christians. The information about Masao Nagano came from the records of the Asahikawa church and an old man who remembered him and had become a Christian through his influence.

Mrs Miura points out that 'Nobuo Nagano' is not the same person as Masao Nagano, although she has used the same common surname. Nobuo and Fujiko are her own. This book in the original Japanese has done much to remove prejudice and to introduce Christianity to her own people.

The publishers are indebted to Mrs Miura and her

translators, Bill and Sheila Fearnehough, and to World
Wide Films for the opportunity to make this book avail-
able to all who enjoy the film and read the story, and for
their generous co-operation.

1 The Looking Glass

'THERE'S no getting away from it, you're just like your mother – not only in looks but in character as well.'

Nobuo Nagano's grandmother, Tose, was in a bad mood whenever she spoke like this. Nobuo knew that when she said he resembled his mother who, according to Tose, had died two hours after his birth, she was far from flattering him. He had been born in Hongo, a high-class suburb of Tokyo, in 1876, the tenth year of the reign of the Emperor Meiji.

'I wonder what sort of person my mother was?' he thought, as he knelt in front of the mirror, peering closely at his face – the round, well-shaped eyes, the straight nose, the firm well-defined mouth . . . 'My mother must have been quite good-looking.'

Ten-year-old Nobuo didn't notice his own mischievous expression as he raised his thick eyebrows. 'Why is it such a terrible thing to take after my mother, I wonder?' But he could not hope to understand what was going on in his grandmother's mind.

He pulled down the corners of his mouth and wondered if his mother's face had ever looked like that. Shutting one eye, he raised his eyebrows and glared fiercely into the glass. The effect was rather frightening. His lips pursed into a wry smile. 'Perhaps my mother used to smile like that,' he thought. He tried another smile. This time he opened his mouth wide and studied his teeth, gleaming white, and with not a single bad one among them. He gazed intently at his uvula hanging down the back of his mouth. 'I wonder what that's for?' he thought. As he

13

imagined his mother with a funny thing like that too,
Nobuo was struck by a strange new emotion. As a rule he
did not think much about his mother, but now he was
suddenly overcome with the tenderest of feelings towards
her. As he put his finger in his mouth and tried to touch
his uvula, he felt himself on the verge of tears. Before he
could stop them, they were spilling down his cheeks.

'Nobuo, why are you crying?' his grandmother Tose's
voice came from behind him. She was a heavily built
woman and when she got angry she was far more frightening than Masayuki, his father. Nevertheless, generally
speaking she made a fuss of Nobuo and he didn't dislike
her. Only he hated the way she became bad-tempered
whenever the subject of his mother came up.

'I put my fingers in my throat, and made myself cry.'
His reply was true enough, but she sensed that in fact
there was another reason for his tears.

'Stop playing the fool. Only the common people let
themselves be seen crying. We are of *samurai*[1] stock, so
you mustn't do such a thing.' As she said this she knelt
down close to Nobuo.[2] He had never seen his grandmother
kneeling except in a meticulously correct way with her
knees together and her feet tucked neatly underneath her,
so he supposed that all women sat as she did. However,
only a few days before he had found that this was not so.

There was a fellow called Roku, a hawker, who was
always in and out of Nobuo's home. Roku sold combs,
tasselled ties for men's kimonos,[3] cuff protectors, thread,
scissors and so on, in a set of lacquered boxes which he
carried slung over his shoulders in an enormous cloth
patterned with arabesques.

'Your ladyship' was what Roku called Tose. Roku had

---

[1] The *samurai* were traditional warriors, vassals of a feudal
lord.
[2] It was customary to kneel on the floor in all Japanese homes.
[3] A kimono is a loose robe with wide sleeves, fastening with a
sash.

moved to Tokyo from Niigata only two or three years before. Tose had been born there too, so she and Roku always had plenty to talk about. He would hang about the kitchen for hours discussing such things as Western fashions, as though he were a complete authority on the subject.

Nobuo always looked forward to Roku's visits. Not that he liked Roku particularly, but he sometimes brought his boy Torao with him. (Torao means 'Tiger'.) Torao was only eight, two years younger than Nobuo, but because there were so few boys of his own age and class in Hongo, Nobuo enjoyed Torao's visits immensely.

On one occasion Roku took him to play at Torao's home. Stepping across the rickety plank over the gutter and entering the doorway, Nobuo was astonished to find that it opened straight into the living room. But all the more astonishing was the sight of a woman of about thirty, with her breasts exposed, kneeling at a table with her legs stretched out to one side.

'I didn't know that anyone behaved so badly,' thought Nobuo in disgust.

Now, as his grandmother knelt beside him, with her feet tucked properly out of sight, Nobuo found himself thinking again of Torao's mother.

'On no account must you let people see you crying,' repeated Tose.

'No,' he nodded; then, putting his hand on Tose's knee, he said, 'Grandmother, open your mouth and let me look inside.'

'What do you mean, open my mouth?'

'Do you know you've got a thing like this at the back of your throat?' Nobuo opened his mouth wide and showed her what he meant.

'It's a disgrace for a woman to open her mouth like that.'

There was nothing further to be said on the subject.

Masayuki Nagano, Nobuo's father, was an amiable man.

One could hardly imagine that he had been raised in such a strait-laced environment. He held a position in the Bank of Japan and had the refined bearing of someone brought up in court circles. Leaving his son in the care of the unrelenting Tose, he hardly ever interfered with his upbringing. Thus Nobuo thought of his father neither as a particularly awesome person, nor as a particularly kindly one. But then something happened; he was severely reprimanded by his father for the first time in his life.

It was a warm Sunday towards the end of March, and Roku and Torao were visiting the Nagano household. Nobuo and Torao were lying on their stomachs, sunbathing on the outhouse roof, about eight feet from the ground. Torao's name, 'Tiger', did not suit him. He was a lovable child with large round eyes, like two black beans.

From the house next door the sound of an organ wafted faintly, the tune of the children's song, 'Butterfly, butterfly'. Nobuo strained his ears to listen. Somehow he fancied that the person playing the organ was Miss Yoko Nemoto, his teacher whom he adored. She had a fair complexion and soft almond eyes. Nobuo thought that, with her russet coat fastened at the throat and her sprightly step, she was altogether a different kind of being from other women in the neighbourhood.

Every year Miss Nemoto taught the beginners' class. In his first year at school Nobuo had been in her care. She often used to stroke her pupils' heads. Even the most mischievous little monkeys became self-consciously well-behaved when she did that. She had a lovely scent too, quite unlike the oil his grandmother used to keep her hair in place. When he held her hand, he felt as if it was somehow melting into his own.

Once, in his first year at school, he had suddenly become anxious, fearing that Miss Nemoto had left to get married.

'Maybe when I go to school tomorrow she won't be there any more,' he thought. 'I know what I'll do. I'll marry her, then she'll never go away.'

This struck him as a marvellous idea. The next day when the bell rang for break and the children all streamed out to the playground, Nobuo hung around the classroom.

'What's the matter, Nagano, aren't you going out to play?'

Nobuo nodded without saying anything. The teacher went over to him, surprised.

'Is your tummy sore or something?'

There was that lovely smell again.

Nobuo shook his head.

'Well, you ought to go out and get some exercise.'

'Teacher . . .' Nobuo faltered.

'What is it?' Miss Nemoto peered into his face.

'When I . . . when I get big I'm going to marry you. So don't go away, will you?' Nobuo spoke boldly now, without stopping for breath. Having got the words out at last he did not feel the least bit embarrassed.

'Marry me!' Miss Nemoto was overcome with surprise. At last she spoke. 'I understand.'

Then, with a solemn face she gave a brief tug to straighten the shoulder of his kimono.

'Promise you'll wait for me and not go away?'

As if to reassure him she grasped Nobuo's hand and gave him a knowing smile. Nobuo was overjoyed.

'Now she'll not go away,' thought Nobuo, and ran noisily down the corridor to play outside, his face wreathed in smiles.

Now he was in the third grade and had forgotten that he had ever said such a thing to Miss Nemoto, though he liked her as much as ever. Whenever he met her in the corridor he bowed to her even more politely than he would to the headmaster. Meeting her in the corridor really made his day for him.

'Your teacher is lovely, isn't she, Torao!' Torao was in the first grade.

'Uh-huh. But my mother chases me with a ruler.' Torao

was more afraid of her than of his teacher. 'Does your
grandmother ever hit you with a ruler, Nobuo?'

'No, she never hits me.'

The organ music stopped.

'Hey, Nobuo. Do you know what is at the other end of
the sky?'

Seen from the roof the sky looked different.

'Dunno,' said Nobuo flatly.

'What, do you mean to say you're in the third grade
and you don't know what's at the other end of the sky?'
Torao's round eyes sparkled with merriment.

'How should I know? I've never been there.' Nobuo
raised his eyebrows crossly.

'I know, and I haven't never been,' Tarao lapsed into
his back-street way of speaking.

'O.K. What is there then?'

'There's the sun.'

'What, don't be stupid Torao. The sun is in the sky.'

'That's not true. It's at the other end of the sky.' Torao
stuck to his guns.

'The place where the stars and the sun are is *in* the sky,'
Nobuo repeated firmly.

'That's a lie. When you draw a picture the sky is on top
of the roof, isn't it. This is the sky.' Torao waved his hands
about in the air above the roof, where he was crawling.

'That's the sky, over there.' Nobuo wasn't giving in.

'That's a lie. That's the other side of the sky.'

The two of them forgot where they were. They stood
up on the roof looking daggers at each other.

'I tell you it's a lie.'

Torao gave Nobuo a push. Nobuo lost his balance and
slid down the roof. Both of them screamed as Nobuo
tumbled over the edge and fell to the ground.

But he was lucky. That day Tose had taken off the
mattress covers and laid out all the old wadding to air in
the sun. Nobuo landed on top of the wadding. He expected
to fall on his head but only his ankle was hurt.

'I'm sorry, Nobuo!' Torao came scrambling down from the roof almost in tears.

'You didn't make me fall off the roof. Understand?' Nobuo grimaced with pain as he rubbed his ankle.

'What?' Torao could not see what Nobuo meant.

'Don't you tell anybody that you pushed me off the roof.' Nobuo spoke rapidly in a commanding tone. Torao gazed humbly at him.

Roku had heard the yells and was the first to arrive on the scene. 'What happened, sonny?' His face was ashen as he glared at Torao standing helplessly.

'It's nothing, I was playing on the outhouse roof and fell off.'

'The roof!' Roku exclaimed. Then turning suddenly on Torao he gave him a savage swipe.

'Torao, it was you, wasn't it?'

Torao began to wail.

'What has happened?' It was Grandmother Tose.

'I'm terribly sorry, madam. This Torao here . . .' Roku began to explain, but before he could say any more Nobuo broke in.

'That's wrong! I fell off the roof myself.'

At Nobuo's words, Roku pulled a face, 'Sonny!'

'What's more important is whether he's hurt himself or not.' Tose was unruffled.

She examined the colour of Nobuo's face and said to Roku, 'There doesn't seem to be very much wrong, but take him to the doctor just to make sure.'

Almost falling over himself with haste, Roku heaved Nobuo on to his back and carried him to the nearest doctor. He had sprained his ankle but there were no bones broken. All the same, when he got back and lay on his bed for a while, Nobuo felt tired out.

'It's a good thing it wasn't more serious,' said Tose as Masayuki came into the room. She stood up and stepped aside for him, and then went off to the kitchen. Seeing

Masayuki, Roku bowed his forehead down to the floor in confusion.

'I'm terribly sorry. Torao has done a terrible thing.'

Torao hung his head dejectedly.

'I keep telling you, it wasn't Torao,' Nobuo said irritably.

'What happened exactly?' said Masayuki mildly.

'As a matter of fact this urchin of mine pushed . . .'

'I see. He pushed Nobuo off the roof?'

'Yes.' The perspiration was streaming down Roku's nose.

'No, he didn't. I fell off by myself,' shouted Nobuo excitedly.

Masayuki smiled knowingly and nodded two or three times. He was overjoyed to think that Nobuo had it in him to try to protect a boy younger than himself.

'Oh, so you fell off by yourself, did you?'

'Of course, do you think I'd let a slum kid push me off the roof?'

When he heard this, Masayuki's expression immediately changed.

'Nobuo! Will you repeat what you have just said?'

Roku flashed a glance at Masayuki's face, and Nobuo blinked at the cold tone in his father's voice. He spoke stubbornly and unfalteringly.

'I said, "Do you think I'd let a slum . . .?"'

Before he could finish the sentence, Masayuki's hand landed a heavy blow on his cheek. Nobuo could not understand what he had done to make his father so angry.

His grandmother had always reminded him, 'We Naganos belong to the aristocracy. We are different from the common people.' So how could he admit, even if forced, that a commoner's boy had pushed him off the roof?

Nobuo scowled at his father. 'Why didn't he praise me instead?' he wondered.

'Torao, I want you to let me see your hand,' Masayuki smiled understandingly at Torao. Sheepishly he held out his dirty little hand.

'Nobuo, how many fingers does Torao have?'

'Five.' His cheek still stung.

'Right, then how many fingers does Nobuo have? Six, I suppose.' Nobuo bit his lip.

'Nobuo, what is the difference between a boy from the aristocracy and an ordinary boy? See if you can tell me.'

'He's right, what is the difference anyway?' Nobuo thought. Looking at it this way he could see no difference. But Grandmother always said they were different. 'Yet there's a difference somewhere,' he could not help but think.

'There is no difference. Both have two eyes, both have two ears. Right, Nobuo? Professor Yukichi Fukuzawa said, "Heaven makes neither one man above, nor one man below another". Do you understand, Nobuo?'

Nobuo had heard of Professor Fukuzawa many times.

'Right, people are all the same. The common people are not necessarily baser than the aristocracy. On the contrary, if for some reason either should commit a murder or do something like that, the aristocrat would be more responsible and guilty.'

He spoke harshly. Nobuo had never thought that his father could be so severe. But most of all the words, 'the aristocrat would be the more responsible,' struck him. Nobuo had grown up to believe that aristocrats were undeniably superior beings, as obvious a fact as that snow was white, fire was hot. 'Can it really be true, that all people are the same?' Biting his lip fiercely, Nobuo buried his head in the pillow.

'Nobuo, apologise to Torao and Roku,' commanded Masayuki gravely.

Nobuo could not yet bring himself to make an apology.

'Doesn't Nobuo know how to apologise? Don't you know what an awful thing you have said?'

Without waiting any longer, Masayuki placed his hands together on the *tatami* matting[1] with grave formality and

---

[1] Japanese homes are mostly floored with mats of woven straw.

bowed his head deeply before the trembling Roku and Torao. He remained in this position for what seemed an eternity. The sight of his father in this attitude was unforgettably engraved on Nobuo's mind.

2 The Chrysanthemum Dolls

IT WAS a fine Sunday in the late autumn, and wisps of white cloud, gleaming in the sun, floated across the clear sky. On the verandah, Masayuki gently puffed at his pipe as he sat gazing at the clouds. His glance fell on Nobuo, who sat beside him with his brow furrowed as if he were thinking about something.

'A penny for your thoughts,' said Masayuki with a smile.

Ever since Nobuo had fallen off the roof in the spring, Masayuki had felt that it was not right to leave the boy entirely in Tose's hands. This was not because of the fall, but because hearing his son say 'Do you think I'd let a slum kid push me off?' had greatly upset him. Now he tried to keep an eye on Nobuo as inconspicuously as possible. Having up till now left everything entirely to Tose, he could not take over from her abruptly, for Tose had an excitable nature and had to have her own way.

'I'm thinking about Miss Yoko Nemoto,' said Nobuo.

'Miss Nemoto?'

'Uh, she was my teacher when I was in the first grade.'

'What about her?'

Judging from Nobuo's rather dejected look, Masayuki thought she must have reprimanded him for something.

'She's going to give up teaching and get married,' said Nobuo in a disgruntled voice.

'Isn't that good news?' asked his father.

Tose, who was sitting nearby, sewing, broke in suddenly, 'Not a bit of it!' she said.

Only yesterday Nobuo had heard that Miss Nemoto had

left, and he felt lonely at the thought. School would be unbearable without her. He would miss her friendly smile and the exchange of bows in the corridor. He didn't know why, but his heart felt empty. Putting down her sewing, Tose rebuked him.

'What's the matter with you, Nobuo? What does it matter to you if the teacher of another class leaves?'

Nobuo scowled at Tose. How could she understand how terrible he felt?

'A boy ought to have other things to think about, than a lady teacher.' Tose bit off a thread with her blackened teeth.

Somehow Tose's words gave Nobuo an uncomfortable feeling. He wondered why it should be wrong for a boy to think about a lady teacher.

'Mother, isn't it a good thing for a child to be fond of his teacher?' reasoned Masayuki. The motherless Nobuo, adoring a lady teacher – the pathos of it stung Masayuki's heart. He knew that Grandmother Tose could never take the place of Nobuo's own mother.

'It's shameful for a boy to have a crush on a lady teacher, Masayuki! No matter how much I keep on about it you seem to have no intention of getting married again. But if you don't, Nobuo will keep on having these crushes. You mark my words.'

Nobuo could sense the spite in her voice. He looked up at his father.

'We'll have to see about that,' said Masayuki with a bitter smile. He knocked the ash out of his pipe. 'How about going with your father to see the chrysanthemum display, Nobuo?' he said, getting up.

'Do you really mean it, Father?' They hardly ever went out together. Forgetting about Miss Nemoto and everything else, he hurried after Masayuki. He was so happy, he had trouble getting the thong of his sandal between his toes.

'What's all this about? It's unseemly for the child of a

samurai to be in such a hurry.' At the sound of Tose's voice Nobuo glanced at his father for reassurance.

'Goodbye, Grandmother. See you later,' he shouted, completely forgetting that failure to observe the proper procedure of putting the hands together on the floor and bowing politely was sure to make Tose livid.

'The chrysanthemum display is at Dango Hill, isn't it, Father?'

Walking along with his father, it seemed to Nobuo that even the familiar houses looked somehow different. Even the persimmon trees behind the fences looked fresh and green.

'Father, what are the chrysanthemum dolls like?'

But Masayuki was lost in thought and did not reply. Nobuo was satisfied just to be walking beside him.

'Are they figures decorated with chrysanthemums, or are they real people dressed in chrysanthemums?'

'Hm . . .' Masayuki suddenly stopped. 'Nobuo,' he began.

'What?'

Masayuki hesitated. 'It doesn't matter . . . Would you like me to buy you a fizzy drink after we've seen the display?'

Even at the end of autumn, the Tokyo sun was warm enough to make people perspire when they walked far.

'A fizzy drink! I'd love that.' Grandmother said that fizzy drinks gave people a stomach ache, but Nobuo had longed, just once, to push the stopper down with his finger, and drink the fizzy liquid as it foamed out. Seeing the happiness on Nobuo's face, Masayuki was happy as well.

'Let's have a cake too,' he said.

Nobuo was in heaven, he was going to see the chrysanthemum display with his father, and have a fizzy drink. This was more than anything he could have hoped for.

Just then a pretty little girl of about five or six came running out of a side street. No sooner had Nobuo thought, 'What a sweet little girl,' than she caught sight of

Masayuki and her face lit up. 'Daddy!' she cried and, throwing her arms out wide, embraced Masayuki tightly. Masayuki said nothing but took hold of her hand. Nobuo could hardly believe his ears.

'That's my father, not yours,' said Nobuo. It infuriated him to see this girl hugging his father in a way that he himself had never done.

'Oh, no, he's my father, not yours,' she countered with a hostile glare at Nobuo.

'That's a lie! Father, that's a lie, isn't it?'

'No, it's not, Daddy, it's not!'

Masayuki looked from one to the other in perplexity. Then he laid his hand gently on the little girl's shoulder.

'Machiko, did you come all this way by yourself? You'd better go home. Don't get lost.'

His tone was kindly, and Nobuo pouted enviously.

'Yes, I will . . . That boy, Daddy . . . Who is he?'

The little girl was still clinging to Masayuki.

'Hmm . . . He's Machiko's . . . Look out!' He snatched her out of the path of a rickshaw carrying a middle-aged man with a straggly moustache.

'Now, off you go, your mother will be wondering where you are.' Masayuki patted her on the shoulder and she started off reluctantly, but after two or three steps she turned round, looked daggers at Nobuo, then turned away and walked straight home.

'What a strange girl!' muttered Nobuo gazing after her disappearing figure. Masayuki's face was clouded as they set off again.

'What a silly creature, saying my father was hers!' But as they walked away, Nobuo forgot the incident in the excitement of going to see the chrysanthemum dolls.

The nearer they got to the marquee where the show was being held, the denser the crowds became.

'Father, the chrysanthemum dolls must be very interesting. Just look at all the people!'

Nobuo gazed in wonder at all the people coming and going up and down the hill.

'Father, even though there are so many people, they all have different faces.'

'If all faces were the same you wouldn't be able to tell who was who, would you?'

There were women in kimonos with the fashionable black neck bands, women in western dress carrying little parasols, men in gay splash-patterned kimonos, old folk wearing shawls, and among them there was a cripple.

'Father?'

'What is it?'

'Is that cripple as important as a *samurai*?'

Nobuo half-remembered his father's quotation, 'Heaven makes neither one man above, nor one man below another.' Although he had forgotten the words, he had not forgotten that his father had said that all men are equal.

'Yes, he is. Even if people have no arms and legs, or if they cannot see or hear, they are all equally human beings.'

'Hm . . .' Nobuo could not understand how they could be the same if they had no arms or legs.

'So long as they have hearts, they are all the same—human beings.'

'Yes, but there are people whose hearts are good and people whose hearts are bad. I think the people with good hearts are better than people with bad hearts.'

'That's rather a difficult question. Nobody can really say whether another person's heart is good or bad. When all's said and done there's no mistaking the fact that heaven makes nobody above or below anybody else.'

Nobuo was still only half convinced.

By the time they reached the top of Dango Hill he was bursting with excitement. Jostled and shoved by people on all sides, at last they managed to get into the enclosure. There were so many people inside that there was scarcely room to move. To Nobuo the discomfort of being in such a throng was a pleasure in itself.

Seeing the famed chrysanthemum figures for the first time in his life, Nobuo thought they were absolutely wonderful. The ones which appealed to him most were Kintaro, riding on a bear, his battle axe slung over his shoulder; and Momotaro, with his retainers, the dog, monkey and pheasant, fighting with the giants.

'What a pity we didn't bring Grandmother,' said Nobuo when they came out of the marquee.

'Mmm,' said Masayuki without enthusiasm.

'But if Grandmother had come, I couldn't have had a fizzy drink,' thought Nobuo. He had not forgotten about that.

They went into a tea booth, with its screens and doors of woven reeds, and Nobuo had his first fizzy drink.

'Ah, that feels better! It tastes good, doesn't it, Father?'

'Mm,' Masayuki sat with his arms folded, looking at Nobuo thoughtfully. 'Nobuo,' he began. 'About that little girl we met . . .'

'Little girl?' For a moment he did not understand what his father was talking about. Then he remembered. 'Oh, you mean that cheeky little thing?' he said irritably.

'I don't want your grandmother to . . .' Masayuki did not finish. He hesitated to ask the child to swear secrecy.

Just at that moment a boy near by was showered in foam as his fizzy drink frothed up and Nobuo's attention was distracted.

Coming out of the booth they walked through the crowds once more. Nobuo was completely happy.

The evening meal was waiting for them when they got home. Tose expected they would be hungry after all their walking.

'Grandmother, have you ever seen the chrysanthemum dolls?' asked Nobuo, picking up his chopsticks.

'Do not talk during meals,' came Tose's rebuke. The meal was early, but Nobuo was hungry and in no time he had finished. He ate so fast that he couldn't even remember what he had eaten.

'Do you know what we saw, Grandmother? We saw Kintaro and Momotaro.'

'Did you, that's good. Were they pretty?'

'Mm, they were beautiful. Even the dog and the monkey and the pheasant had kimonos made of chrysanthemums. I used to imagine that the chrysanthemum dolls would have faces made out of chrysanthemums too, but I was wrong.'

'They can't make faces out of chrysanthemums! What else did you see then?' Tose was in the mood for conversation.

'The forty-seven *ronin*[1] were there too, weren't they, Father? There was one beating a war drum in the snow. That was Oishi Kuranosuke, I suppose.'

'Oh, you saw the forty-seven *ronin*, did you? Grandmother would have liked to see them too.'

'Yes, but there were so many people, you'd have been crushed to death. It would have been too much for you, Mother,' said Masayuki.

Nobuo did not look up. 'That's right,' he ventured. 'Grandmother gets tired quickly if she goes out. Maybe her shoulders would get stiff too.' Tose went to have her shoulders massaged every two or three days.

'My goodness. Was it as crowded as that? You must have met some people you know, then?' She began to rub her shoulder vigorously as if to relieve the stiffness.

'They were all people we didn't know, there were children and grown-ups and women in Western dress and all sorts of people.'

Tose raised her eyebrows. 'Women in Western dress?'

'There was a sort of foreign-looking woman, wasn't there, Father?'

[1] The *ronin* were faithful *samurai* who avenged the death of their lord.

'Well, well! And what other kinds of people were there?'

'Let me think. I'm not sure. There were so many people, you see. Oh, yes, of course . . . we met a strange little girl too, but . . .' Neither Nobuo nor Tose noticed the colour drain away from Masayuki's face.

'A strange girl? Was she a beggar, then?'

'No. Not that.'

'How was she strange, then?'

'Well, she came up to Father and held on to him and called him "Daddy".'

'Eh? What was that? Nobuo! What did you say?' Tose's attitude was threatening. At the bottom of his heart Nobuo realized that he had said something he ought never to have said. He looked enquiringly at his father. Masayuki was kneeling in a formal position, his eyes downcast.

'Nobuo, where did you meet this girl?' Tose's mood had changed completely.

'Where was it? . . . I've forgotten exactly . . .' Nobuo became flustered. He did not know what had enraged Tose, but he felt very uneasy.

"Well, then, what sort of child was she? How old?'

'She was younger than . . .'

'I apologise.' Masayuki pressed his palms firmly on to the floor.

'I thought there was something strange going on . . .! Behind your mother's back . . .! You . . . you . . .' Tose's nostrils flared.

'I understand how you feel, but you'll do yourself harm if you get so angry.' Masayuki spoke in a calm voice. This only made Tose furious and her body trembled uncontrollably.

'You . . . You . . .!' Her shoulders shook. 'I don't want to hear anything about such a . . . And a child too!' she gasped.

'Yes, but . . .'

Tose would not listen. She shook her head vigorously.

'You . . . You unfilial son!' she shouted, and at that instant she swayed and fell with a thud on the *tatami* matting.

Tose died that night of apoplexy.

3   Mother

AFTER the funeral, when Masayuki and Nobuo, together with Tsune, the newly-hired maid, began to settle down to their life together, Nobuo suddenly began to miss Tose. When he came back from school, the house seemed empty without her and he was unbearably lonely. When he played in the garden, and his kimono got dirty, he would glance up at the verandah, thinking, 'Grandmother will be cross,' and then he would burst into tears.

He remembered many of the bedtime stories she had told him, how she had put him to bed each night, and how even if he had coughed just once in the middle of the night, she would get up and cover his shoulders to keep him warm. As time went on, only Tose's good points remained in his memory. But as he puzzled over why she had got into such a rage and died, it seemed to him that he was to blame because he had mentioned the little girl, and his heart grew intolerably heavy.

Another year had begun, and the remembrance service held for Tose on the forty-ninth day after her death had passed. One evening Masayuki was inexplicably late in coming home. While Nobuo was passing the time playing cards with Tsune the maid, they heard the sound of a rickshaw stopping outside the front door. Running out to see, Nobuo saw his father stepping down. Behind him another rickshaw was just coming through the gate. 'Who can that be?' he wondered.

His father never brought friends home late at night. When the shafts were lowered and the front cover taken off, a refined-looking woman, her head covered with a hood, got down smoothly from the rickshaw. Seen by moonlight, her lustrous eyes were strikingly beautiful. As the rickshaw moved off the woman put her arm around Nobuo's shoulders.

'Nobuo!' she said.

Nobuo did not know what to do. He felt shy and at the same time annoyed. Struggling to free himself, he pushed against the woman's chest and made her stagger back. Without thinking, he showed the intense dislike he suddenly felt for both of them.

Masayuki laid his hand on Nobuo's shoulder. 'Well, let's go inside anyway,' and led the way in.

The woman turned to Masayuki and bowed ceremonially, her hands touching the *tatami* floor.

'Thank you for allowing me to come.'

When they were in the living room, Masayuki beckoned to Nobuo and sat down beside him.

'Nobuo, this is your mother!' His voice was low and trembled somewhat.

'You said my mother had died.' Nobuo looked at the woman whose face was rather ghostly now, by the light of the lamp.

'That's right.'

The woman was about to say something too, but before she could begin Nobuo replied angrily, 'I don't need a new mother.'

Masayuki and the woman exchanged glances.

'Nobuo, I am your real mother.' As she said this the woman drew close to Nobuo and took his hand.

'That's a lie, my mother is dead,' Nobuo cried, shaking his hand free.

'She isn't dead. Look carefully at her face. Doesn't she look just like you?'

Nobuo stared at the woman once again. Now that he came to think of it, there was a resemblance. And she was far more beautiful than the mother he had visualised when he looked at his own face in the mirror long ago.

'Perhaps she does look like me,' he thought, 'but . . .'

'Nobuo!' The woman stretched out her hand and took Nobuo's. Her dark eyes were full of tears.

'. . . . You were alive all the time?' Nobuo had such a strange feeling. It was unbelievable that his mother, whom he had so long believed to be dead, should be holding his hand and talking to him.

'Of course I was alive, always thinking about you . . .' She was about to embrace Nobuo, but he drew back.

'If you were alive, then why didn't you live in this house?'

'Your grandmother, you see, didn't care for Kiku. That's your mother's name. She didn't care for your mother so she sent her away,' explained Masayuki.

'Then, why didn't you tell me about it, Father? Why didn't you let me meet my mother? Why didn't you tell me . . .? Why didn't you tell me my mother was alive?' Before he could stop himself Nobuo's voice faltered and he was crying.

Masayuki sighed deeply. 'You've had a hard time of it.'

'Grown-ups are liars! You tell me not to tell lies . . . but you and Grandmother, you've told me a great big lie.' Nobuo burst into sobs.

In spite of the fact that with Tose he had not been utterly lonely, he had longed for his mother. Looking up to the sky, he had thought, 'My mother, she's turned into that star up there.' As he had watched other children with their mothers, he had thought enviously, 'If only I had a mother too.' Why hadn't she come then, when he needed her? Now the thought tormented him.

'Nobuo, why are you crying? Oughtn't you to be glad that you've met your mother?' said Masayuki rather severely.

'Don't be hard on him, dear. Poor boy, he doesn't know whether to be happy or angry. What else can you expect? The one who has suffered most all this time has been Nobuo.'

Hearing her say this, Nobuo was unable to control himself and began to wail loudly. He was overjoyed to think that this person who was protecting him so gently was his own mother. But it was not only joy that he felt. He was conscious of a sense of miracle that his mother, whom he thought had been dead for so long, should be alive and here beside him.

'It's all right. It's all right now. You needn't cry any more.' Masayuki patted Nobuo on the shoulder.

'So now, do you understand? That little girl you met one day, she's your sister. She's called Machiko.'

Forgetting all about crying, Nobuo looked at his father. 'Is that cheeky little thing my sister?' he thought as he recalled watching her scamper up the hill.

Nobuo had often wanted a younger brother or sister. That was why he had been so fond of Torao. 'I bet she's a tomboy, that girl.' At the very thought of this Nobuo's joy knew no bounds. As he imagined himself taking her to play with him in all sorts of places, his heart leaped.

'But why did Grandmother send Mother away?' he asked. The word 'Mother' slipped out naturally. Nobuo didn't feel at all embarrassed.

'I am the one to blame. It wasn't your grandmother's fault.'

His mother gently wiped away Nobuo's tears. 'How strange,' thought Nobuo, 'Grandmother put her out of the house, but she doesn't say anything bad about her.' As Nobuo was puzzling about this, Masayuki spoke.

'Perhaps you'll understand all the difficult things when you get older but, you see, your mother . . .' He broke off and glanced at Kiku's face. Kiku smiled gently and nodded.

'Your mother is a Christian. Your grandmother disliked "Yaso", as she called him, more than anything else.[1] "I

---

[1] 'Yaso' is a derogatory word for Jesus.

won't have a Yaso daughter-in-law in this house!" she said, and told your mother to get out.'

'Did you say "Yaso"?' Nobuo suddenly looked scared.

He did not know who Yaso was, but he remembered Tose having said that he sucked human blood and ate people's flesh. He could not forget how she had told him that Yaso was an evil creature who did all sorts of frightening things such as deceiving people by magical powers in order to destroy Japan.

So, to Nobuo, Yaso was an unforgivably wicked person. When he heard that his mother was a follower of this Yaso, a creepy sensation came over him. In spite of her gentle exterior, he was convinced that she must be guilty of something terrible. He began to see why it was that his grandmother had told him that she was dead. Taking a stealthy glance at his mother, he felt that it was better to have no mother at all, than to have a follower of Yaso for a mother.

'Yaso, Yaso, born in a stable! Ya! Ya! Ya!' Nobuo knew how the children sometimes made fun of the open-air preacher, with this song, a parody of the respectful greeting to a royal prince.

'Ah, now you've come,' the preacher would begin. 'To-day I want to tell you an interesting story.' No sooner had he said these words than the children would start to run away, shouting.

'Anyway,' he thought, 'Yaso can't be any good.'

'I don't like Yaso.' Nobuo pulled a face.

Masayuki and Kiku said nothing but looked tenderly at him.

'I'll be coming to live with you from tomorrow,' said Kiku as she went away that night.

Masayuki remembered the time when Kiku had had to go. She was the daughter of a friend of Tose's, and as Tose favoured her as a bride for Masayuki, he had married her. But after they had been married for a year or so, Tose

had found out that Kiku was a Christian. Tose had called
Masayuki and had given him a piece of her mind.

'Masayuki, didn't you discover before now that Kiku
was a follower of Yaso?'

He had known. Masayuki had grown up to have liberal
and progressive views, in spite of, or maybe because of
Tose's strict upbringing. He could not understand how
Tose should look upon Christian believers with such hatred.
He could not understand her 'Yaso, Yaso' attitude.

'Yes, I knew about it.'

'What, do you mean to tell me that you knew all along,
yet thought nothing of becoming man and wife?'

Such a thing, in Tose's mind, was far beyond the limit
of decency and reason.

'There's nothing specially wrong with being a Christian.'

Masayuki had inherited his father's mild personality,
and he had never answered her back or provoked her
before. He knew too well that when she got worked up
there was nothing he could do to control her. But today
things were different. Masayuki had to stand up for Kiku.

'Do you know what you are saying? How can you stand
there and talk to your mother like that? This proves that
you have been bewitched by Yaso, without a shadow of
doubt!' Tose was in a rage.

'Bewitched? There's no such thing in this civilized
scientific age. I can't bring myself to think that Christians
are particularly bad.'

'Japan has always had Shinto and Buddhism. We don't
have to worship a foreign god! Don't you understand
what a shameful thing it is for a Japanese to do?'

'Mother, this Buddhism which you believe in came from
a foreign country during the Nara Period, you know.'

Masayuki had had about enough.

'Masayuki! Are you still answering me back? Whatever
happens I will not have a Yaso daughter-in-law in the
Nagano family. Kiku! I want you to leave this house.'

'That's inhuman!' shouted Masayuki, glaring at his mother. 'Kiku hasn't done anything wrong.'

'In that case, put your mother out of the house, then. Masayuki, you throw your mother out and spend the rest of your life with this Yaso, Kiku.'

Tose was getting worked up. Kiku, who until then had sat with her head bowed, suddenly looked up.

'Mother, I beg you to forgive me.'

In those days there were many instances when even sons were disinherited and disowned by their parents because they became Christians. It could not be said that only Tose was bigoted. If someone explained, 'My daughter-in-law was a "Yaso", so we disowned her,' people would only say, 'Well, there really was no alternative, was there?'

'Kiku, when you asked to be forgiven, did you mean that you were prepared to give up Yaso?' Tose looked doubtfully at Kiku. Tose had heard that people who had become Christians would never turn back, even if they were burned at the stake.

As she expected, Kiku bowed her head and did not reply.

'Kiku. Please leave this house!' There was a note of finality in her words. Kiku turned pale.

Masayuki broke the silence. 'Mother, you don't have to go so far. We have Nobuo to think about too. I will speak to Kiku myself.' He put his hands on the mats and bowed.

'You! What makes you think you can make her listen? If you think you can influence her now, why didn't you speak to her before? Kiku! Is Yaso so important to you? Even if it means leaving this house, aren't you prepared to give up Yaso?'

Kiku's stubborn attitude made Tose angrier than ever. She had hoped that just the mention of being disowned would make Kiku change her mind and ask to be forgiven, if only for the child's sake. But she just sat there without speaking, her head bowed, and Tose thought she was impudent beyond words.

'Whoever denies me before men, I also will deny before my Father who is in heaven.' Kiku pondered these words of Christ, repeating them over and over again. 'I believe. Even if it means being killed, I cannot deny Christ,' she thought.

Kiku thought of Christ, persecuted and nailed to the cross. 'Father, forgive them, for they know not what they do.'

Now, Kiku felt sorry for Tose. A mother-in-law who had to order her out of the house, leaving her beloved husband and child, deserved pity more than hate.

For Kiku the thought of being separated from her husband and Nobuo was worse than death. For Nobuo's sake she had many times thought of recanting and saying, 'I won't believe in Christ any more'. But even if she were to recant, it would be only words, it was impossible for her really to deny Christ. That would be to deny God and deceive her mother-in-law at the same time.

'But I shall have to leave Nobuo, and what kind of life will he have without his mother?' She did not know what to do. 'As things stand now, there's nothing I can do but commit him into God's keeping.' As she thought of Nobuo, just learning to walk, she began to weep.

'Just as I thought, Yaso are all fools. You don't care even if you are parted from your own children, your own husband.' It did not occur to Tose that in driving Kiku away she herself was the fool. Under no circumstances could Tose forgive anyone of the upper classes who believed such a perverse religion.

'Mother, I don't want to divorce Kiku,' began Masayuki.

'Silence! Kiku is the daughter-in-law of the Nagano family. As long as I live I will not have a Yaso daughter-in-law here. If you must have Kiku here, then I will leave. Whatever will our ancestors think if I allow a Yaso daughter-in-law to remain here.'

Kiku and Masayuki went out into the room where

Nobuo was peacefully sleeping, and peeped at his face, neither of them saying a word.

At last Kiku placed her hands together and bowed to Masayuki. 'I am very sorry.'

'Not at all, Mother's a bigot. Please forgive her.'

'No, no. It has all been my fault. Perhaps it would have been better if I had just said I don't believe any more, but . . .'

'Kiku, you stick to your convictions.' Masayuki had often heard these words from his father. To his way of thinking, the tiny minority of Christians in Japan were worthy of respect. They possessed a sure faith which the present world seemed unable to receive. Although he himself did not possess it, he wanted to let his beloved wife follow it completely.

'Once Mother has had her say, there is no turning back for her,' he went on. 'But still, it's hardly likely that she will go so far as to make out divorce papers. So long as you leave this house, Kiku, you are free to do as you please. For instance, suppose you were to start living with some man . . .'

'A man? I resent that.'

'No, wait until I've finished. Supposing that the man were to be me, how would that be? What do you think, Kiku?'

'Well, of all the things . . .' Kiku was weeping.

Tose would never allow her to take Nobuo with her, but Masayuki thought it possible that in due time Tose might let her come back again, when she saw how miserable her grandchild was.

As soon as a house had been found for her, midway between Masayuki's place of business, the Bank of Japan, and the family home in Hongo, Kiku left the Nagano home. Her own family gave their unofficial consent.

Even supposing that he had gone against his mother and kept Kiku in the house, Masayuki knew the Nagano home would no longer be a place where Kiku could live in peace.

When Kiku left the house, Tose had her last insult ready. 'I will not allow that woman to be called Nobuo's mother. Anyone who prefers this Christ to her own child has no right to be called a mother.'

So Tose brought up Nobuo to believe that his mother was dead.

'What does it matter if it's hard for the moment? Time will show that this was the right thing to do. Since God is a living God, He will surely care for Nobuo too.' With this thought, Kiku had been able to bear the separation for nearly nine long years, until Tose died.

4 Under the Cherry Tree

THE following day, Kiku and Machiko became members of the Nagano household. Nobuo came home from school to find Machiko playing near the gate, drawing something on the ground.

'Hey! This is my house!' proclaimed Machiko, leaping to her feet when she saw Nobuo. She stretched out her arms so that he could not pass.

'So this is my own sister,' thought Nobuo as he studied the little figure, her mouth closed in a defiant line, her arms spread out to block the way.

Machiko's skin was fair, her eyes were large and she had a rounded face. Her tightly closed lips gave her a cheeky yet lovable expression. Nobuo was thrilled to think that this was his sister, but tried to slip past her without saying anything. She would not give way.

'You mustn't come in here! This is my house,' she shouted.

'Huh! She's just a cheeky little kid,' thought Nobuo. He longed to say, 'I'm your big brother, silly!' But he looked down at her without saying a word. The top of her bobbed head barely reached his shoulder.

'Ah, Nobuo, you're back.' It was Kiku appearing at the door. Nobuo blushed and bowed deeply.

'Machiko! What do you think you are doing, getting in your big brother's way?' Kiku scolded her gently.

'What? Is he my brother?' Machiko burst into happy giggles. 'My brother! Machiko didn't know you were her brother. I say, Machiko has a big grown-up doll. Let's play with it, shall we?' she said, pulling him by the hand.

Her chubby little hand, strangely tickly, gave him a pleasant sensation. All the same, he felt inexplicably shy and all he could say was 'Huh', as he darted into the house.

'Nobuo, it's lunch time.' Kiku came up to him and put her hand on his shoulder. She smelt lovely, like Miss Nemoto, and Nobuo was delighted. When he sat down at the table, Machiko put her hand on his knee and whispered in his ear, 'Let's play with bean bags afterwards, shall we?' Thinking 'What a little flirt she is,' Nobuo picked up his chopsticks, said the customary words of thanks and began to eat.

Machiko looked thunderstruck. 'Hey, brother! Don't you pray before meals?'

'No, I don't pray or anything.'

'That's funny. Fancy not praying to God, Mummy.'

'No, but that's all right for your brother, just now.' After she said this Kiku began to pray quietly. Nobuo stared at his mother and Machiko, with their hands together, their heads bowed.

When the prayer was over Machiko said a loud 'Amen'. All of a sudden Nobuo felt he was a lonely outsider. When Grandmother was alive, they had managed all right without praying, he thought unhappily.

Nobuo had no idea what the yellow crescent-shaped object on his plate might be, for neither Grandmother nor Tsune the maid had ever produced anything like it. Watching Machiko eating it with evident relish, Nobuo concentrated on eating the accompanying pickles.

'Ah, Nobuo. Don't you like omelette?' asked Kiku. Nobuo ate without replying. 'I don't know whether I like it or not. I've never eaten the stuff before,' he said to himself, picking impatiently at the omelette with his chopsticks. But when he tasted his first mouthful he got a surprise. He could not believe that such delicious food existed in the whole world. 'So this is omelette, is it?' he reflected. He had heard of it before, but had no idea what

it would be like. 'To think that Machiko had been enjoying omelette all this time!' he thought enviously. Grandmother Tose had eaten neither meat nor eggs, so they used
to have nothing but fish and boiled vegetables with their
rice.

When their father Masayuki came home in the evening,
Machiko greeted him with outstretched arms and entwined
herself around him, just as she had done the time they had
met in the street. Forgetting his customary words of greeting, Nobuo looked on numbly. Then, catching sight of him
standing there, Masayuki laid his hand on Nobuo's
shoulder.

'What's up?' he asked. 'You don't look very well.'

'Nothing,' replied Nobuo sulkily, avoiding his father's
eye.

At supper, Nobuo was just about to pick up his chopsticks when he stopped short, noticing that Masayuki, Kiku
and Machiko were all sitting with their heads bowed. Kiku
began to pray.

'What's it matter?' he thought, 'I'm not a Yaso,' and
picked up his chopsticks. When Kiku had finished giving
thanks, Masayuki and Machiko both said 'Amen'. Hearing
Masayuki's 'Amen', Nobuo felt betrayed. What did this
mean? His father had never even prayed before, let alone
say 'Amen'. Nobuo felt a twinge of dislike for him.

It was a cold Sunday morning. Nobuo awoke to find
Masayuki and Machiko already up and about. After breakfast Machiko put on her best crêpe shawl and said, 'Come
on, big brother, let's hurry and go to church.'

'What's church?'

'Oh, church is where you pray and hear stories and sing
songs.'

'Hmm,' Nobuo gazed in silence at Machiko as she
hopped excitedly around the room on one foot.

'Would you like to come with us too, Nobuo?' Kiku was

dressed in a black kimono which Nobuo thought looked very well on her.

'No, I'm not going.' Secretly Nobuo would very much have liked to go with Kiku, but the idea of church did not appeal to him at all. In fact it gave him that slightly creepy feeling.

After they had gone, Masayuki began reading a book, warming one hand over the charcoal heater. Nobuo wondered about going to fly his kite, but that somehow did not feel right. So he resigned himself to sitting vacantly beside Masayuki.

'What is it?' Masayuki turned from his book to Nobuo.

'Does Mother always go to church on Sunday?'

'Yes, I suppose she does.'

'Why, when she could easily have given up Yaso?' He sounded exasperated.

'Nobuo,' Masayuki laid his book down on the *tatami*. His tone was serious.

'Yes,' replied Nobuo, also in a serious tone.

'Human beings are creatures who must have something to cling to, even if it costs them their very lives. Do you understand?'

It was difficult for Nobuo to grasp.

'When you are big, I'll explain it to you sometime. But you see, your grandmother hated Christianity, so she turned your mother out of the house. You were just a baby.'

'Why didn't she take me with her?'

Bright rays of sunshine were warming the room.

'Because your grandmother would not allow it.' Masayuki doubted whether Nobuo could understand such an explanation.

'Well, then, she could have given up Yaso and stayed here instead.' Nobuo could not hide his anger.

'But you see, Nobuo, there are some things that people can give up, and other things that it is impossible for them to give up.'

'Do you mean Yaso was more important to her than I was?' Nobuo could not be expected to understand Kiku's attitude.

'Perhaps so. I don't think your mother would give up her faith even if it meant being crucified.'

'Crucified? What does that mean?'

'Let me see . . . Just a minute. Masayuki got up and went into the bedroom, returning with a small card in his hand.

'Nobuo, that is what being crucified means,' he said, handing the card to the boy.

Nobuo took a glance at the card and gasped. It was painted in the most beautiful colours he had ever seen, but what he saw depicted on the card was brutal. The emaciated form of Christ was hanging on a cross, his hands and feet pierced by nails, and blood flowing from his side. For a moment Nobuo held his breath while he stared at the picture.

'So that is what being crucified means! What if Mother were to be stripped naked and crucified in such a cruel way?' The thought made Nobuo shudder. It horrified him to think that his mother was not prepared to give up Yaso, even if it meant such a fate.

'This person did something very bad, I suppose, Father?' Nobuo spoke hoarsely. He was only ten and the effect of the crucifixion scene was overwhelming.

'Not at all. This Jesus Christ didn't do anything bad at all. He healed people who were ill, and told people about God and loved people.'

'Was he crucified even though he did good things? That's terrible! That's not fair.'

Among the senior boys at school there were several who would take small boys like Nobuo by surprise as they walked along the corridors, suddenly giving them a punch or hitting them in the back.

If anyone so much as gave Nobuo a jab, he would flare up and fight back, even against a boy twice his size. Now

he got more worked up than ever at the thought of a
person who had not done anything wrong being crucified
like this. It was so unjust; he was almost in tears.

'It's terrible, isn't it?' said Masayuki, taking the card
and studying it himself.

'I bet this Jesus was angry, wasn't he?'

'No, he wasn't angry at all. On the contrary, he prayed
for those who nailed him to the cross. "God," he said,
"please forgive them. I am sorry for them because they
do not know what they are doing." '

'Hm. What a strange person this Yaso must have been!'
Nobuo still could not help thinking that Jesus did not get
angry because he really had done something wrong. But
the only lasting impression he received was the horror of
the crucifixion.

It was the first hot day in spring and the cherry trees
in the school garden were in full bloom. Nobuo was now
in the fourth form and was the class monitor. He had
stayed behind to help the teacher, and coming out of
school he saw about ten of his classmates in a huddle
under the biggest of the cherry trees, holding a whispered
discussion. When Nobuo walked up to them they exchanged glances and made room for him.

'Has something happened?'

'Haven't you heard? They say there was some woman's
hair in the seniors' cloakroom. And blood all over the
place.' It was Matsui, the spokesman of the class, who
answered with a serious face.

'I didn't know.'

'That's not all. They say that at night you can hear a
woman crying. What if it's a ghost?' added the vice-
monitor, Otake, in a frightened voice.

'Tell me exactly who it was who heard the crying.'
Nobuo remained calm.

'I don't know. I don't know who heard it, but there
doesn't seem to be any doubt about it. What do you all

think?' Matsui looked round the group. They all nodded together solemnly. Nobuo laughed at the absurdity of it all.

'That's all just made up, it's not true.'

'How do you know it's not true, Nagano? Everybody says there really are ghosts.' At Matsui's words the other boys nodded.

Nobuo was at a loss, but he spoke up again. 'But my father says there are no such things as ghosts.'

'Oh yeah, well my father says that ghosts really do exist.'

One by one they all had their say. There was no denying the fact that even among grown-ups there were many who believed in the existence of spirits and ghosts.

'There's no such thing.' Nobuo was resolute.

'Is that so? All right, just to prove whether there is a ghost or not, how about meeting under this tree at eight o'clock tonight?' said Matsui. Everyone fell silent and some of them furtively began to drift away.

'What about it? Are we going to meet then?' Matsui pressed for a reply. The wind blew and scattered cherry blossom on the nodding heads of the boys.

'We'll all come, so there will be nothing to be afraid of.'

'Right. We'll meet here in the dark,' Otake agreed.

'I expect Nagano will come too,' said Matsui with an 'I'm not going to let you escape' look on his face.

'Of course, I'll come. We meet here at eight o'clock tonight, you said?' Nobuo spoke as calmly as would be expected of a class monitor, and nodded his assent.

'That's settled then. Everybody comes, no matter what happens. O.K.?' Matsui looked around the group. Each one agreed.

At supper time it began to rain a little, and around seven o'clock the wind was blowing and it was raining hard.

'Mother, is it all right if I go to the school this evening?' asked Nobuo. He had been looking out of the window for some time.

'Gracious me! What business do you have at school this time of night?' Kiku stared at Nobuo in amazement.

'It's not important really, but . . . let me think . . .'.

'If it's not important, what's the point in going?'

Nobuo looked outside again. The rain was making a furious noise.

'Is there something the matter?' Masayuki looked up from his newspaper.

'They say you can hear a woman's voice crying in the seniors' cloakroom at night. We're all meeting tonight to see if there's a ghost or not.'

'What, a ghost? There aren't such things!' Kiku laughed awkwardly. 'There's no need to go out in all this rain for the sake of such a thing as that. What do you say, dear?'

Masayuki sat with his arms folded and looked rather stern.

'It's all right. I won't go. It's obvious that nobody will turn up if it's raining like this,' Nobuo said.

'Is that so? You don't have to go, but tell me, Nobuo, exactly what kind of agreement was made?'

'We were to meet at eight o'clock tonight under the cherry tree.'

'So you promised to do that, did you? Are you telling me you are thinking of breaking your promise?' Masayuki looked Nobuo steadily in the face.

'I promised to go, but it doesn't matter if I don't go. What does it matter if there's a ghost or not?' Nobuo had convinced himself that it was not worth his going out in such heavy rain.

'Off you go, Nobuo,' said Masayuki quietly.

'All right . . . but look at the rain!'

'Oh, did you agree that you needn't go if it was raining?' Masayuki's tone was severe.

'No, we didn't decide what would happen if it rained,' replied Nobuo, looking up fearfully at his father.

'If you break a promise you make yourself lower than

a dog or a cat. Dogs and cats don't make promises so they never break them. That makes them wiser than humans, it seems to me.'

Nobuo pouted. 'All this fuss about a silly promise?' he thought. As though he could read his thoughts, Masayuki continued. 'Nobuo, if it's a promise you needn't keep, you oughtn't to have made it in the first place.'

'Yes,' said Nobuo, but his knees were knocking.

'I'll go with you,' said Kiku, getting up. Machiko had been asleep since before supper.

'Kiku. Nobuo is ten. There's nothing to stop him going by himself.'

The school was half a mile away. Kiku looked at Masayuki uncertainly.

Nobuo had not gone very far before he was drenched to the skin. He had to feel his way along the pitch-dark road. Although it was not as windy as he had imagined, being soaking wet did not help him to make progress. He'd walked this way every day for four years, but it seemed completely different from the road in daylight. Staggering along, Nobuo told himself over and over again what a fool he had been to make such a stupid promise.

'I don't suppose there'll be anyone there after I've made all this effort,' he muttered, feeling very aggrieved about his father's treatment.

Sloshing through muddy puddles, he pressed on, half walking, half stumbling. Although this was called spring rain, his drenched body began to feel very cold indeed. So promises were made to be kept, even though it meant going to such lengths to keep them! The journey of a mere half-mile felt more like two or three, and Nobuo wanted to cry.

When he arrived at the school at last, as luck would have it the rain had turned to a light drizzle. The pitch-black school grounds were silent. He listened but could hear no voices and it felt as if at any minute the woman's ghostly sobs would break out.

Nobuo stealthily approached the rendezvous under the cherry tree.

'Who's that?' a voice hissed. Nobuo nearly jumped out of his skin. 'It's me, Nagano.'

'Oh, it's you is it, Nobuo?' It was the voice of Osamu Yoshikawa, who sat in front of Nobuo in class. Yoshikawa was not an outstanding boy, but he was sensible and got on well at school.

'Ah! Yoshikawa. You surprised me, coming in spite of this downpour.' Having been quite sure no one would be there, Nobuo was flabbergasted.

'But it was a promise.' Yoshikawa's almost blasé reply had a very grown-up flavour.

'It was a promise.' Nobuo repeated Yoshikawa's words silently. Then a strange thing happened to him. The clear-cut weight of the word 'promise' came home to him. 'To think that I had no choice but to come, just because my father told me to—not because of my promise.' As he considered this, Nobuo suddenly felt ashamed of himself.

He thought that Yoshikawa must be the finest person in the world. He felt disgusted with himself for being proud of being class monitor.

'It looks as if nobody else is coming,' he said.

'Mm.'

'In spite of the fact that they promised to come, no matter what!' Nobuo had already half persuaded himself that he had come because he had promised.

'Yes, but it's raining, remember!' said Yoshikawa. There was no trace of self-righteousness in his tone.

Nobuo thought that Yoshikawa must be a remarkable person.

5 Hide and Seek

'WHAT are you going to be when you grow up, Nagano?'
Osamu Yoshikawa asked Nobuo.

On that rainy night they had been the only ones to
meet in the school grounds and, ever since, their classmates had thought of them together as 'Nagano and
Yoshikawa'. Naturally they had grown close to each other.

It was June, and Nobuo was paying his first visit to
Yoshikawa's home. Osamu was the only one in. Unlike
Nobuo's, the house had neither gates nor garden. It was
not even a third the size of the Nagano mansion, just a
three-roomed semi-detached house. Yoshikawa's father
worked in the Post Office. Reed blinds screened the little
projecting bay window, full of pot plants, and people
passed by just outside. This was a novelty for Nobuo.

'When I grow up?' Nobuo studied Yoshikawa's calm
round face. It amazed him that he had grown so fond of
Yoshikawa. No, he was amazed that he had not become
Yoshikawa's friend long before now. But from Nobuo's
standpoint, Yoshikawa's existence began that stormy night
when he had suddenly become aware of his presence under
the cherry tree. Until then he had never particularly
noticed him. He was a slow-speaking, inconspicuous sort
of person.

Nobuo parried his question. 'What are you going to be,
Yoshikawa?' he asked.

Nobuo himself had never really thought about it. He
had no boyish dream of becoming a soldier. For a start he
could not imagine what it could be like to be a grown-up,
and he even felt that the day would never come.

'Me? I think I'll be a Buddhist priest.'

'What, a priest?' shouted Nobuo in amazement.

'Mm, a *bonze*.'

'What makes you want to be a *bonze*? You'd have to have your hair all shaved off and chant long Buddhist *sutras*, you know.' While his grandmother Tose had been alive, a priest had come once a month to read the *sutras* in their home. Now, it struck Nobuo that the priest was not much in evidence these days.

'Yes, I know. What do you want to be, Nagano?'

'Well, come to think of it, perhaps it might be good to be a school-teacher.' Nobuo found himself thinking about the fair-complexioned Miss Yoko Nemoto again. It would be much better to be a teacher in a school than a priest in a temple. Both pupils and parents stopped and bowed respectfully to a school-teacher.

'A school-teacher? There's something to be said for that, too.' Yoshikawa hung his head meditatively, then continued, 'But a school-teacher can't teach grown-ups, can he? I want to be a priest so that I can teach both children and grown-ups.'

'Mm.' Yoshikawa sounded terribly grown up.

'Have you ever thought you would like to die, Nagano?'

'What did you say?' Nobuo had never in his life thought that he would like to die. Somehow Yoshikawa's conversation was getting rather frightening. He could not make out what he was driving at. At the time of Tose's death the thought of a person who had been so alive until that moment, just dying before one could realize what was happening, had filled him with panic. It was a strange feeling. Tose's death did not seem to have been brought about by illness; it was as if something had suddenly deprived her of life. The memory of it was enough to fill Nobuo with dread. He could not conceive of death except as a sudden unexpected visitor. He could not imagine dying as a process in which the victim lay ill for a long time, gradually getting thinner, suffering pain and then

finally breathing his last. Occasionally, he would glance
behind him in the dark, haunted by the fear that Death
would suddenly reach out for him.

'Of course, I don't want to die. I want to keep on living
for ever. Do you want to die, Yoshikawa?'

'Mm, sometimes I think I'd like to die,' Yoshikawa said
with a sad little laugh. Nobuo had been gazing fixedly at
him, but now he turned his glance to a potted rhododen-
dron. Four or five children were running past the window.

'But aren't you afraid of dying?'

'Yes, maybe I am afraid, but when my father gets drunk
he kicks my mother.'

'Eh? Does he kick her? That's terrible.' Nobuo thought
of his own father, who rarely even raised his voice.

'That's right. He is so cruel to my mother that sometimes I want to die and leave a letter saying, "Please don't
hurt my mother any more".'

'Mm.' Nobuo looked solemnly at Yoshikawa. What an
amazing person! He felt envious of Yoshikawa for caring
so much for his mother.

'But when I think of Fujiko, I feel it would be cruel to
her.'

'Fujiko? Is that your sister?'

'Yes. She's slightly lame. She's been lame ever since she
was born. When she goes outside people make fun of her
and call out, "Look at the cripple!" It would be very hard
for her if I wasn't around to stand up for her.'

'Mm.' Nobuo felt that he was very much a child compared with Yoshikawa. Up till now, whenever he had gone
to play at a friend's house, they had played tag or wrestled
with one another. But Yoshikawa preferred talking to
playing. It seemed that he had lots of things he wanted
to talk about.

'Well, well. How nice to see you. You are always so kind
to Osamu.' The front door opened and Yoshikawa's mother

came into the house. Although she had never met Nobuo before, she greeted him affectionately.

'Could this be the person who gets kicked and punched so cruelly?' Yoshikawa could not have been speaking the truth when he said he wanted to die because his mother was so badly treated.

Then Yoshikawa's sister, Fujiko, bounced into the room behind her mother, and her merry eyes caught sight of Nobuo. 'Hello!'

'Good afternoon,' replied Nobuo, bowing deeply. Fujiko was suddenly overcome with shyness and tried to hide behind her mother. But no sooner had Yoshikawa said, 'What's up, Fujiko? Are you shy or something?' than she got over it.

'I'm not shy any more,' she said as she walked unselfconsciously across the room. She had some bean bags in her hand. As she walked she kept hitching one shoulder up because of her lame leg. But although her shoulder moved up and down with each step, it looked as if she was doing it just for fun.

Fujiko could play 'bean bags' the best of the three, and Yoshikawa was fairly good too, perhaps because he was used to playing with her. Nobuo was the worst, but whenever he did a little better Fujiko's round eyes sparkled with delight.

When Nobuo got home and saw his own sister, all he could think of was Fujiko. He found it hard to believe that when Fujiko went outside she was made fun of by other children. Surely what Yoshikawa had said about his mother being punched and kicked, and about Fujiko being teased, was all made up. His mother was much too kind a person and Fujiko was such a lovable girl.

'I'm going to offer some rice on the family altar, Mother.' Nobuo held out his hand to his mother.

'What, to the ancestors?' Kiku looked questioningly at Nobuo. He had never suggested such a thing before.

'Yes.' Nobuo had begun to feel very uneasy that Kiku did not pay her respects at the family altar. Just recently, when he had been visiting the Yoshikawa's home, the priest had called and chanted some *sutras*. Seeing the sacred flame alight on the altar, and the smoke of burning incense filling the room, Nobuo became aware of the fact that the doors of the family shrine at home had not been opened for a long time.

He remembered how, when his grandmother had been alive, there had been offerings of rice and lighted candles on the altar every day. Suddenly Nobuo began to think of his mother as a cold-hearted woman. Many times he had heard Tose say something like this, 'Masayuki, when I die, you'll at least burn an incense stick for me, won't you?' So Nobuo felt that his grandmother was being cruelly neglected. Could it be that his mother never even gave a thought to her?

It was not that he disliked his mother. He could see that she was kind beyond words. But at mealtimes he felt strangely hostile towards her. It was always the same – Kiku praying aloud, his father and Machiko with their hands in an attitude of prayer. Each time Nobuo felt an outsider and would stare at them until they finished. Often this feeling of loneliness would persist throughout the meal. Prayer took a lot of getting used to. There were some times when he felt like joining in, but for some reason or other he could not make himself take part. 'It wouldn't make any difference even if they didn't pray,' he said to himself. Whenever the time drew near for the next meal Nobuo would start reasoning like this and feel utterly miserable. Today he felt specially bad.

'Mummy, tomorrow shall we go to Mino's house and see the fish?' Machiko had been pestering her mother about this for some time.

'Mino's father is ill, remember. We'd just be in the way,' Kiku replied time and time again, but this had not persuaded Machiko.

'Mummy, let's go to Mino's house tomorrow to see the fish,' she persisted.

Listening to all this made Nobuo miserably lonely, too. He had no idea who Mino was, or what kind of a house she lived in, and he could not imagine what kind of fish they had, but his mother and Machiko knew. So he felt jealous. And envious because he was not his mother's only child. Then he thought, 'It doesn't matter. I'll take care of Grandmother, anyway,' and this was a comfort to him.

'Mother, can I have some rice to offer on the family altar,' he repeated, his face revealing nothing of what he was thinking. Looking perplexed, Kiku was about to say something when Machiko broke in.

'I say, Mummy, isn't Daddy going to be home for supper?' she asked, giving her mother's knee a shake, and ignoring the fact that Nobuo was waiting for Kiku to reply.

'I'm afraid he'll be coming home late this evening,' she answered, giving Machiko a smile.

'Do you think he'll bring me a present?'

'We'll have to wait and see.'

It struck Nobuo that perhaps he was not really his mother's child after all. What his grandmother had told him was probably true, that his real mother had died two hours after he was born. Glancing at Kiku and Machiko, Nobuo got up and went into the kitchen. But he had no idea where the special dishes and trays for the altar were kept.

Grandmother Tose had strictly forbidden him to set foot in the kitchen without permission. 'Menfolk should not meddle in the affairs of the kitchen,' she had said, laying down the law with a classical proverb. ' "Each to their own rôle, man to man's, woman to woman's. To be loyal to his ruler and bring honour to his family is enough for a man." '

Now, having broken that taboo and entered the kitchen, Nobuo remembered Tose's stern words. It would surely grieve Tose if she knew where he was now, he thought, but on the other hand he could not just walk out of the kitchen empty-handed.

'Nobuo!' Kiku was calling. Nobuo did not reply but stood gazing at the floor. All of a sudden tears began to fall.

'Nobuo, we're going to start supper now.' Kiku came into the kitchen.

Machiko followed her, and seeing Nobuo she exclaimed, 'Why, you're crying!'

'Tell me, what's really the matter?' Kiku asked, bending over him. Nobuo turned his head away and, slipping out of her grasp, escaped into the room where the family altar was. As he knelt in front of it an inexplicable sense of desolation came over him, like a cold mist in his heart. He could not make out whether he was sorry for his grand-mother or just for himself, but the tears kept spilling down his cheeks all the same.

'Nobuo. You're angry because I don't offer rice on the family altar, aren't you?' Kiku came and laid her hand on his shoulder.

'B . . . b . . . but, I . . .I feel so sorry for Grandmother!' Nobuo sobbed.

He pulled away from his mother's hand.

'You've forgotten about Grandmother, so you don't offer her any rice.'

Kiku sat down, rigidly straight in front of Nobuo. He had never seen her look so stern before. But he went on.

'And another thing, why don't you burn incense to her?'

'But . . . that's because . . .'

Nobuo made no effort to listen to what Kiku was begin-ning to say, but kept on talking.

'From the beginning you didn't like Grandmother.'

'What a thing . . .'

'Grandmother drove you out of the house, so therefore you don't burn incense to her.'

'Well . . . I . . .'

Aghast, Kiku took Nobuo's hand, but he dragged it away and shouted, 'It's cruel to Grandmother now she's dead!'

'Nobuo . . . I . . .'

Kiku tried to calm Nobuo, but having once unburdened himself, he found it impossible to calm down.

'When I grow up I'm going to be a priest in a Buddhist temple.'

Nobuo amazed himself with the words he had just said without thinking. Up to that moment he had had no thought of becoming a priest. But now he had said it, he felt that it had become the expression of his true feelings. 'That's it,' he told himself in all seriousness. 'I'd really like to become a priest and offer up *sutras* in thanks for Grandmother.'

'You want to be a priest?' Kiku's glance shifted from Nobuo to the Buddhist altar.

'Yes. Yoshikawa wants to be a priest. Me too.' Nobuo could imagine himself and Yoshikawa, with round tonsured heads, chanting *sutras* together.

Kiku nodded without saying anything. Her head was bowed as she quietly tried to keep back her tears.

That night, when Nobuo went to bed he could not sleep, for he remembered his mother's tears. He realized that many of the things he had said had wounded her. 'I wish I had never said them,' he thought.

'Hey, Nobuo, there's a friend to see you.' Machiko ran up to Nobuo as he was watching an ants' nest in the garden.

'Who is it?'

When Nobuo stood up Machiko whispered to him. 'He's come with the lame girl.'

Nobuo scowled at Machiko. 'Don't you let me hear you calling her "lame girl" any more,' he shouted over his shoulder as he ran towards the gate.

Osamu Yoshikawa was standing, holding Fujiko's hand. 'It's hot, isn't it?'

Nobuo returned the greeting. 'Yes, isn't it?' Fujiko gave a shy laugh.

Soon Machiko and Fujiko had spread a straw mat in the shade of a tree and began to play house together just like old friends.

'You be the father and Fujiko can be the mother,' Machiko told Nobuo.

'That's right, then Osamu and Machiko can be the couple next door.'

Nobuo and Yoshikawa looked at each other and laughed.

'Welcome home, dear,' Machiko bowed in imitation of her mother, hands together on the ground in front of Yoshikawa.

'You must be tired today, Papa.' Fujiko too gave a good imitation of her mother.

'That's no good, you're not saying anything at all.'

Nobuo and Yoshikawa fled, guffawing loudly. They climbed the gingko tree behind the garden shed. From there they could see Machiko and Fujiko playing.

'Yoshikawa, I'm thinking of becoming a priest too.' Recently Nobuo had often wanted to tell Yoshikawa, but he had missed the chance. Now, having climbed up the tree, he found he could speak freely.

'Hmm . . .' That was all Yoshikawa replied as he sat astride a branch, feet swinging. Nobuo thought it would have pleased him, and he was disappointed.

'Where have our husbands gone,' said Machiko.

'They must have gone out drinking again. They're awful.' When he heard Fujiko's reply, Yoshikawa's feet stopped swinging.

'Nobuo, it's tea-time.' Kiku was calling.

Her voice rang out clearly. From their vantage point in the gingko tree, Nobuo and Osamu could see Kiku's slim figure on the verandah. She was facing in the wrong direction as she called them.

'O.K.' Nobuo shook the branches of the gingko tree roughly as he replied. Kiku's fair face turned towards them.

'Is that your mother?'

'Yes.'

Nobuo felt a swelling of pride. 'She is a beautiful mother. I wouldn't be ashamed to introduce her to anybody,' he thought.

'Nobuo, it's tea-time.' He could hear Machiko's high-pitched voice.

'Let's go.'

'O.K.'

The two boys climbed down and ran to the verandah. When Yoshikawa saw Kiku, he hung his head and blushed to his ears as he bowed.

'It was clever of you to find your way here,' she said, acknowledging his greeting formally, with her hands pressed on the verandah floor.

'What a pretty sister you've got,' she added.

Yoshikawa scratched his head shyly.

'Yes, isn't she nice. I like her very much, Mummy.' Machiko looked up at Nobuo. 'What do you think, Nobuo?'

'Yoshikawa, let's go and wash our hands.' Nobuo ran off like lightning. He was surprised at himself. Why hadn't he been able to say that Fujiko was pretty?

'I'm a boy, that's why.'

He went to the well and took a cool drink of water from the bucket. 'We're boys, aren't we?' he said.

'Well?' Yoshikawa looked surprised. 'Of course; that's obvious.' And he laughed.

They seated themselves on the verandah, and ate salty crackers from a heaped plate. Kiku was nowhere to be seen.

'Your mother seems very kind.' Yoshikawa had been quietly munching. He gave the impression of having wanted to say it for a long time.

'Yes, I suppose so.' Nobuo looked across to Machiko sitting on a mat with Fujiko, in the shade of a small tree.

'Mother is kind, but . . .' Nobuo lowered his voice.

'What, isn't she?' Yoshikawa, who had been nibbling a cracker, raised his voice sharply.

'Well, you see, although Grandmother is dead, she doesn't offer rice or incense on the altar for her.' Nobuo came out with what was troubling him most.

'Is that so?' Yoshikawa put a piece of bean candy into his mouth with a gesture of disbelief. His mother lit the lamps on the Buddhist altar and prayed there without fail every morning.

'My mother and grandmother didn't like each other, you know. So now Mother doesn't even burn incense for her.' Nobuo did not know why he was saying this. He had not intended to say anything bad about her, but whenever he heard anyone say she was kind his antagonism was aroused.

'However much you dislike a person, when they die they become a venerable spirit, don't they?' Yoshikawa sounded very surprised.

'That's what I think. Anyway, she doesn't even burn incense. I'm really sorry for Grandmother.'

'Hmm . . .' Yoshikawa seemed lost in deep thought.

'So I want to be a priest and chant *sutras* for Grandmother.'

Yoshikawa looked searchingly at Nobuo. 'Nagano, you really want to become a priest?'

'Yes, I give you my word of honour.'

Nobuo stretched out his little finger, and linked it with Yoshikawa's stouter one, sealing the promise.

'Hi, Nobuo, what are you making promises about?' Machiko came running up.

'What's the promise about?' Fujiko came limping along after Machiko, going as fast as she could.

'It's a secret.' Yoshikawa tried to send them away.

'Tell us, tell us.'

Machiko gave Yoshikawa's knee a shake. Yoshikawa put his finger to his tightly sealed lips, and Nobuo nodded.

'It's a secret, a secret, do you hear?'

Fujiko laughed affectionately, looking up at Nobuo. What a strange feeling it gave him, somewhere in his chest.

'My, you are having a good time! What's the secret? I'd like to know about it too.' Kiku had suddenly appeared on the verandah. Startled, Nobuo gazed at his mother, feeling guilty about what he had been saying.

'Mother knows already,' he answered brusquely.

'What can it be, I wonder?' said Kiku, smiling as she stroked Machiko's head.

The sky looked threatening, ready to release a downpour at any moment. Nobuo was walking to Yoshikawa's house. The wind suddenly ceased completely, and the trees and grass in the gardens were motionless. 'The summer is going, holidays are over,' he thought. For some reason Nobuo always stopped under a particular tree, which stood in an empty plot of land where the road turned towards Yoshikawa's house. When he saw the tree, he knew he was nearly there but he always stopped, even though he intended to go on. When he reached the tree he would begin to wonder whether Yoshikawa was in, but after a moment or two he would run on cheerfully.

'I've got something to show you.' Yoshikawa had been looking forward to Nobuo's coming.

'Something interesting? What's that?'

Yoshikawa's house was spotless everywhere, the shoes in the porch were always cleaned and arranged as if for display, never left untidy.

'Everything spick and span,' Nobuo always thought. Since he had become class monitor Nobuo had had to write the marks for classroom cleanliness and order on the blackboard. At those times he remembered Yoshikawa's house.

'If you guess right, I'll give it to you.' Yoshikawa laughed.

Fujiko and her mother were not at home. 'It'll be raining any minute now,' Nobuo thought as he replied. 'What can it be . . . a top?'

Yoshikawa laughed again and said, 'Not that. It's not a kid's toy.'

'Well, is it something for grown-ups?'

'It's something both kids and grown-ups can look at.'

'Something to look at . . . Is it a picture book?'

'Yes, that's it.'

Yoshikawa took a book from a drawer below the Buddhist altar. When they opened it Nobuo's eyebrows shot up. The first page had a picture of emaciated spirits of the dead being pursued by green and red demons over a needle-studded mountain.

'What do you think of this, eh?'

'It's frightening.'

Yoshikawa adopted a superior air. 'Rather awe-inspiring, don't you think?'

Nobuo turned over the page. In this picture men were sinking and floundering in a crimson lake, crying for help. Those trying to crawl out at the edge were being pushed back by demons with iron clubs.

'How awful!' A strong feeling of horror swept through Nobuo.

'There's no hope for them. They are the people who did evil things during their lives. That's the sea of blood.'

'The sea of blood?' Thoughts of clammy, slimy blood flitted through Nobuo's mind.

'Yes, these people murdered and shed the blood of others, so they are put in the sea of blood – so my mother says.'

'Hmm.'

The next picture showed a crowd of people in a huge cauldron with upraised hands screaming for help. Flames licked around it.

'Horrible, isn't it?' Nobuo was becoming more and more depressed.

'There's nothing to be done for them. Hell is a place where evil men like them must be thrown.' Yoshikawa looked at Nobuo and grinned. 'If you do something bad, that's where you go.'

Nobuo felt wretched. 'What if I do something bad?' he thought.

Seeing Nobuo's gloomy face, Yoshikawa quickly flipped over a number of pages. Elephants, rabbits and lions giving children rides on their backs and romping and playing with them, appeared. Nobuo could not help breaking into a smile. Yoshikawa smiled too.

'That's a picture of Paradise.'

'Paradise is a wonderful place, isn't it?'

The next picture showed a group of men with peaceful faces, gathered around the Buddha listening to his teaching.

'Are these all good men?'

'That's right.'

Nobuo cautiously turned back to the picture of the boiling cauldron. 'Yoshikawa, the people who go to hell, are they people who have done only one thing wrong? I suppose they did wrong things every day?'

'Maybe . . .'

'Perhaps they never did a single good thing in their lives?'

'Maybe. I think so.'

'Then . . . in that case Paradise is for those who never did an evil thing.'

'Maybe that's it.'

Yoshikawa looked in surprise at Nobuo's earnest face.

'Yoshikawa, do you think you will go to hell?'

'Well . . . I don't know. What about you Nagano?'

'I've never done anything really bad, but . . . is having a quarrel with your sister bad? I've had lots of quarrels.'

'Now you mention it, I have quarrels too. When my

father gets drunk and violent I often want to knock him down.'

Yoshikawa showed Nobuo his clenched fist.

'Yes, but are Paradise and Hell real places?'

'The priest says they are.'

'The priest wouldn't tell lies would he?'

The two nodded agreement. Nobuo once more turned to the pictures of Hell. There was a rumble of distant thunder.

'There's an evening shower coming,' said Yoshikawa, leaning out of the window.

Glancing at the picture of the souls trying to scramble out of the sea of blood, Nobuo suddenly remembered the picture of the crucifixion, which his father had showed him.

'What about him?' he wondered. 'Did he go to hell, or did he go to heaven?' It struck him that the crucifixion picture was a picture of hell, too.

The last day of the summer holidays finally arrived. Tomorrow they would have to go back to school.

Towards the south, gigantic columns of cloud were piling up against the sky. Nobuo had been to the woods at the Yushima shrine to catch cicadas. When he got home he could hear the sound of Fujiko and Machiko singing. As usual, the pair of them were kneeling on a mat spread out beneath a little tree. He caught sight of the back view of a boy beside them, but it was not Yoshikawa. Who could it be?

As Nobuo came up to them, all three turned round.

'Well, I never, if it isn't Torao!'

Sure enough, it was Torao, who used to accompany Roku the pedlar on his visits when Tose was still alive.

'Nobuo, where have you been?' As always, Torao's eyes sparkled impishly like a pair of black beans. He looked a little shy.

'To the Yushima shrine, catching cicadas. Why haven't you come round to play recently, Torao?'

'But . . . since her Ladyship . . . died . . .' Torao called Tose 'her Ladyship', just like his father.

'That's right, it's because "her Ladyship" is dead now, isn't it, Torao?' Machiko said this with a perfectly straight face. With her open nature she had already become friends with Torao.

'Is Roku here too?'

'No, he doesn't come round the Hongo district these days.'

When his joy at meeting Torao after such a long time had subsided Nobuo looked at Fujiko. 'Has Yoshikawa come?'

'He's talking to Mother in the house.' Machiko broke in instead of Fujiko.

'With Mother?'

Nobuo started to go inside but suddenly lost heart.

'Nobuo, let's play hide and seek.' Machiko stood up and Torao followed her. They tossed up by playing 'scissors, stone and paper' to choose who would be the seeker, and Torao lost.

'He's bigger than he was,' thought Nobuo, looking at him.

'Six . . . seven . . . eight . . .'

From his hiding place in the garden shed Nobuo could hear Torao counting slowly, a pause between each number. The garden was silent, apart from Torao's counting, and nothing broke the peace of the early afternoon.

'Nine . . . ten. . . . Ready everyone?'

'Not yet, wait a bit.' Fujiko called back, slightly flustered, as she opened the shed door. Then, cheerfully, 'All right, I'm ready now.'

'Fujiko, don't shout so!' Nobuo whispered.

'Oh . . . Are you in here too?' Fujiko got a fright when she saw Nobuo.

'Hide behind me.'

With a little nod, Fujiko came beside Nobuo. Below the

hem of her kimono her bad leg stuck out a little. It was withered and shrunken.

'Found you, Machiko.' Torao's sharp voice rang out. Inside the shed, in the dim light, Nobuo and Fujiko exchanged glances, then lowered their heads. Nobuo wanted to hug Fujiko to him then, with a strangely painful longing.

'Fujiko?' Nobuo whispered.

'What?' Fujiko answered softly. Her clear eyes under their soft eyelashes held a question too.

'It's all right, nothing really.'

Nobuo hoped that they would never be found. He thought it was wonderful to be hidden away, just with Fujiko. Up till now, Nobuo had never experienced such bitter-sweet happiness as this, playing hide and seek. He gazed fixedly at Fujiko's withered foot.

Next it was Machiko's turn, and after that Nobuo's.

'Ready?' Beside the gingko tree Nobuo counted ten and then opened his eyes. The cicadas were singing now. Nobody answered him. Nobuo tiptoed quietly towards the shed. There was no one inside. He walked on quietly towards the back door. He could hear Kiku's voice in the living room, and Yoshikawa's voice too, saying something. Nobuo stopped and looked in through the window. Kiku had her hand on Yoshikawa's shoulder, and Yoshikawa was gazing downcast at the floor. Nobuo suddenly felt that a hole had opened in his chest and loneliness had flooded in. He felt that Yoshikawa had replaced him in his mother's affection, and his mother had replaced him in Yoshikawa's. Nobuo started from the window at once, but he could not restrain himself.

'Yoshikawa!' he shouted.

'What . . . have you come back?' Yoshikawa put his head out of the window, and Kiku stood behind him.

'Nobuo, Yoshikawa has come to say goodbye.' Kiku's eyes were wet with tears.

'Goodbye?' Nobuo had not heard anything about that. 'I'm going to Ezo.'

Yoshikawa looked steadily at Nobuo, his customarily calm face troubled, as if it would soon break into tears.

'What . . . to Ezo?'

'Yes.' As he nodded, tears welled up visibly in Yoshikawa's eyes.

From songs he had heard, and from the saying 'Even the birds do not fly to Ezo Island', Nobuo knew it as a distant, lonely place. The news was too sudden, and Nobuo could only look blankly at Yoshikawa.

6 The Second Term

THE second term had begun. The first day at school after the long summer holiday was always something of a novelty. Nobuo was glad to meet his teachers and fellow pupils again, but felt a bit shy. All his friends were a little reserved at first too, but soon they were talking away happily like old times, and starting their quarrels again. Everyone had so much stored up inside them that they wanted to tell, and the noise was terrific. But Yoshikawa was nowhere to be seen. Even if he had left school, one might have expected him to come to the school playground.

'He's late,' Nobuo thought, but just then the vice-monitor, Otake, who was standing close by, shouted loudly, 'Hey, everybody. Do you know that Yoshikawa has left school?' All eyes immediately turned towards Otake.

'What, Yoshikawa left? What happened?'

The school bully, Matsui, came up to Otake with a look of surprise. 'I bet his family have done a moonlight flit.'

Otake had never liked the idea of Nobuo and Yoshikawa being friends. The fact that Nobuo should prefer Yoshikawa to him, the vice-monitor, made him angry.

'A moonlight flit, eh?' Someone shouted in a hysterical tone and everybody laughed. Nobuo felt as if he were being laughed at too.

Another boy burst out, 'No, they didn't do a flit. Yoshikawa's pa drank too much *sake*,[1] and they've had to borrow a lot of money, I hear.'

[1] rice-wine.

'Shut up, stupid. They borrowed a lot of money, and couldn't repay it, so they cleared out. That's what's called a moonlight flit.' Otake laughed in a superior, adult way.

'No, someone said that he got drunk and had a quarrel and stabbed someone in the chest or shoulder or something.'

'My grandmother says they've gone to Kyushu.'

'No, I was told they'd gone to Niigata.'

Everybody told what they had heard. Having picked up the story by acute listening to their elders, they were discussing the matter just as excitedly as grown-ups.

Lessons began, but Yoshikawa had still not arrived.

'Have they really flitted? I'm sorry for them,' thought Nobuo. He felt lonely as he gazed at Yoshikawa's empty seat in front of him.

'Why is Yoshikawa absent?'

Mr Takura, the teacher, who was waiting for them, glanced over the pupils' desks.

'Yoshikawa's family have done a moonlight flit,' Otake announced triumphantly.

'A moonlight flit?' said Mr Takura, and lapsed into silence.

When lessons were over, he called Nobuo to the staff room. It was a hot afternoon, and somewhere a cicada was singing.

'Nagano, do you know where Yoshikawa has gone?'

'I don't know.'

Nobuo thought that Yoshikawa could only have gone to Ezo. But today, according to what his friends said, it could have been Kyushu or Niigata or anywhere. So Nobuo could not say for certain. And even if it was true that Yoshikawa had gone to Hokkaido, Nobuo was in no mind to tell anybody else. He remembered that Tose had once said, 'Hokkaido is the place for the penniless and people who have done wrong and have no other place to run to.'

'What? You and Yoshikawa are good friends and yet . . .

Well, children are a simple lot. Fancy him not telling you where he was going,' said Mr Takura, laughing.

Now Nobuo felt that both he and Yoshikawa were being laughed at and he became angry. The teacher opened his fan sharply and began to fan himself vigorously.

'Er . . . Yoshikawa's gone to Ezo,' Nobuo blurted out without thinking.

'What? . . . Ezo? Hokkaido? I might have guessed. But surely they could have found a place to run away to without going as far away as Ezo. Nagano, who told you this?'

'Yoshikawa.'

'Is that so? But in that case, you, the monitor, have been telling lies, Nagano.' Mr Takura fanned himself even harder.

'Telling lies?' Nobuo wondered, biting his lip.

Seeing Nobuo's doubting face the teacher continued.

'Well, that's true, isn't it? I asked you where Yoshikawa had gone and you said, "I don't know," didn't you? Why didn't you tell me straight away that he had gone to Hokkaido?'

'I'm not a liar,' thought Nobuo.

'You know the saying "a *samurai* is true to his word". Now the Meiji period has come and the *samurai* have cropped their hair, people have become a lot less truthful. But you as a monitor should set an example.'

Whether it was the sultry heat or the fact that one of his pupils had left without saying anything to him, Mr Takura was in a bad mood.

'If I had said that Yoshikawa had gone to Hokkaido, it would have been hard on Yoshikawa, so I said nothing,' thought Nobuo, as he stood listening to the teacher with downcast eyes.

'Don't let me hear any more lies from you. You may go.' The teacher turned back to his desk. Nobuo bowed and left the staff room. 'I didn't tell a lie,' he said to himself.

He looked at the slightly frayed band of his kimono.

'But, even though I didn't tell a lie . . .' Nobuo thought

with deep distress. It was not that he felt any animosity to the teacher, but he was worried that he had not been able to explain properly.

'Grown-ups, they can explain things all right. I wish I could turn into a grown-up quickly.'

Often afterwards this thought came back to him, and it was a long time before the strong-willed Nobuo could forget his feeling of frustration.

That day was unusually hot and sultry, as if the sun had fallen right down to the earth.

'It looks like rain this evening.'

Kiku was lighting the mosquito smoke coils on the verandah near Masayuki.

'Yes.' Masayuki gently fanned himself.

To Nobuo, his father always looked calm. However hot it was, he never used his fan in the energetic way that Mr Takura did. Until recently Nobuo had felt affectionately towards his father, but his feelings were changing. At meal times, for instance, it irritated him to watch Masayuki slowly munching pickles and sipping his tea. When his father spoke he was tediously slow, it was difficult to communicate with him. Nobuo did not dislike him, but the more he wanted to speak to him the more irritating he found his father's air of composure.

'Father,' he called.

Masayuki gently fanned himself for a moment before looking at him and replying. 'Yes, what is it?'

Nobuo wished he would reply more quickly.

'Well . . . What do you do when you want to make clear to somebody all you're thinking about?'

Masayuki blinked a little and replied, 'That's a big question.' Then he changed the subject slightly.

'What grade are you in now, Nobuo?'

'The fourth grade.'

'Hmm, the fourth grade. Next year you will be in the first

grade of high school. Well then, you should be able to speak for yourself on most matters.'

'But I can't.' And he described how he had been unable to explain when Mr Takura had said he was a liar.

'Is that so?' Masayuki gazed out over the garden for a while. 'As I thought, it's going to rain.'

Masayuki's conversation was punctuated with the usual pauses. Nobuo, waiting for an answer, was growing impatient.

'Nobuo, even when you grow up, you will find it difficult to express everything you feel, either in speech or in writing. But you must make your listeners understand more than you actually say. As well as the courage and effort needed in trying to make others understand, something else is needed. What do you think that is?'

'I don't know.' Nobuo cocked his head on one side.

'It's sincerity. A sincere heart shines out of your words and passes on to others through your face,' said Masayuki, and gently plied his fan again.

A sincere heart, courage, effort. Nobuo pondered this and began to understand a little.

'But, Father, there are times when sincerity won't work, aren't there?'

'Yes, there are.' Masayuki thought of how Tose had never understood about Kiku's faith. 'But it can't be helped, people's natures are all different. There are some people who do not understand what you are feeling, and others that you can't understand. The world is full of different types of people.'

But the thought still nagged Nobuo, 'It's terrible to be thought a liar.' He looked at the thin smoke rising from the mosquito coil. 'I'll read more books. If I do that perhaps I'll be able to say what I think.' From then on he concentrated on reading, and the books gave him something of themselves.

Two or three days after this, when Nobuo returned from school, he saw three large pieces of luggage lying on the verandah. Kiku's nephew, Takashi Asada had come from Osaka to enter university. He looked at Nobuo.

'Hmph . . . You look intelligent enough, but you are as skinny as grass growing in the shade,' he said, not mincing matters.

His body and voice were big, but his eyes were smiling and Nobuo liked him from this first meeting. At supper time he came to like him more.

'Thank you, now I'll start.' As soon as he sat down Takashi took his chopsticks and began to shovel rice into his mouth.

'Hey, we say grace here, Takashi,' Nobuo nervously jogged his cousin.

'What's that?' After he said this Takashi looked up at everyone for the first time. Kiku began to pray as usual, but Takashi just went on calmly eating his food. When Kiku had finished praying, he said, 'That's it, my aunt's a Yaso.'

As he said this, he thrust his rice bowl, which he had emptied in three mouthfuls, across to Kiku to be refilled.

'Well, I'm not a Yaso. I don't pray.' Takashi announced cheerfully. Nobuo gazed at him in amazement, and Machiko's eyes opened wide as she watched him.

'If that's so, just do as you please,' Kiku said simply. Takashi's statement had been unopposed and nobody had taken offence. Nobuo was impressed. But he was astounded at Takashi's next statement.

'Ugh . . . these vegetables are too salty.'

Grandmother Tose had always taught that men should not say what they were thinking. Nobuo knew the saying, 'A *samurai* should never show his feeling even when he is suffering.' A man should never admit that he was hungry or lonely or that life was hard. To swallow down and conceal one's feelings was the first step in becoming a truly resolute person. Tose had said, 'Don't let your thoughts appear on your face. A real man still laughs when he is weeping in his heart.' She had also taught that it was only low-bred people who commented on whether their food was tasty or not. So when Takashi criticized the vegetables in such a casual way, Nobuo was completely dumbfounded.

'Oh, I'm so sorry. I suppose Kansai people like a different flavour?' Kiku waited on him as if nothing had happened. The ways of Kiku's family and the Nagano family were completely different.

'It must be good to be able to say what you are thinking,' thought Nobuo as he watched Masayuki silently using his chopsticks.

At the next meal too, Takashi ignored Kiku's prayer and began to eat straight away. But it would be wrong to imagine that he created a strained atmosphere by doing so. On the contrary, since Takashi had come to the Nagano home, it could be said that things had become brighter.

'I like cousin Takashi,' said Machiko, sitting on his big knees.

In Takashi's room a great number of books were arranged in an orderly manner. 'I arrange them myself. If they're just put in anyhow, it's the very limit finding them,' he said.

'If you can find a book here you can read, go ahead. You're just the right age for books, so read anything you like,' he told Nobuo.

Takashi bought a magazine called *The Children's Garden*, a cheap paper-back called *Tales of Famous Warriors and Heroes*, and *Robinson Crusoe* for Nobuo. He even borrowed some girls' magazines from somewhere for Nobuo to read. In one of them Nobuo discovered that there were women who on their own initiative wrote articles and stories. He had thought that women only worked in the house like Tose and his mother, so this was a great discovery for him. The stories of the heroes were interesting, but what gripped him most was *Robinson Crusoe*. The endurance of Robinson Crusoe, cast up alone on a desert island, never giving up hope, held him spellbound.

'What would have happened if it had been me?' he thought. 'Probably I would not have been able to live like Crusoe. If it had been me . . .'

He had learned that books could transport him far away.

Then he read Shoyo Tsubouchi's book *The Spirit of the Modern Student* and other books like it. For Nobuo, who from quite a small boy had been taught the Analects of Confucius, reading adult novels was not difficult. From the novel *The Spirit of the Modern Student* Nobuo picked up several English words and badly wanted to put them to use – words like 'books', 'watch', and 'useful'. He began to feel he had grown up, and was becoming a little too cocksure. However, one day when he saw the German and English books that Takashi was reading, this cocksure feeling evaporated. He could not read a word of them.

'Takashi?' Nobuo asked determinedly.

'What?'

'Please teach me English.'

'Do you know what you're saying?'

'Please teach me German and English and things.'

'You're just a kid. What grade are you in?'

'The fourth grade.'

'No. It's not possible yet.'

'Why's that?' Nobuo was not giving up.

'You'll study that when you go to high school.'

'But in America and England, little children use English, don't they?'

'Of course.'

'Well then, Japanese children can learn to use as much English as American and English children do,' Nobuo said flatly.

'You're an interesting kid, you are.'

'Japanese children aren't less intelligent than foreign children, are they?'

'No, but *they* live in a country where English is used

every day. Of course they learn it naturally. They repeat words again and again, and learn them that way.'

'If you can learn words by using them again and again, there's nothing so hard about that, Takashi.'

At Nobuo's words, Takashi looked keenly at him. 'You're a scrawny little thing, but you've got a wonderfully strong character!'

From that day, Takashi's opinion of Nobuo changed, and Nobuo began to learn English.

7 Yearnings

NOBUO was now in the third year of high school, and Machiko in the third year of junior school.

'Hurry up, or we'll be late for school,' she called to him from the entrance hall. Nobuo was lingering in the house, putting his books into his satchel and taking them out again.

'Did you hear me?' Machiko sounded as if she was on the verge of tears.

'I don't mind if you go without me,' shouted Nobuo, and Machiko set off alone. Nobuo followed slowly after her at a distance.

Now that he was fourteen, for some reason or other Nobuo disliked going to school with Machiko. She always spoke in such a loud voice, things like, 'Look! Nobuo! What is that red flower called?' or, 'Don't you think that girl is pretty?' He had never thought anything of this habit of hers before, but now he found it unbearably embarrassing.

For example, a few days before, at the school entrance, a pretty girl had come up to them. "Nobuo, this is Keiko Miyakawa. Don't you think she's pretty?' Machiko had said in a loud voice, and Nobuo had blushed scarlet, as if his whole body had been set on fire.

Altogether, he felt that Machiko's voice was far too loud. She was quite without reserve, and made friends with people in no time, not just with the girls of her own class but with senior girls as well. So whenever he went to school with Machiko he would find himself surrounded by a horde of girls. No wonder he hated going with her these days. Gazing at her back as she tripped along, he thought what strange creatures girls were.

Even when mention was made of a woman in books he was reading, he felt a sort of choking feeling. If the woman was beautiful, this feeling was mysteriously heightened so that he could hardly breathe. As he tried to visualize the beautiful woman, if she were a married woman the face he would see in his mind would be his mother's. If she were an unmarried girl, strangely enough he would imagine the girl who had gone away three years ago, Yoshikawa's sister, Fujiko. He told no one about this.

He could not understand how it was that Fujiko who, when he had seen her last, had not even started school, should appear to him as the beautiful young woman in the book. In Nobuo's class there were several beautiful girls. The daughter of a wealthy shoemaker, whenever she passed Nobuo in the corridor, would blush deeply, lower her eyes and hide her face in the sleeve of her kimono. Nobuo's heart would throb violently, but she was nothing like as beautiful as Fujiko, whose face he saw whenever he read a novel.

'I wonder where old Yoshikawa is now?' he asked himself.

Since the summer in the fourth grade, when he had whispered that he was going to Hokkaido, there had been no news of Yoshikawa. Nobuo had no idea whether he had gone to Hokkaido as he supposed, or where he was. Hokkaido seemed too far away for there to be much chance of ever meeting again.

'Yoshikawa used to say he was going to be a priest,' he recalled. He still remembered how he himself had made a pact with Yoshikawa to do the same. He would look at his own little finger and think how it had been linked with Yoshikawa's thick one, symbolic of their promise. It all seemed such a long, long time ago, yet interestingly enough, Yoshikawa and Fujiko themselves were still fresh in his memory.

'Nobuo, how about a spot of flower viewing?' Takashi suggested one Saturday afternoon. Nobuo enjoyed an outing with Takashi, but he found little pleasure in flower viewing or festivals these days.

'I've got to study,' was his excuse for refusing the invitation.

'Hmm.'

Takashi's face reminded Nobuo of the famous Takamori Saigo. His eyes were always laughing and he gave the impression of being able to behave like a spoiled child without any qualms.

'Have you really got work to do?' Takashi opened his eyes wide in disbelief and Nobuo felt that he could see into his very soul. He shook his head and laughed in confusion.

'You scoundrel! You've changed lately.' Takashi lowered himself heavily into a cross-legged position in front of Nobuo. Nobuo instinctively sat up straight.

'There's no need to go all formal,' Takashi smiled.

'Do you really think I've changed?'

'Well, I suppose it's your age. You've become an adolescent.' Nobuo flushed at the use of the word.

'Why do you think it is that you don't go around with Machiko these days? It's because you've reached adolescence. For the next two or three years you'll feel shy about visiting other people's houses. I can remember the feeling of not being interested in going to see the cherry blossom any more.' Takashi bowed his head.

'Do you mean to say there was a time when you hated to go out too?' asked Nobuo with a touch of relief in his voice. Takashi liked nothing more than going out, if he had the time. There was no one like Takashi for being able to supply details of where a new house was being built, whether the cherry blossom buds were swelling, whether the food at such and such a place was tasty or not, and so on.

'There was indeed. I never went anywhere, but stayed in my room and got more and more introspective, wondering if I'd live very long. As a result, I'd down about seven or eight bowls of rice at one meal.' Takashi guffawed.

Nobuo was surprised, not by Takashi's coarse laughter, but by the fact that these days he himself felt that for some reason or other he would not live to old age. He would puzzle for hours over why human beings had to die. Sometimes he would have a vivid memory of the face of his grandmother Tose in death, and would wonder what kind of death he would have.

'Takashi, why do human beings die?' Nobuo's face was serious.

'They die because they're alive, I guess.' Takashi's expression was calm.

'They die because they are alive?' That seemed a logical explanation; but Nobuo felt that he had been given an evasive answer.

'If a person is living, wouldn't you expect them to go on living for ever?' he said.

'There's something in that. I've wondered, too, why people don't live for ever. Nobuo, do you know this saying, "Living we die, meeting we part"?'

'Yes, my teacher taught it to us. It means that living things must inevitably die and people who meet must part.'

That made Nobuo think of Osamu Yoshikawa. In a couple of years from now the friends in his class would all be scattered, and he would have said goodbye to his teacher. And this Takamori Saigo's double, Takashi, would have to go away when he finished university. And inescapably the day would come when he, Nobuo, would be separated from his father, his mother and

Machiko. Whenever he contemplated these things, Nobuo felt that life was an empty, melancholy thing.

'If meeting means parting, surely it would be better not to meet anyone in the first place,' he told himself, and felt a bitter desolation at the bottom of his heart.

'That's right. It's just as your teacher said, "Living, we die" means simply that people who are alive die. As to why they die, no matter how hard people think about it, nobody knows the answer. All I know is that some day I'll die, and some day you'll die too.'

'Is that so?' Nobuo wondered. 'Can it be true that no one knows why people die?'

'Aren't you afraid of dying?' he asked his cousin.

'It's a frightening thought. Even if I knew I was going to die, I'd want to live just a moment longer, but I suppose there's no getting away from it.'

'So it's impossible to live for ever under any circumstances?'

'That's asking too much. It's true that your mother believes in eternal life and all that, but . . .'

'Eternal life?'

'Uh, that's what Yaso followers believe.' Looking at Nobuo, he continued, 'Nobuo, I bet you'll turn Yaso one of these days,' and laughed.

Nobuo was indignant. 'Me? I'll never turn Yaso. I'd sooner die,' he declared.

'There's no need to make such categorical statements. Swearing that you will never do such and such is not so straightforward as people think.'

'Yes, but . . .' Nobuo felt uneasy.

'You see, human beings don't necessarily live their lives as they plan them. Take me for instance. I had an ambition to come to Tokyo, keep my nose to the grindstone, and come out top of my class at Imperial University. But look what's happened. I lose my head over every girl I meet. Rather than wanting to study I just can't wait to play around with girls.'

When Takashi got on to this subject, Nobuo started to blush.

'How about you? Don't you ever dream about girls?' he asked, blowing a cloud of tobacco smoke over Nobuo. Nobuo got redder and redder. His body was already a man's body. He had many a time dreamed of a woman, though where she came from he did not know.

'You dream of a woman, and feel you want to hold her hand. That's because you're a man. I think a lot about women. There's nothing wrong in that. There are some fellows who will tell you that it's unmanly to think about women. That's all a big lie. A woman is a man's indispensable living companion. Thinking about women is neither unmanly nor dirty,' Takashi concluded. His face was serious.

Nobuo thought of Fujiko's face. He pictured her, not as the little girl she had been, but as a teenager like himself.

Needless to say, the day slipped away without either of them going to see the cherry blossoms.

Since Takashi had come to live with them, Masayuki had begun going to church with Kiku, but recently his church attendance, even on Sundays, had become rather spasmodic.

'It must be my age. I don't know why but I feel tired,' he would say, and spend the day pottering about the house.

'You've just turned forty. That's no age at all. You'd better see a doctor at once, or else . . .' Takashi was plainly anxious, but both Masayuki and Kiku were unconcerned.

'You've been working hard. I expect you are tired. Just take things easy on Sunday,' Kiku would advise. She seemed unaware that there could be something wrong with Masayuki. All the same, Nobuo felt uneasy when he saw his father looking so haggard.

'Mother, don't you think it would be better if father

saw a doctor?' he asked. He did not say it in as many words, but he implied that his mother was to blame for going off to church and leaving his father at home. Come rain, come snow, she went to church every Sunday morning. Whenever the two of them and Machiko set off together, Nobuo could never get used to his feeling of emptiness at being left behind.

Since the arrival of Takashi there had been English lessons, outings together to Asakusa and so on, so that, although his parents were out on Sundays, Nobuo had plenty of activities of his own. Nevertheless, at the sight of them going off with Machiko, his old feeling of envy would return.

'Nobuo's right, Aunt Kiku. Why don't you give church a miss sometimes. Nobuo always looks lonely on Sunday. Even more than have you call a doctor, Nobuo would like you to stay at home.' As usual, Takashi spoke without restraint.

'That's not the reason. It's just that father is . . .' Nobuo was thrown into confusion.

'I don't need a doctor. Off you go, Kiku,' urged Masayuki, his head pillowed on his arms. Nobuo was afraid his father was purposely rebuffing him.

'But . . .' Kiku was less concerned about Masayuki's health than she was about what Takashi had just said, and looked at Nobuo anxiously. But Nobuo pretended not to notice and opened the book he was reading.

'Nobuo's not a child. He's in the third year of high school,' Masayuki said persuasively.

'Don't forget to buy us lots of tasty things to eat on your way home,' joked Takashi.

'Trust you to think of that! All right then, I'll see you later . . .' Kiku answered, smiling at Takashi.

Nobuo was unable to share in this sense of intimacy between Takashi and Kiku. His mother seemed closer to Takashi than she was to him.

'I wish Nobuo would start coming to church with us too,

don't you, Mother?' Machiko looked at Nobuo with the expression she always adopted when she went to church. He could not stand her on these occasions. He hated this condescending attitude, but the way she seemed to look upon her mother as her exclusive possession aroused his anger even more.

'Nobuo, why the vacant expression?' asked Takashi, almost crushing his shoulder with his grip as he led him into his own room. Once there he continued, 'The trouble with you is that you are too reserved towards your mother.' He never minced words.

'It's nothing of the kind, it's just . . .'

'Is that so? Then do you mean to tell me that you dislike her?'

'Dislike her?' Far from disliking her, Nobuo held her in the deepest adoration. It was just that somehow he could not feel at ease with her. He would like to be able to unburden himself, to confide in her, tell her all he was thinking, but, as was to be expected, he found it hard to express himself.

'Do you know, Mother, the dog next door smiles when it sees me!' Machiko would make nonsensical remarks like this to her mother.

'Do dogs smile?' Kiku would laugh in amusement.

'Of course they do. "Machiko," he says, "something wonderful is going to happen to you today. I'm sure of it." That's why he smiles.'

'That's good, isn't it?'

Nobuo envied Machiko's ability to say such things. Why couldn't he say things as easily?

'Mother, I was dreaming about you last night. You were carrying armfuls of pretty flowers.' Machiko would talk on about her dream. Nobuo had dreams about his mother too, but he could not talk about them.

'You've got to learn to say what you are thinking, clearly. Even parents and children aren't so transparent that they understand each other without communicating.

Isn't that what words are for?' Takashi insisted. Then he added with a smile, 'You'll have a lot of trouble when you fall in love, because you're too shy to say what you think.'

At the very mention of the word 'love' Nobuo's heart started to thump and he lowered his head in embarrassment.

The weather had been damp and sticky for days on end. One day when Nobuo came home from school Machiko came running out to meet him.

'Something terrible has happened!'

'What's the matter?' Perhaps his father had been taken ill or something, but Machiko was obviously just teasing. Her face was covered in smiles.

'Guess what?' she urged him.

'What? I've no idea.' Nobuo purposely ignored her and walked into the house. Machiko ran in after him and held out a letter under his nose.

'Take a look at this.'

Nobuo had never received a letter in his life. He turned it over in amazement. 'It's from Yoshikawa,' he exclaimed. Dropping his books, he tore open the envelope. His fingers trembled.

'*Dear Nagano,*' it began. '*I've been such a long time in writing to you. Are you well? I expect you've grown a lot. It's three years since I came to Hokkaido. My mother and sister and I are well, but my father died suddenly a short time ago. He coughed up blood and died. They say it's because he drank too much and damaged his stomach. While he was alive I thought he was a terrible father because he was cruel to my mother, but now he is dead I feel very sad. Death is a strange thing. I wonder that we don't feel more resentment about it.*

'*Fujiko is well. She reads a lot of books these days and is quite grown up. Perhaps it's because of her bad leg, but she seems much more grown up than other children of her age.*

'*Before coming to Hokkaido I thought it was an awful place, but once I actually came to live here I felt as though I'd never lived anywhere else. Sapporo is a fine place. I was surprised to see so much snow in the winter; the surface of the snow is above the level of my head and it piles up right to the roof. But the scenery is wonderful with the pure spotless white of the snow.*

'*Perhaps you have completely forgotten about me. My father left Tokyo heavily in debt, so he said that I mustn't write to my teachers or friends. That's why I've not written to you. I can't tell you how much I would like to meet you again.*'

Yoshikawa's rounded handwriting gave Nobuo a nostalgic feeling. Still standing, he read the letter through once more, then he sat down and read it again. Hokkaido suddenly seemed very near. Nobuo was no longer aware of the rainy season and the unpleasant sticky heat of Tokyo; he felt a new strength rising through his body, just through reading Yoshikawa's letter. He seated himself at his desk, intending to write an immediate reply, but his heart was thumping strangely.

He sharpened his pencil industriously.

'*Dear Yoshikawa,*' he began. '*How time flies! I cannot tell you how thrilled I was to receive your letter.*'

Reading over what he had just written, Nobuo realized that it struck him as rather peculiar. Seeing that Yoshikawa's letter had told him about his father's death, he would sound a cold-hearted creature for saying he was thrilled. 'Nevertheless, I am thrilled,' he told himself.

He read through Yoshikawa's letter once again – for the fourth time. The more he read it the more keenly he felt how terrible it must have been for Yoshikawa to lose his

father. 'What if my father were to die?' he thought. These
days the sight of his own father's ailing body filled him
with anxiety. 'Just supposing Father were to die now' – the
thought of what would happen to Nobuo himself was
enough to upset him badly. First of all, who would go out
to work so that they could keep body and soul together?
It was unthinkable that his mother Kiku would work. He
knew that there would be no alternative but for him to get
a job. As for that, he could think of nothing except getting
an apprenticeship in a big store. 'And how lonely Mother
and Machiko would be.' As he chewed over these possibilities he realized how Yoshikawa must be feeling his
father's death, and hated himself for saying he was thrilled.
Trying to picture the kind of life Yoshikawa must be living
now, Nobuo picked up his pencil and began again.

'*Dear Yoshikawa,*
   '*How the time has flown! Ever since the day you left
for Hokkaido, I have wished very much that I could
meet you again. Sometimes I have studied the map and
wondered where you were.*
   '*Today when I received your letter I was so excited
that my fingers couldn't keep still as I tried to open the
envelope. Then, when I read your letter, I was so sorry
to hear that your father had died. It must have been
very sad for you. Now that he has gone, I wonder who
will work and provide for your family. I can hardly bear
to imagine how terrible it must be for you to have to
work. You are just fourteen, the same age as I am. But
do keep on at it and don't give up.*
   '*So even Hokkaido is "home" to those who live there,
is it? I was surprised to hear that the snow piles right up
to the roof. It must be terribly cold.*
   '*I am just the same as usual. My cousin from Osaka
is living with us while he attends university here. He is
an interesting person and is teaching me English.
Machiko is bursting with health. School is much the*

*same as usual, but the teacher who was in charge of our
class when you left is not there any more. Well, I'll write
again some time. Goodbye.*

Nobuo Nagano.'

Nobuo read over what he had just written. The truth
was that he really had been thrilled to receive Yoshikawa's
letter, and his words of sympathy over the death of Yoshikawa's father somehow sounded insincere.

'It's strange,' he thought, putting the letter back on the
desk and gazing out of the window. It was drizzling outside. The little paper doll that Machiko had made as a
charm to keep the rain away, hung limply from the eaves.

'Yes, it's strange,' he thought again. Nobuo was still fond
of Yoshikawa. It was true that he had sometimes wished
he could meet him again. Yet in spite of this he found it
impossible to enter genuinely into the grief that Yoshikawa
must be feeling.

Nobuo read his letter through once more. As he did so,
something else struck him. There was nothing in it about
Fujiko. Although from the beginning he had meant to
mention her, he had succeeded in giving the impression
that no thought was further from his mind.

'I've written nothing but a pack of lies!'

So even in a simple thing like a letter it was difficult to
express oneself without reserve. And even if he had expressed his true feelings, it seemed to him, his letter would
hardly sound sincere. Either way, it would be uncon-
vincing. So Nobuo was filled with apprehension at the
thought of Yoshikawa reading what he had written. To
think that his friendship with Yoshikawa depended on such
an uncertain link! At length, however, in spite of his
misgivings, he posted the letter.

When he awoke on Sunday morning, Nobuo had a
shivering sensation in his back. In the rainy season the
bedding did not get a chance to air properly, and this was

probably why he had caught a chill. His throat ached and his whole body felt limp.

As usual, Machiko had been up and dressed in her Sunday best for some time, and was dancing around the house. 'What a peculiar creature, getting so excited about going to church. She seems to prefer church to school,' he thought to himself with distaste, and turned over in bed.

'Breakfast's ready, you know!' Machiko came to wake Nobuo. But he just lay there with his eyes shut, as if it were too much of an effort to speak.

'You sleepyhead!' she teased, whisking his quilt away. His body trembled and he instinctively curled up to keep warm. 'You're making me cold,' he croaked at her.

'Oh!' Machiko got a fright when she saw the anger on his face, for it was genuine. 'Sleepyhead!' she called again, fleeing into the living room. Nobuo pulled the quilt around himself again, but he still felt cold and miserable.

'What's the matter? Aren't you up yet?' enquired Masayuki, who had just finished washing. Nobuo looked up at his father without replying.

'I say. You're not looking very well.' Masayuki knelt on one knee and placed his hand on Nobuo's forehead. 'Kiku. Kiku!' he called urgently. He did not get flustered as a rule.

'What's happened?' No sooner had Kiku entered the room than she placed her own forehead against Nobuo's. Nobuo blushed with embarrassment and joy. He had often seen Kiku press her cheek against Machiko's, but he had never had it pressed against his. The day when he met Kiku for the first time, she had hugged him closely, but since then she had done nothing more than lay her hand on his shoulder occasionally. Now the fact that his mother unhesitatingly placed her forehead on his, gave Nobuo a feeling of deep peace at the bottom of his heart.

The doctor was called at once. Kiku watched closely while he examined Nobuo. Looking up at Kiku's anxious face, Nobuo fell asleep again.

Everything was so dark. He was walking barefoot along a pitch-black road. His feet were unbearably cold. He was on the way to school, but somehow he was lost. If only his feet were not so cold. They were cold, but strangely enough his head was hot. 'Those sparks are flying towards me.' Wondering why his head was so hot, he turned around and saw that somebody's house was on fire. His body felt so heavy. 'I'm tired, so tired.' He crouched down and fell asleep on the spot.

After a while Nobuo suddenly opened his eyes. The light bulb was a yellow ball above his head.

'Nobuo?' Kiku was bending over to look at him. He smiled a faint smile of amusement at the anxious look in her eyes.

'You've been asleep for hours.'

'So that's it. I've been asleep, dreaming,' he thought. He looked at his mother in a daze.

'Does your head ache?' Kiku wrung out a cold cloth. From somewhere outside came the sound of the wooden clappers of the night watchman. Nobuo realized to his surprise that it was the middle of the night. He looked at Kiku and tried to say something, but before he could form the words he fell asleep again.

He was conscious of someone feeding him with gruel, and he imagined that the doctor came and said something. He was aware, too, of having his night clothes changed. The thing that he was most conscious of was the searing pain in his throat. It was not until the middle of the following night that Nobuo became fully conscious.

'Nobuo.' Kiku's face was close to his. 'Everything's all right now. Was your throat terribly sore?'

'Mm,' Nobuo nodded docilely. 'Mother, please go to bed now. How long have I been asleep?'

'Ever since yesterday morning you've had a high fever and scarcely opened your eyes.'

'Since yesterday morning!' Nobuo looked at his mother in amazement. She must have been sitting by his side all the time! Nobuo looked at her, with her ornamental waist-band neatly fastened, sitting so correctly.

'Mother, haven't you been asleep at all?'

Kiku shook her head. 'I was worried about you being so ill,' she replied gently.

'Does Mother care for me as much as all that?' he wondered in amazement. An inexpressibly sweet sensation of joy welled up within him.

His mother was so beautiful and gentle, he even had a yearning love for her. But never before had Nobuo felt that he could utterly trust her. He had always felt there was something in her that he had to be on his guard against. He had been unable to accept the fact that his mother had something more precious to her than he was.

'Can there be a mother in the whole wide world who would do such a thing as desert her child as she did?' he had asked himself miserably when he was younger. Such wretched feelings could not be healed in just a few years. Nobuo desperately wanted to know whether his mother really loved him. Now, as he realized that she had been so anxious about the outcome of his illness that she had not slept since the morning of the day before, this unutterable joy and relief swept over him.

'So she really is my mother after all. She's not just Machiko's mother,' he thought.

He was absolutely delighted. 'Mother . . .' He wanted to express this joy in words but by saying her name he at once felt he had adequately expressed all that he wanted to tell her. He had never felt like this before in his life.

'What is it Nobuo?' Kiku's eyes were wet with tears.

'What's the matter, Mother? Why are you crying?' The old Nobuo had never been able to ask about things as gently as this.

'I was so worried that your illness might grow worse. You see, your temperature was so high for such a long time. But now it's such a relief to see my Nobuo awake again.'

'Are you crying because you are relieved, Mother?'

'It's funny, isn't it. Whether we are happy or sad, we can't help crying.'

Kiku softly wiped the corners of her eyes with the edge of her kimono sleeve.

'My mother is happy because I'm not going to die. She really is my mother,' Nobuo reminded himself again.

'Nobuo. Isn't it wonderful! It's really wonderful!' Machiko was leaning over and gazing at him. It was the following morning.

'Yes?'

He had sometimes been jealous of her intimacy with their mother, but it was quite different this morning. Machiko's round eyes were very appealing as she looked down at him.

'I'm still a child, you see, so Daddy and Mummy said "Go to bed" when it was night.' She took her doll, which was by her side, and held it out to Nobuo. 'But this doll sat by your side all the time and didn't sleep. She was so anxious for you. Instead of me, you see. I promised the Lord Jesus that I would let you have this doll if He made you get better quickly.' Then Machiko put her hands together to pray.

'Dear God,' she said. 'Thank you very much for hearing Machiko's prayer. Thank you very much indeed. Now Nobuo is able to eat his food again. I will truly give him this doll to keep, so please don't let him get sick again. In Jesus' Name, Amen.'

This was the first time that Nobuo had heard Machiko pray. He was moved.

Machiko's doll was about eighteen inches high, wearing a red flowery kimono with long sleeves. Usually Machiko took such great care of it that she would hardly even let her mother touch it. Needless to say, no matter how much her friends pleaded with her, she would not so much as allow them to hold it. It was unbelievable that she should be wanting to give this precious doll to Nobuo.

Nobuo wondered if he would be prepared to give his most treasured possession, a paper-weight inlaid with mother-of-pearl, to Machiko. He could hardly bring himself to think of such a thing. So, as he realized what it meant to her, he saw how much she cared for him. To think that this little sister of his was capable of doing something which he felt incapable of doing – it suddenly struck Nobuo that Machiko was a remarkable person.

'Thank you, Machiko. But I'm a boy, so I don't need a doll,' he said gently.

'Never mind, I'm giving it to you because I promised Jesus I would.' Machiko's face was earnest.

'That's all right. This doll is your own very, very special doll.'

'Well then, Nobuo. You pray to Jesus then. Say, "I'm giving the doll back which she said she'd given to you, and please don't be angry with her".'

'Pray! I'm not a Yaso. I don't know how to pray.' But no sooner had he said this than he thought of how she had prayed, giving up her doll for his sake, and he suddenly felt ashamed of saying 'Yaso' in such a hateful way.

'If you don't know how to pray, will you let me teach you?'

Nobuo did not know what to reply to this. He had said he could not accept the doll, and he was unable to pray. He was at a complete loss for words.

8 At the Gate

DURING Nobuo's final year at high school, his cousin Takashi came from Osaka on a visit. Takashi was now helping his father in the wholesale drapery business.

'It's no fun being a salesman, you have to work twice as long as an office worker and kowtow to everyone,' he said; but even as he said it, Takashi did not look as if it were as bad as all that. It was a time of general depression following the Sino-Japanese war, so what he said was not without justification, but with his characteristic optimism he showed no sign of feeling it very deeply. Nobuo envied him.

'Nobuo, you're beginning to look quite handsome.' Takashi slapped a large hand on Nobuo's shoulder.

'Machiko's quite a beauty too,' he went on tactfully, but she replied primly, 'I don't want to be flattered, cousin Takashi.' She knew that it was Nobuo who had the greater share of their mother's good looks.

After a welcome dinner given for him, Takashi persuaded Nobuo to go down town with him, to 'see the lights'.

'Nobuo, you've graduated, I suppose.'

'Yes.'

'Well, today, to celebrate your leaving school, I'm going to take you somewhere really good.'

Takashi led the way, walking rapidly; but sometimes he had to stop.

'Tokyo's changed, I don't know where I am.' He turned and faced Nobuo, lowering his voice unconsciously.

'Have you ever had fun with a girl?'

96

'Fun with a girl . . .?' At first Nobuo did not understand.

'Well then, have you ever been down to the Yoshiwara and had fun?'

When he heard the word 'Yoshiwara', Nobuo blushed scarlet. He was overcome with such a rush of feeling that he did not know what to reply.

'What's up?' At the sight of Nobuo, Takashi roared with laughter. He was thirty, with a wife and children.

'Anyway, it's an experience a man has to have for the first time sooner or later. And tonight I'm treating you. Celebrate your graduation!'

Nobuo stopped and took two or three steps backward. He had heard about the Yoshiwara and knew what it stood for. He imagined that there must be hundreds of women there, more beautiful than he had ever seen. And as for having fun with one, Nobuo knew from his school friends what that meant.

It would not be true to say that he did not want to go, yet within him there was a feeling of reluctance. Somehow it was a place Nobuo was afraid of. He was like a child, torn with curiosity to have a look inside a haunted house and yet at the same time afraid. As far as Nobuo was concerned, women were a closed book. The fact that there were only two sexes, men and women, filled him with amazement.

His mother – she certainly was a woman; and Machiko too was now an unsophisticated young woman of sixteen. Even with these two blood relations with whom he lived, waking and sleeping under the same roof, he sometimes felt ill at ease. Sometimes when Machiko came close to him, he would suddenly become confused and shift away from her. Why he felt this aversion to her when she was his sister, he did not know. Afterwards he often had feelings akin to love towards her, which he could not express. There was no reason in it; one minute he would feel antagonistic, and the next loving. So Nobuo was afraid of women who could awaken such feelings in him.

One night he had a dream in which a strange woman appeared in a place he did not know. Since then he had not been able to forget her. The general impression had been rather vague, but he was strongly aware that it was a woman and it unnerved him to think about it. Sometimes, even when he was talking to his friends at school, his feelings about her would suddenly well up and he would blush scarlet right down to his neck, much to his friends' surprise.

One evening he had seen a woman riding in a rickshaw, leaning forward in a charming attitude, and Nobuo felt that her warmth had passed directly to his own body. That night he could not escape from his mental image of her. Nobuo was strong-willed and did not wish to be swayed by his emotions, but once this thing had started there was no breaking free from it. The fact that a woman could completely rob him of his freedom, filled him with fear and a sense of mystery, yet in spite of it he felt a longing for the very thing which was such a trouble to him.

In those days, before becoming a soldier, it was the accepted custom that a man should have had sexual experience of women. More than half Nobuo's school contemporaries had proudly boasted about their own. That Takashi should be leading Nobuo to take this step in life would not have been considered either remarkable or immoral.

'What's up, are you scared?' said Takashi, giving him a push in the back. Nobuo started walking again, trying to control his rapid breathing. He neither saw the street nor the people walking by. He felt himself getting tenser and tenser and taking many deep breaths.

'Nobuo, women aren't anything to be scared of. Once you get to know them there's no problem.' As he said this

Takashi himself grew excited at the thought of pleasures ahead, and his voice grew even louder than before.

As he walked, for no apparent reason Nobuo remembered Yoshikawa.

'I wonder if Yoshikawa has had anything to do with women yet?' he thought. Memories of Yoshikawa's face flashed into his mind, the face of a ten-year-old, of the time when they parted, but it looked very adult and full of deep wisdom.

'Yoshikawa wouldn't play around with women,' he thought, recalling his friend's letters in which he told of his regular visits to the Buddhist temple. Yoshikawa, in Hokkaido, working on the mining railway to support his mother and Fujiko, and going to hear the priest's teaching, would have neither opportunity nor inclination to go after the girls, he believed.

'Yet I'm doing what he wouldn't do.'

Nobuo considered going home by himself, but his feet followed Takashi as before.

'Why can't I turn round and go home?'

Even though he wanted to he was not able to stop. Sensing the gaiety of Yoshiwara, which he had not yet seen, he walked on, musing, 'What sort of women are they, I wonder? What sort of things should I talk about?'

Imagining one thing after another, Nobuo silently kept up with Takashi.

'Look, Nobuo. See that big archway? Beyond that's the Yoshiwara. We're nearly there.'

When Nobuo looked in the direction of Takashi's pointing finger his heart began to beat wildly. Then, after he had pulled himself together a little, he began to notice numbers of men riding in rickshaws, dressed in fashionable clothes, overtaking them with smiles of anticipation on their faces. Five or six students were singing, 'Even if I had ten thousand foes', waving their hands and shouting. Somehow their silhouettes seen in the dark shadows inside the arch left a sharp, burning impression in Nobuo's mind.

'There are lots of people going in, aren't there?' Nobuo noticed that his own voice was wavering and strange.

'That's right, real men.' Takashi threw the words back with a smile.

Thinking of himself as one of this large crowd of men, Nobuo felt suddenly lonely.

'Where am I going?' He suddenly began to hate himself. To get himself a woman would certainly not be considered bad, but neither was it a thing to be praised. In his heart he was convinced that it was not good.

'If it were Yoshikawa, he would be ashamed to come to such a place.'

Looking at one of the bright pictures in the Yoshiwara from a distance, Nobuo still could not make up his mind to go back.

The thought that the soft-skinned woman of his dreams could here become a reality was a persistent attraction.

'Hey, what are you doing? Act like a man!'

No sooner had Takashi said this than Nobuo came to himself with a start. 'That's right!' he said to himself. 'I'm not behaving like a man at all.'

He made a tremendous effort of will. 'About turn!'

By the time he realized that he had turned round, he had broken into a run. He did not spare even a glance for Takashi shouting behind him, nor the scornful looks the people thronging in turned on him.

Nobuo kept telling himself, 'Keep going! Keep going!' again and again as he ran.

At home and in bed he pinched himself hard and repeatedly as a punishment for his weakness in being led as far as the entrance of the Yoshiwara.

'What if Yoshikawa had seen me?' he thought. Yet the turmoil in his heart would not abate. He got up and switched on the light. He sat down at his desk and took out some writing paper, for he had to write and tell Yoshikawa. Maybe in the morning, when he re-read the letter, he would tear it up, but he felt compelled to write something immediately.

  'Dear Yoshikawa,
   'It's ten o'clock at night, and something has happened that I want to tell you about. Yoshikawa, human beings are not free, are they? Tonight, for the first time I came to know the painful fact that men are captives. Even in middle school I prided myself that no one was my intellectual superior. I may be thin, but I have reached second standard at the judo hall. In fact, I confess I have always secretly prided myself that I was superior to most other people. Comparing myself with other young people, I thought I was more discerning and stronger willed than they. So I used to apply the saying, "Man is the Lord of Creation", to myself without any qualms.'

When he reached this point, Nobuo wondered whether to go on. The question, should he or shouldn't he tell everything about his weakness to Yoshikawa, away in Hokkaido, knowing nothing, flitted into his mind. Yet Yoshikawa was not merely a friend. Nobuo always thought of him as walking one step ahead of him, or perhaps as living at one level higher than himself. And it was not just because he was far away.
  Nobuo started writing again.

  'Dear Yoshikawa,
   'I'm ashamed to write this. Tonight I was on the way to the Yoshiwara, where the prostitutes are, and, persuaded by my cousin, I went as far as the outskirts, but when I was nearly there I turned round and ran home. It was because of you. When I thought that you would not go to a place like that, I suddenly felt ashamed. If you were not such a fine person, I would now be sharing a pillow with a prostitute. I want to thank you,

Yoshikawa. Even though you are far away in Hokkaido, you saved me in a crisis.

'*It's wonderful to have a good friend. If I hadn't known you, what an awful thing I might have done, without even thinking. Yoshikawa, when I spoke about being a slave, I was speaking about my problem with women. If I discovered a hundred yen for instance, I would not pocket it myself. You could say I am free from the love of money. But if, for instance, a woman took hold of my hand in a place where there was no one to see me, I don't feel I could shake her off and go away. To put it bluntly, sexual desire is my biggest problem. Yoshikawa, in this area of life I don't feel I'm a free man. Many times I have an uneasy feeling that sex is going to be my downfall. Please don't laugh at me. I wonder if you can teach me the way to freedom. This is a strange letter, but for me, at twenty,[1] this is a great problem. Don't laugh, but help me, I beseech you, and reply as soon as you can. Today, when I saw the lights of Yoshiwara I turned and ran back, but I could not trust myself to do the same again.*

Nobuo Nagano.

'*P.S.   Please burn this letter immediately. I would be very embarrassed if your mother or Fujiko should read it.*'

When he had finished writing, Nobuo felt a little calmer. But as he wrote Fujiko's name he could not help but recognize a feeling of love in his heart.

Two or three days after Takashi returned to Osaka, though it was still January the sky had been clear since dawn and the day was as warm as April.

'It's almost warm enough for cherry blossoms,' said Kiku.

---

[1] In those days education began at seven.

'Yes, but it's not healthy to be as warm as this,' replied Masayuki.

'What's the matter, Father, are you ill?' Machiko looked at Masayuki, her plaits swinging in a white ribbon.

'Hmm . . . My shoulders are stiff.' Masayuki looked across to Machiko, now quite a young woman, and gave a faint smile.

Nobuo wanted to say, 'If you're not well, go to bed,' but he kept silent. Those days he had many things to say but checked them just as he was about to speak. After all, if it had no real importance, it was better left unsaid. He had begun to realize the emptiness of merely exchanging words with people.

'Are you all right?' asked Kiku.

'It's nothing much.'

Nobuo looked at his father as he changed into his suit. 'You know, he really ought to go to bed,' he wanted to say.

Masayuki's face looked drawn, but Nobuo said nothing. He had no right to tell his father what to do, and his father had more sense than he had.

Looking up at Nobuo, Masayuki said, 'Your work for the examinations is going all right, isn't it? You look a bit tired; don't wear yourself out.'

Nobuo blushed. It was sex that was getting him down, not his exams. He dreamily went to the gate to see his father off in a rickshaw.

'I'm off now.' Machiko, clutching her books, slipped past Nobuo.

'Uh-huh.' At Nobuo's absent-minded reply Machiko turned back. The pleats of her skirt swayed softly. 'Nobuo, why do you look like that on such a lovely day?'

'What? . . . Oh, it's nothing.'

'You can say that if you like, but both you and Father don't seem well and it makes me feel bad too.'

Machiko swung out of the gate, without looking back. Nobuo ambled after her. Up till now, Machiko had always wanted to go with him wherever he went, but she did not seem to want to any more. Even when they set off for their schools, which were in the same direction, Machiko always started a little before him. Nobuo stood at the gate and watched her now, striding energetically half a block away. The impression she gave, bright and fresh, without a care in the world, was pleasing to him, even if she was only his sister.

Nobuo followed, and had gone only a little way when he heard a man shouting wildly behind him. Looking round, he saw the regular rickshaw man who only minutes before had called for Masayuki. But he was not pulling the rickshaw now. Cold shivers ran down Nobuo's spine. Something had happened to his father. Gradually the rickshaw man's words became intelligible. Nobuo hurried home as fast as he could, but his legs were trembling so that anybody would have thought him very slow.

Masayuki had been unconscious in hospital for six hours, and was snoring heavily. Kiku, Nobuo and Machiko could only watch him in a fever of anxiety. Nobuo bitterly regretted that he had not urged his father to go to bed, when he had seen his tired face that morning.

'Why wasn't I able to say a single word?' he wondered, and bit his lip so hard that the blood began to run.

'Father, Father!' Machiko cried out from time to time in a voice choked with tears. For Machiko, who had grown up without any real problems, this was unbearable.

As might be expected, Kiku was the most composed of the three, but in that half-day her beautiful cheeks had become pinched and haggard.

Nobuo unconsciously had both hands tightly clenched. 'What if Father should die now?' he thought. Even to think of it was unbearable. The only thing to do was to kneel down and pray something as he had seen Machiko and his mother do with their hands together in an attitude of prayer. How he envied them. But secretly Nobuo be-

lieved that the God of Yaso would answer them. He kept
thinking of his father and of the time when he had slapped
him, as a small boy—'when Torao pushed me off the outhouse roof, and I said, "No slum kid ever pushed me off
the roof".' Now he was twenty, Nobuo understood his
father's feelings. 'He did right to hit me,' he thought. With
Masayuki's unconscious form in front of him, he appre-
ciated the value of what his father had said. 'I need my
father,' he groaned. Perhaps it was only a desire to return
to the past, but he longed that his father should live on.
Even if he only slept, only breathed, so long as he could
live, Nobuo would be grateful. But it was not to be, for
Masayuki died that evening.

Nobuo had never imagined that there could be a funeral
other than a Buddhist one. To all the relatives it was the
only thing that could be done. So when Kiku suggested a
Christian funeral everyone suddenly became hostile and
excited.

'How can you do such a shameful thing?'

Tose's younger brother declared that if there was to be
a Christian funeral he would go home. 'We know you're
a Yaso, but that doesn't mean to say that you must go so
far as to give Masayuki a Yaso funeral.'

All kinds of criticisms were levelled at Kiku. Most people
had not approved of the way things had worked out over
Tose. It had only been because of Masayuki's peace-loving
nature and Kiku's kindness that their complaints had never
been brought out into the open. For Kiku to suggest a
Christian funeral, therefore, invited their hostility all the
more.

But when someone declared, 'No, we can't send Masayuki off with such a funeral,' Kiku produced a sealed letter
for all to see.

'These are my husband's last wishes,' she said, and bowed
politely.

'Last wishes? When did my father write them?' Nobuo
wondered in amazement.

The paper was read by Tose's younger brother.

'*All men must die, but no one can foretell the day of their death. In this letter there is nothing new that I want to write. Kiku knows everything I have requested. What I have said to Kiku, Nobuo and Machiko in everyday conversation, and what I have done, I wish you to think of as my legacy to you. With such a plan in mind I have lived each day. In the distress that comes with my death, may this note be a comfort to you.*

(1) I wish you, Nobuo, as the eldest son of the Nagano family, to take care of your mother, guide your sister, and become a worthy head of the family.

(2) However, that does not mean that I want worldly success for you. Learn from your mother how men should live.

(3) Nobuo, I want you to think very seriously about the fact that you were born a human being, and make special efforts to realize your humanity to the full.

(4) I consider myself fortunate to have lived as the husband of Kiku, and the father of Nobuo and Machiko. All this has been given to me by God.

(5) You may have some financial problems after my death. Do not let this disturb you, surely God will supply your needs.

(6) I wish to have a Christian funeral.

'*Here I close, I have recently been feeling very tired. Just in case anything should happen I have written this.*

Masayuki
January 14th

For Kiku, Nobuo and Machiko.'

When the will had been heard all present just nodded and hardly anyone discussed it, even in a whisper. To them, a will was nothing more than a bequeathing of property. This will, without any such statements, left them at a loss. But there was one thing that was definite – no one could oppose the Christian funeral any more.

After the funeral was over, the house seemed suddenly very lonely. Whenever Nobuo lay on his bed and closed his eyes, he sensed that the word Death, written large, was pressing in on him. Both his grandmother's and his father's deaths had been sudden. They had been extreme cases, leaving no time for anything, no conversation, not even a last entreaty. If there could only have been two or three days taking care of them, and the ones dying had had a chance to speak to those being left, it might have been easier to bear the sadness. But his father and grandmother had lost consciousness immediately, and had died while they had all watched helplessly.

'It really isn't fair.' Nobuo felt so resentful that he wanted to complain to someone about it.

'Maybe I'll die suddenly too, like Grandmother and Father.' The thought frightened him. Shortly before his father's death it had been the problem of sex that had occupied his thoughts. But now his biggest worry had become death. The problem of sex seemed to hold greater possibilities for discussion and solution; there was a way out, But death was an irrevocable, clean-cut loss of life – a predicament from which there was no escape.

'I don't know when or where or what the cause will be, but one thing is sure, I'm going to die.' Nobuo opened his eyes and stared hard at his two hands. Looking at his pale palms, he thought, 'These hands are alive. But one day they'll be completely cold, unable to move.' Starting with his thumb, he bent his fingers one by one and then opened them again. At that moment the sharp realization that all men have to die came starkly home to him.

'Why is it that I've never before realized so clearly that death, the end, is one of the most important facts of life.'

Nobuo thought highly of his father. Admittedly, when he had been alive he had struck him as being too peaceful, and this sometimes irritated him. But then, he had written

in his will, 'What I have said to Kiku, Nobuo and Machiko
in everyday conversation, and what I have done, I wish
you to think of as my legacy to you.' This was the attitude
of a man who had come to be prepared for death at any
time. During his peaceful day-to-day life, he had nevertheless wrestled with this great problem.

'Would I be able to live a model life every day like that,
so that it could speak like a will for me?'

His father's death grieved Nobuo, but it left another
even more lasting impression on him. It was at the funeral
that Nobuo first set foot in a Christian church. The slightly
gloomy building, with its high ceiling, was not the suspicious place that Nobuo had imagined it to be. The people
he met there were neither forbidding nor particularly
strange. But a funeral, without the chanting of *sutras*, or
burning of incense, just an organ playing hymns, seemed
to Nobuo to be very unfeeling. He could not get used to
the minister praying, and everyone, including himself,
uniting in a hollow-sounding 'Amen'.

'But if my father and mother believe so deeply in this
religion, it can't be too bad,' he began to think. Even so,
he could not imagine himself going there all his life.

As a result of Masayuki's death, there was an immediate
down-to-earth problem to be faced : whether or not Nobuo
should go to university. As a banker, his father had had a
good salary, and there would be enough for them to live
on for the two or three years he was studying. But Nobuo
did not think that as head of the family he should live off
the family savings. Of course he longed to go to university.
But he stubbornly concluded that he could get up to
graduation standard by himself. As he took this step into
manhood he could be prouder of supporting his mother
and sister than of a university education.

'Yoshikawa only went to junior school, but he supports
his mother and sister,' he reminded himself. Now that he
realized what a big thing it was, he respected Yoshikawa

even more. The day after the formal week of mourning for his father was over, Nobuo wrote to Yoshikawa.

'*Dear Yoshikawa,*

'*I suppose my other letter reached you. Recently, my father died very suddenly, a thing I never thought could happen. Yesterday was the seventh day of mourning and, to tell you the truth, I still cannot fully realize that it has happened. When I wake up in the morning, it's like the end of a long dream and I feel that my father is still alive. Afterwards the feeling of desolation is terrible. You have lost your father too, so I think you will understand. Father died of a stroke in no time at all. Man may be the "Lord of Creation", but I still wonder why people should have to die in such a miserable manner. My grandmother died of a stroke too, so when my father died suddenly of the same disease, I came to think of death as a sudden, awful, surprise attack. Of course, I don't suppose anyone thinks of death without revulsion, but to be attacked without warning, and struck down by a single blow, is something unbearably frightening. I have been thinking a lot about death, and there are several questions that puzzle me about it. It's amazing, isn't it, you and I both had a father and mother and a sister, and we have both lost our fathers. I feel that your destiny and mine are similar. Even if it is just wishful thinking I would like them to be the same. Anyway, even though you lost your father in junior school days, you are living a very worthwhile life now. I must try to do as well as you, my senior.*

'*This is not a very logical letter, but I just had to write one. Please forgive my previous strange letter and don't laugh at me.*

Nobuo.'

He had wanted to write, but now he felt he had written

nothing worthwhile. He longed to speak to Yoshikawa, even if only a few words. Since entering high school Nobuo had made many friends, but for some reason there was no one with whom he could have a heart-to-heart talk. Maybe it was because Yoshikawa, far away in Hokkaido, was the one to whom he could talk most easily. But then, if they met now, it was quite possible that even they would not be able to talk freely. Perhaps it was because he was unable to see Yoshikawa's face that Nobuo was deeply bound to him through letter writing.

The day after Nobuo sent the letter off, another arrived from Yoshikawa. Under the illusion that it was a reply to his letter of the day before, Nobuo opened it joyfully. Just to look at the familiar rounded handwriting and widely spaced words was to be comforted.

'Dear Nobuo,

'I've read your letter over and over again. To tell you the truth, I did not think that you were the sort of person who could write such a letter. I'm sorry; that sounds a bit rude. But I have always looked upon you as being rather proper and reserved. I never thought you would write to me about your sex problems. But you know, I'm human too. Any way you look at it I'm just an average person. Even though I go to hear the priests, in my heart I'm not in the least different from you, Nagano. But after reading your letter I was relieved and felt a new respect for you. I've burned my fingers badly over sex too. But this is the worst of being human; we can't help it, can we? As human beings with many sufferings, we need the teaching of the Buddha. Have you read any religious books? It does not look as if you have yet.

'Losing my father early, and having many hardships in life, I have found the priests' teaching to be a help and comfort. According to several sermons I have heard, men cannot live without making blunders, and I have *increasingly come to realize that this is so. To do what we feel we ought to, and to refrain from doing what we feel we ought not to do, would be good – but it doesn't work. Just as you have written, men have no freedom. My sister Fujiko, with her crippled leg, is like this and people think of her as disabled. It's easy to laugh at the physical cripple you can see, but it is harder to realize that in our hearts we are all helpless cripples. Yet, even though that is so, it's good that we have been able to talk freely about sex. I think we ought to drink a big toast to that. I'm only sorry that the letter did not seem like your usual self.*

'Talking about drinking, I have started to drink a little sake *recently. The winters here are colder than you could ever imagine and I've taken to having a glass now and again. But having had to put up with my father's drunken rages, I'm determined not to become a heavy drinker like him.*

'As the old proverb says, "A friend from afar is a great joy". When are you going to come to Hokkaido, so that I can meet you, and we can have a drink together? Whatever you say, you are really fortunate, having both your parents, and getting ready for university. I pray that good fortune will accompany you throughout your life. Even though I say this, it doesn't mean that I consider myself unfortunate. My father's drunkenness and early death, and the fact that I could only go to junior school, by and large I think of as trials that fate has apportioned to me. If you once succumb to self pity, there's no end to it. As soon as you enter university, do write to me.

Osamu Yoshikawa.

'P.S. That little terror Fujiko has grown up so rapidly. She even looks quite pretty. The relationship with one's sister is a funny thing, isn't it? Though they are women and the opposite sex, they don't seem like that to me. This brother-sister relationship, no one

*without an elder or younger sister could understand it,
could they?'*

When Nobuo had read the letter through, he heaved a
sigh of relief. 'Yoshikawa doesn't know about my father's
death yet,' he murmured to himself as he read it again.
'Yoshikawa lost his father a long time ago.'

Nobuo now realized the significance of the life Yoshikawa had been living for years. The feelings he had had
when he wrote about his sex problems, now struck him as
a luxury. Yoshikawa had neither envied Nobuo's good
fortune nor resented it, but had always written cheerfully,
as if he himself were blessed with good fortune.

'And now I have no father.' Nobuo began to weep, but
his tears were not for his father's death, they were tears of
gratitude for Yoshikawa who, though much less fortunate,
had by his wonderful spirit been a constant inspiration to
Nobuo.

'One thing is certain, I'm not unfortunate either. Being
unable to go to university is no misfortune at all.'

9 Shackles

ON LEAVING school, thanks to one of his father's senior partners, Nobuo obtained a job as a secretary in the law courts. One rainy day, about a month after he started work, Nobuo went out of his room, carrying some papers. As he turned into the corridor, he bumped into a young man being escorted by one of the court policemen. Up till now, when he met a prisoner in the corridors, he would always avert his eyes and step out of the way. Feeling strangely disturbed as they passed each other, he would wonder whether the man had a mother and father, or wife and children, and what had happened to bring him to this place. But today when he turned into the corridor and bumped into the man, he had no time to avoid him.

The prisoner was wearing a deep hat of woven reeds, but he lifted his head and looked reproachfully at Nobuo. Seeing his face, Nobuo nearly cried out, for it was Torao, the boy with whom he had played as a child.

'Little Torao!' Nobuo swallowed the exclamation he was about to utter and looked blankly after Torao, who lowered his head and tried to avoid being recognized.

'Maybe I was mistaken,' Nobuo thought.

Those round eyes, like two little black beans, surely they were Torao's. He remembered affectionately the argument they had had on the roof of the shed, and how Torao always came with Roku the hawker. Torao was a quiet, good-natured boy. What had happened to him afterwards that he should now have his hands tied behind his back? Nobuo was unsettled all day.

Before leaving work he scanned the bulletin board

113

outside the courtroom and found that it was Torao for
certain. He had been accused of theft and assault.

Even when he got home and started his evening meal he
still felt unsettled. He did not notice the sound of the rain
dripping from the eaves.

'What's the matter, Nobuo?' Machiko looked at him in
surprise.

'Huh, what's that?'

'What's wrong with you? You've just been breaking up
the bean curd with your chopsticks.'

Punctilious Nobuo would never break up the cubes of
bean curd; he ate them as they were. But when she spoke
and he looked at his plate, there was the bean curd all in
bits.

'Well, I never, so he has. Nobuo, that's not like you at
all.' Kiku had noticed something strange about Nobuo even
before Machiko, but this was the first mention she had
made of it.

'Are you feeling ill?' she asked, hiding her anxiety. She
was more concerned that something had happened at his
work than for his health.

'Not really, but today's rainy and I'm a bit cold.'

Nobuo was uncertain whether to tell them about Torao
or not. Although he was only a childhood friend, Torao
had shown that he did not want to be recognized, and
therefore Nobuo decided to keep silent about the incident
if he could. But he also thought he ought to reveal something to Kiku and Machiko, as they were anxious about
him. Since his father's death, Nobuo had been filled with
an overflowing love and concern to share everything, both
joys and sorrows, with his mother and sister. He seemed
to have awakened to his position as mainstay of the family.
Now he had lost his father, Nobuo was zealous in his care
for them, and in doing so he became an adult.

After they had finished the meal, Nobuo spoke.

'Mother, do you remember Roku the hawker?'

'Roku, who was he, I wonder?' Kiku's face showed that she did not know anything about him.

'Well, wasn't there a hawker who sold combs and thread and cuff-protectors and things?'

'A hawker?'

'Yes, he used to bring a little boy called Torao along with him. He once pushed me off the outhouse roof.'

When he said this Kiku remembered. 'Of course, that was when your grandmother was still alive. Your father told me about it.' Kiku nodded. She was not going to be drawn too far.

'Ah, Torao, that nice dark-eyed boy.' Machiko clapped her hands as she remembered him. 'I remember playing hide and seek with him. But did Roku ever come to the house?'

Then Nobuo remembered that after his grandmother's death Roku had stopped coming for some reason or other. Two years later it had been just Torao who had come unexpectedly to play and then disappeared again.

'What happened to Roku, I wonder?' Kiku brought the conversation back to the main subject.

'I don't know, but today, in the corridor at the office, I ran slap bang into Torao, my friend when I was a little boy.'

'Fancy that. Where does he live now? He must be grown up by now,' said Machiko.

'It's not like that . . . he had his hands behind his back.' Nobuo showed them, with both wrists together. Kiku and Machiko both raised their voices, 'Well!'

'What happened?' Kiku frowned.

'He's being tried for robbery and assault. It shocked me that such a good-natured fellow would do such a thing. Just to think of it is depressing.'

At Nobuo's words, Kiku and Machiko nodded.

'Now that you mention it, I've seen Torao recently, at Asakusa. There was a man, drunk since noon, with some woman hanging on to him. It was about a fortnight ago.

At the time I thought I'd seen his face before, and after I had gone a little way I realised he looked like Torao.' Machiko was thoughtful.

'That's impossible.' Nobuo could not even imagine what Torao would look like, drunk.

'But at the time I only thought it looked like him. I couldn't really think that it was Torao.' And Machiko looked as though she remembered something else that happened at the time.

'Even if people are good as children, can they really turn out like this?' Nobuo asked his mother, who had been listening intently to their conversation.

'Nobuo, there are times when people change more than they ever imagined they could.' Kiku spoke quietly, her hands folded in her lap. Nobuo had a thought that made him blush. 'I could turn into the kind of person I'd never imagined myself being.' Up to the day he had gone to the Yoshiwara he had never imagined himself as doing such a thing. It was certainly not what he would have done on his own. Until now Nobuo had thought of his true self as the one which had run away. But this was the first time the ugly truth had come home to him, that when he had hurried towards the gate of the Yoshiwara it had also been his true self. Then there were the times when he was beset by mental images of a woman's body and could not sleep. This was a side of himself he would have been ashamed to admit to anyone. So now he was thinking, 'Surely at these times too it's your true self, Nobuo Nagano.'

If the seemingly mild Torao were the real Torao, the real Torao also went about assaulting people and doing things like that. Come to think of it, however much one might say that Torao had just been a child, the fact that he had pushed him off the roof showed that even then he had been capable of doing such things in a fit of temper. Nobuo changed his mind about Torao.

'People are frightening things. There are situations and

times when I'm very kind, but at other times I'm so ill-natured I hate myself.'

Machiko gave a little shrug. Her shoulders had recently taken on a very feminine outline. 'Mother's just the same, you know.' Kiku smiled.

'What! Mother?'

Nobuo had come to think of his mother as always kind and peaceful. 'Where in his mother's life could there be that kind of contradiction?' he thought, looking at his mother's face.

'Don't look so surprised, Nobuo. Your mother's human too. I easily get depressed, and hate people and get angry.'

'That's impossible, it can't be true. I can't imagine you ever hating anyone or getting angry,' Nobuo broke in.

'Nobuo, just because you can't see a person is angry, it doesn't mean they are not. If you think your mother is never angry you're greatly mistaken.'

She had only to remember the time when she was forced to leave Nobuo and get out of the house. Her attitude then towards Tose, who had driven her out, was hardly excusable.

'Pray for those who persecute you.' Kiku's conscience always pained her when she heard these words in church.

After he went to bed, Nobuo thought about what his mother had said. 'Just because you can't see a person is angry, it doesn't mean that they are not.' And, 'There are times when people change more than they ever imagined they could'. He could not say with certainty that in the decades that lay ahead he would not, like Torao, commit some crime. Whatever the circumstances, he did not think he would become a thief. But if he was living in a boarding house and there happened to be a young girl there and he was alone with her some time, he could not deny that desire might turn him into a maddened wolf. Even if she happened to be someone's wife, Nobuo was still afraid that something would happen. Whether he laid hands on somebody's wife or an unmarried girl, it would still be a crime.

'But even if it did not involve breaking the law, it would still not be right. It's not only breaking the law that is wrong.' Nobuo shuddered at the thought.

In their respectable district the evenings were short. There were no sounds, as if everyone was already asleep. Somewhere far away a dog was howling; its voice increased his feeling of loneliness.

He thought about one of his superiors at the office, a most evil-natured man, who would give his juniors vague instructions to bring him certain sets of papers, and scold them severely because they brought the wrong ones. Nobuo had come to the conclusion that he did this deliberately in order to have the opportunity of telling people off. This man was committing no crime, but the effects of his unpleasantness were far more serious than the crime of stealing a few apples. As he wrestled with all this, Nobuo had to make a new assessment of himself.

'Making people unhappy, that's a serious sin too.'

This word 'sin', the more he thought about it, the more points cropped up which he could not define.

'Perhaps the best I can do is to keep from harming anyone else.'

Then another thought struck him. 'Someone like me, always plagued with thinking about women, people don't know what I'm thinking but . . . that can't be wrong too, can it?'

When he tried looking at it in this way, surprisingly it seemed to come closer to being sin than hitting someone in a fight. It was nothing that anyone could see, it threatened no one, but Nobuo was amazed by the strong sense he now had that harbouring such thoughts was sin.

'Can it be that sin is developing right in the depth of my heart, where no one knows about it?' Nobuo was still thinking about this when he fell asleep.

10   The Fig Tree

THE next day, when Nobuo returned from work, he could hear Takashi's loud voice even from the front door.

'Hello. I'm glad you've come.'

He had expected Takashi to be alone, but when he went into the living room, there, sitting on the *tatami* floor, was another guest too, a man of about thirty. His hair hung a little over his forehead and he wore a black kimono and *hakama*.[1] His eyes arrested Nobuo's attention. Only very rarely had he seen such kind and gentle eyes. Nobuo sank to his knees in a formal greeting.

'This is my cousin Nobuo,' said Takashi. 'You know, the fellow with no self-respect who did an about turn and ran away from the Yoshiwara.'

At Takashi's bluntness Nobuo blushed. It was a good thing Machiko and his mother were not there, he was thinking. He had not told them about the visit to the Yoshiwara.

'Hey, stop looking so superior! My friend is a teacher and very knowledgeable. It's a good opportunity to ask him questions – anything you like,' Takashi went on. But Nobuo still had no idea who the man was.

'What sort of teacher?' he asked, still sitting up formally.

'What sort of teacher? He's the best in Japan. He's Harusame Nakamura, the novelist.'

Nobuo had not heard of him. But for someone who enjoyed reading as much as he did, to meet a novelist was a rare treat.

'I'm Harusame Nakamura. Pleased to meet you. I live

[1] Formal dress for a Japanese man.

119

next door to Takashi, and I'm indebted to him in many
ways.'

'He wants to do some research, so he may stay in Tokyo
as long as six months. You could learn all sorts of things
from him in that time,' Takashi said flatteringly. He was
in a good mood. The economy might be in a bad way, but
Takashi's shop at least was making steady progress.

'This is one of my novels.' Nakamura drew a book from
the folds of his kimono and laid it in front of Nobuo. It
was called *The Fig Tree*.

One fine Sunday afternoon, Nobuo picked the book up.
As was his habit when starting a new book, he held it in
his hands for a moment or two, enjoying the feel of its
weight. In the garden the azalea blossoms were scarlet
under the 'eight fingers' tree. It was a very peaceful spot.
A bee, its wings glinting in the sun, seemed to hesitate a
little and then settled on an azalea. Times like this were
the happiest in Nobuo's life. Always, before starting to
read, Nobuo would hold the book quietly and try to
imagine what was in it. Here was a world he had not yet
visited, a story he did not yet know. And this book was a
special one, received directly from the hands of the author.
Just to wonder what sort of novel the gentle Harusame
Nakamura with his smiling face would have written, was
a pleasure. For some reason Nobuo had thought of novelists
as pompous and degenerate. But there was certainly no
pomposity about Nakamura. There was a candid light in
his narrow eyes.

Before he had read many pages Nobuo was completely
absorbed. It was the story of a Japanese named Hatomiya
who went to America, became a Christian and married an
American girl, Emille. But before leaving Japan he had
had an affair with a Japanese girl, Sawa. Sawa was later
married against her will, murdered her husband and was
sent to prison. On his return from America with Emille,
Hatomiya became the minister of a church. But one day

Sawa escaped from prison and came to him. Desperate to spare his wife all knowledge of this affair, he panicked and hid Sawa in a rented room. But then he visited her from time to time and their intimacy was revived.

Emille, meanwhile, made a home for three beggar children. She did not know that one of them, a girl of twelve, was Hatomiya's illegitimate child by Sawa. Eventually Sawa was recaptured and Hatomiya was also sent to prison. His parents resented having a foreigner in the family and made life difficult for Emille, but her Christlike forbearance and forgiving spirit, even when her husband's behaviour became known, finally won them over. When Hatomiya was released, he learned that Sawa had committed suicide in prison and, tormented by the fact that he had been to blame from the beginning, he was unable to forgive himself. He was found on the railway line, killed by a passing train.

Nobuo finished the novel of over three hundred pages at a single sitting. The sun had already set, and everything was tinged with the colours of evening. Feeling disappointed, Nobuo turned his tired eyes towards the garden but not to look at anything. The red of the azaleas was duskier than at noon, and before long the flowers and foliage had almost completely vanished into the dark. 'When peace had finally come to the Hatomiya family, why should this be the tragic conclusion?' he pondered. He could not help but think it a pity.

He felt more sorry for the angelic Emille than for the dead Hatomiya. No matter how much one is oppressed by a sense of guilt and sin, surely it is not necessary to torture oneself to that extent. Thinking about Hatomiya gave him a feeling of self-satisfaction. 'If a man who has faith finished up in such a way, then I who do not believe in anything, am better off.' This was the conclusion he felt compelled to draw. On the other hand, Emille's manner of life was so different. When Hatomiya's parents did not speak to her, or abused her for not dusting the room properly, she never got angry. More than that she often tried to comfort her husband, who had betrayed her, when he was in prison. And when Sawa died she took charge of the body and had it buried with due ceremony. This filled Nobuo with amazement. Wasn't Sawa Emille's rival, her enemy? To keep her rival's child and bring her up kindly would not be at all easy. Nobuo was impressed by Emille's beautiful spirit. He continued to think about the novel even during the evening meal. He felt that it was completely different from anything he had ever read. Just what was different was hard to say clearly, but it left a deep impression.

'You've been studying hard today, haven't you, Nobuo? I went to your room two or three times but you never noticed me.'

'Huh, I was reading an interesting novel.'

'What, a novel?' Machiko frowned a little.

'Machiko, there's nothing wrong with reading a novel.'

'But it's just made up stories, isn't it? You'd be better off reading the Bible.'

When he heard the word 'Bible', Nobuo became silent. He knew that his mother and Machiko had Bibles, but up till now he had had no inclination to read one and judge for himself. Now, when he heard the word, Nobuo wanted to get hold of one. He wanted to investigate the book that Hatomiya and Emille had read every day.

' "There is no one righteous; no, not one." Is that written in the Bible?'

'Hey, Nobuo, when did you hear that? That's one of the most important verses in the Bible,' said Machiko eagerly. Nobuo could not avoid a feeling of respect mingled with jealousy over his young sister, who knew things that he did not.

'Nobuo, what's the title of the novel?' Kiku turned and smiled at Nobuo. Hearing him speak a verse of Scripture, Kiku felt so happy that she wanted to shout out loud.

'It's *The Fig Tree*, by Harusame Nakamura, who came

here with Cousin Takashi the other day :' He had forgotten
to tell his mother about the book.

'Nobuo, is he really a novelist? He's such a quiet,
respectable sort of man.' Machiko stopped eating. It
seemed that she also thought novelists were not like normal
people.

'I heard that Mr Nakamura was a novelist, but does he
put verses of Scripture and things like that in his books?'
Kiku asked in surprise.

'Well, you see, the story is about a Christian minister,
but there are things that I don't understand.'

'About a minister. Then he was a good man, wasn't he,
Nobuo?'

'I don't really know. He was extremely conscientious
and very repentant about something he did over ten years
before, but while he was in this state he did things like
betraying his wife.'

'Well, I don't like that,' Machiko pouted. 'It was only a
novel, you know. A minister would not betray his wife.
Novelists don't know much about ministers.'

'Machiko, I don't think that's quite right. Ministers are
human. As long as you're a human being, no matter how
splendid your faith may be, you can't say that you will not
fall to Satan's temptations.'

'But I think Mr Nakamura is terrible. He's got no right
to write in such a way about a minister.'

'But, Machiko, as far as I'm concerned, I don't know
whether the author is right or wrong.'

'If anyone betrays his wife, that's certainly wrong. A
man as bad as that couldn't be a minister.'

'Machiko and Nobuo, listen to me. You are thinking
that there are two kinds of people, good and bad, but there
is only one kind. It's just like Nobuo said before, "There
is no one righteous; no, not one". In the sight of God it is
quite certain there is no one who is just.' Kiku spoke
quietly but sternly.

'Well . . . maybe. But I think there are some truly honest, sincere, true-hearted people in the world.'

'Nobuo, I used to think that too, but at church the minister says the same as Mother did.' Machiko's expression indicated that for her the matter was decided.

'Then you mean to say it's not impossible that a minister would betray his wife?'

'Yes,' Kiku replied. 'At least I think so. But I don't mean that our minister is like that. Not one in a hundred would be so bad, but such a thing might happen, very occasionally.'

'But, Mother, is it really true that there are no righteous people in the world?'

'I don't think there are any.'

When this was stated so simply and clearly, Nobuo felt ashamed. He had included himself in the category of the good people, and was disappointed that his mother did not think of him as a perfectly upright young man.

'I gave up going to university to take care of her and Machiko, and Mother doesn't credit me with being a good person,' he thought. 'I don't go out to enjoy myself. I come straight home from work. I don't drink. I don't smoke.' Nobuo more and more had a compelling urge to justify himself.

'Nobuo, you don't look convinced. You think that you are so well behaved you must be righteous, I suppose.'

Nobuo gave a wry laugh. His thoughts had been read only too well. The meal had finished, but the three still sat where they were, continuing to talk.

'Nobuo, what sort of man do you think your father was?'

'I think he was a very fine man, much, much better than I am.'

'But your father never said he was a righteous man. He said he was a sinful man. He said he had a tendency to think of himself as better than others. "There is no greater sin than this in the sight of God," he used to say.'

It was only three months after Masayuki's death. Kiku's voice sounded strained and Machiko's eyes filled with tears.

'Is that so? Did Father say that? But he really was a fine man and there's nothing odd about thinking of him as a wonderful person.' Nobuo kept his voice cheerful on purpose.

'No, if anybody thinks they are superior it shows they are not. I don't know if you can understand this at the moment, Nobuo, but I'm sure the time will come when you will.'

That a person who thought himself superior might not be so, was a painful truth for Nobuo. He liked to be praised, whatever he did. The more he considered this idea, the stranger it seemed.

One evening, about ten days after Nobuo had finished *The Fig Tree*, Harusame Nakamura called unexpectedly. Maybe it was the searching look Nakamura gave him, but Nobuo felt as if it was the first time he had met him, and looked long and repeatedly at his face. His hair, without a trace of oil, hung down over his broad forehead as it had done before. The previous time he had called, Takashi had merely introduced them and he had left almost immediately, having said very little.

Nobuo gave him a friendly welcome. 'Thank you for your book. I've read it.'

'What do you think of it?' Nakamura replied, scratching his head shyly.

'Well . . . there are several things that are hard to understand, aren't there?'

'Maybe . . . It's not really a novel for everyone.'

'That minister. Basically he was a bad man, wasn't he?' Nobuo had to ask this.

'Well, you could not say that anyone isn't bad.'

'Recently my mother said something like that. So you do too?' Nobuo was too shy to ask if he was a Christian.

'Are you asking me if I'm a Christian? Of course I am,'

Nakamura replied casually. He was neither boasting nor furtive about it.

'Is that so? You are a Christian too. Then wouldn't it have been better if you had written more in praise of the minister?'

'Why?'

'Well, to be frank, most people don't like Christianity. My mother had to leave me as a new-born baby and was turned out of the house, just because she admitted she was a Yaso. To make people think better of Christianity it would have been preferable to write about the minister's good points, but . . .'

'Oh . . . your Mother suffered that much, did she?' Harusame Nakamura looked in surprise in the direction of the parlour where Kiku was. Takashi had never mentioned to him that Kiku was a Christian or that she had been forced to leave home for her faith. All he had said was, 'You might not think it, but I have a beautiful aunt in Tokyo.' That Kiku was indeed beautiful, had two children and had recently lost her husband, was all he knew.

'Your mother left you here and lived alone, did she?' Nakamura's face showed his keen interest.

'I was told that my mother was dead, and my grand-mother brought me up. She was a real Yaso hater it seems. My father was not the sort of person to oppose her, and so there was nothing for it but to be separated from his wife. But he used to visit her on his way back from work, and my sister was born without my knowing about it.'

'Is that so? Well, then, you, your father and your mother all suffered, didn't you?'

'Maybe, but my grandmother took ancestral Buddhism so seriously that to have a Yaso daughter-in-law was a disgrace and she could not have her in the house.'

Unconsciously Nobuo was protecting his grandmother Tose.

'People still think that ministers and Christians are good-for-nothing people, just as I wrote in my novel.'

'To tell you the truth, I don't like Yaso very much either. It's a Japanese characteristic, copying Western things, using foreign words like "Amen", believing in a foreigner called Jesus as a god, and it doesn't appeal to me at all.' Nobuo spoke frankly. He felt there was no need to be tactful about what he said to Harusame Nakamura. He thought Nakamura's face reflected sincerity. No, it was more than sincerity, it was genuine affection.

'I suppose so, in the beginning I felt like that too.' Nakamura nodded, showing that what Nobuo said was not unreasonable.

'How did you become a Christian?'

'Well, I thought you would ask that. But there are rather many things to explain.'

As if to try and remember something, Nakamura stopped speaking for a moment. Kiku came in with tea and bean paste sweets.

'Thank you for the fine book we received the other day.' She addressed him formally.

'Not at all. I'm really quite ashamed of it!' he answered, bowing. 'But . . . I hear you are a Christian too.' Something like awe showed in Nakamura's manner. He would not have thought she was Nobuo's mother. Yet in her perfumed freshness there was a hint of the grief of bereavement.

'People like me are not really worthy of being called Christians,' Kiku answered quietly, her eyes cast down. Harusame Nakamura looked fixedly at her, impressed by the fact that in this woman there was a faith strong enough to make her leave home.

'That's not so. I've already heard the gist of your story from Nobuo. I hold the same faith, but it makes me sad when I wonder how long it will be until Christians are really accepted in Japan.'

As he heard the two of them talking, Nobuo was amazed

that he should dislike the faith of such worthy people. 'From the beginning I've been prejudiced and never tried to find out what true Christianity is like,' he thought. Why, he did not even know what the Christian teachings were. He had not read the Bible to see what was in it. He was prejudiced because Christianity was a foreign religion and had a Western flavour. Without any good reasons, his dislike for Christianity had grown. Yet there was one thing that Harusame Nakamura and his mother and dead father had in common. That was modesty, if nothing else. If this had developed as a result of their being Christians and was not theirs by nature, it would be worthwhile to re-examine Christianity.

'Mother, how did you become a Christian believer?'

This was the first time Nobuo had asked this question. Seeing his earnestness, Kiku was taken aback. But after a little nod she said, 'All right,' and then paused a moment to think.

'Ever since I was quite small, you know . . . I used to wonder why people were born into this world, what was the purpose of life, and what happened after death. However, one day when we had gone on a pleasure trip to a village near Osaka I saw something terrible. There was some shouting and a disturbance going on in the street and we thought it was a fight, so we went out to see. Everyone was shouting "Yaso priest, filthy priest!" and cursing a young man. He was standing there quietly, but a man came up and said, "If you're a filthy priest, eat this," and took a dipper from the cesspit and poured the filthy stuff over him. Although his head, his eyes and his mouth were all covered with muck, the young man said nothing but went off to the nearby river. The heartless villagers all scattered, but I was just a child and watched him from the bridge. And what do you think happened? When he had finished washing his face and hair, he began to sing at the top of his voice. His face was so radiant that it made an indelible impression upon me.'

'They were terrible villagers, weren't they, Mother?'

'They really were. So after that did you become a Christian?'

'What I saw that day with the impressionable eyes of a child I was never able to forget, but I did not become a Christian immediately. There was no one to teach me. Two years before my marriage a guest who often came to our home began to teach me about Christianity and I soon believed.'

'But you had received Buddhism from your ancestors. There was no need to believe a foreign religion, was there?'

'But Nobuo, I worked it out like this. Everyone was saying that Christianity was a false religion and hating it, but knowing my story you must wonder which is the false religion. Those villagers evidently knew that Buddhism was the religion of Japan, but if they had really followed the teachings of Gautama Buddha, why did they torment a young man who had done them no harm, and cover him with muck? It was the faith of the man who suffered silently and then sang with joy which commended itself to my way of thinking, rather than the faith of his persecutors.' Kiku spoke in an impartial tone and Nobuo listened silently.

'Religion is a pretty troublesome thing, isn't it? In the history of Christianity there have been religious wars which are far from praiseworthy,' Nakamura murmured, with his arms folded.

'That's so. They were Christians but still men, and therefore they were not all righteous. However, for me, an unmarried girl, I think it was a sense of righteous indignation which brought me to faith.'

'Then, Mother, there's nothing particularly bad about believing in Buddhism, is there?' Nobuo asked with a sense of relief.

'If that is the road you choose, then I won't say anything about it.' Kiku and Harusame Nakamura looked at one another and nodded with a smile of understanding. Nobuo felt that somehow he alone was different and cut off from them.

'Mother!' Machiko called out as she opened the sliding doors of the sitting room.

Bring them in here, please.' And Machiko came in, slightly shy, carrying some tea and biscuits.

'Last time I saw you just for a moment. You are a very attractive girl.' Nakamura greeted her with the appropriate courtesies and looked calmly at her as she joined them on the *tatami.*

'Do you write novels?' Machiko's natural friendliness broke through her reserve.

'Do you read novels?'

'No, I don't understand things like novels yet.'

'It would be a good thing if you read Mr Nakamura's *The Fig Tree.*'

'But there's something bad about a minister in it, isn't there? What did you write bad things about a minister for?' She had a slightly resentful note in her voice.

'Are you a Christian too?'

'Yes, I am, and ever since I was small I've been to church,' Machiko replied, folding the sleeves of her purple kimono, patterned with arrows, in her lap.

'Is that so? Then you really can't do anything but scold a man who writes bad things about ministers! I certainly can't claim to have enough faith to become a minister – and even supposing I had, I think I would soon fall, if I was attacked by Satan. I'm only a man. If we are not careful we tend to trust in our own strength, don't you think? Even a minister who is too self-confident may find his faith crumble away. So this novel is a warning to us believers to discipline ourselves. If you read the verses of Scripture at the beginning of the book, you'll understand, I think.'

Nobuo opened the book and looked. The quotation was from the thirteenth chapter of Luke's Gospel.

'Those eighteen upon whom the tower of Siloam fell and killed them, do you think they were worse offenders than all the others who dwelt in Jerusalem? I tell you, No! But unless you repent you will all likewise perish. And he told this parable: A man had a fig tree planted in his vineyard; and he came seeking fruit on it and found none. And he said to the vinedresser, "Lo, these three years I have come seeking fruit on this fig tree, and I find none. Cut it down; why should it use up the ground?" And he answered him, "Let it alone, sir, this year also, till I dig about it and put on manure. And if it bears fruit next year, well and good; but if not, you can cut it down".'

'I know what you're saying; it says in the Bible, "There is no one righteous; no, not one",' replied Machiko. 'But what I say is, if you write bad things about a minister, Christians will be called fools even more.'

'Then I don't know what to say.' Brushing his hair back from his forehead Harusame Nakamura sounded distressed.

'But when I read the book, I thought the wife Emille was a very wonderful person,' said Nobuo. 'For example, when she took some medicine to her mother-in-law and had the medicine cup thrown at her, she bore the pain of the gash with a smile. And then she lovingly cared for the child of her husband's lover. And when Sawa killed herself in prison she had the body buried properly. To tell you the truth, it made me weep.'

'Was she such a wonderful wife? Why did her husband betray her if she was such a fine person?' Machiko picked up the book from where it lay near Nobuo. 'May I have a look?'

'A novel is a complicated thing. The minister who betrayed his wife even when she was so kind and generous, is a picture of ourselves, Christian believers who, although we experience God's love, still fall into unbelief. It's difficult to make my purpose understood by everybody, and

even in my own church some people got quite angry about
it!' Nakamura looked at Nobuo and Machiko in turn.

'That's too bad,' said Kiku, taking a sip of tea.

'I don't know much about Christianity, but isn't this
novel a sort of reflection on teacher Nakamura's faith and
life?'

'Maybe that's so.'

'Even though I don't understand it all, this novel really
stirred me up. It will always leave a deep impression on
me.'

'Is that so? It really spoke to you, did it?' Harusame
Nakamura smiled happily.

Before he left, he told them that he would be in Tokyo
for some time and would call again.

11 A Game of Cards

FROM that time on, Nobuo's thoughts imperceptibly turned to God.

It was a rainy day in early June. Nobuo was opening his lunch box during the noon break. It was a two-tiered porcelain one with a blue floral pattern. Somehow it made him feel aware of his mother. Accompanying the rice there was a slice of omelette, some fried meat with sweet and sour sauce, some boiled 'devil's tongue' jelly and fried bean curd, with two slices of pickled horse-radish as a relish. Nobuo gazed absent-mindedly out of the window as he ate. The window opened on to the quadrangle. A single Empress tree grew tall and straight, and beneath it there was a red rose, drenched with rain.

'Beautiful!' he thought. Then he gasped. 'To think that such beauty should grow out of such dirt.'

How strange this was. Although he had often looked at the garden at home, the beauty of the flowers had never before struck him as particularly remarkable. Every year, in front of his window, the yellow Japanese rose bloomed, the iris came into flower and the tree peony blossomed. These things happened as a matter of course; one took them for granted. But now, looking at the glistening red rose, Nobuo wondered if this attitude was right. It surprised him that he had never before been amazed that white and yellow, blue and red, all kinds of flowers should grow out of the earth.

'That's a beautiful rose, isn't it,' he remarked to his colleague at the next desk.

'Uh, it comes out every year.' His mouth stuffed with

133

rice, he cast only a brief glance at the rose. Looking at him, Nobuo thought, 'What an unfeeling creature he must be.' But on reflection he himself was equally lacking in feelings. Until now he had done no more than comment that a flower was in bloom. If something he had always taken for granted had appeared in a new light, it followed that everything else called for reappraisal.

'It's not just the flowers,' he pondered. 'In the morning a day begins, and then night comes. That can't be taken for granted. There are parts of the universe where it's night all year long, and parts where it's day all the time. And aren't there places on earth where it's twilight all day long?' Nobuo's thoughts rambled on.

'But first of all, I wonder where I came from?' Of course he knew that he came from his mother, but why accept this as a matter of course? His father and mother had not planned to produce this person who was himself. The baby born to them just happened by chance to have his individual personality.

'But wait, was it by chance?' Nobuo remembered the word 'necessity'. Was his existence a matter of necessity or a matter of chance?

His thoughts were interrupted by the office boy calling him. 'Mr Nagano, there is someone to see you.' The office boy turned away and went out into the corridor. Nobuo had been working in the law courts for only a couple of months. Who could possibly wish to see him? He had no idea.

Glancing at his reflection in the rain-spattered window pane, he straightened his jacket and went out into the corridor. There he found a kimono-clad young man standing, a tall, robust fellow with a round face. Nobuo could not recollect having seen him before.

'Well, well, Nagano. It's me, Yoshikawa!' The young man held out a large hand and laughed disarmingly.

'What, are you really? Down from Hokkaido?' Nobuo's voice sounded hollow with surprise.

'That's right. I'm Yoshikawa all right. You're still as pale as ever. I'm sure I'd have recognized you anywhere.' Wistfully he looked Nobuo up and down from head to foot, again and again. Yoshikawa looked easily five or six years older than Nobuo.

'My, Yoshikawa, you really have grown up. Tell me, when did you come to Tokyo?'

'This morning. My grandmother died and my mother said she wanted to attend the funeral whatever happened. But, of course, it was too far for us to be in time. However, it was a question of filial duty, so even though we were too late, the three of us decided to take ten days off and come.'

'The three of you! That must have been quite an undertaking.' Nobuo's heart missed a beat when he heard that all three of them had come.

Promising to visit Nobuo's home later that day, Yoshikawa said goodbye and left.

The drizzly rain continued until the evening. Knowing his friend would be coming, Nobuo was unable to relax. He made innumerable journeys to the front gate and then returned to his room. While he was waiting there was something else on his mind – he was hoping for a chance to meet Fujiko again. Yet it was something he was unwilling to admit to himself, and, of course, would not want anyone else to suspect. As he looked at the stepping stones between the front door and the gate, glistening wet with rain, Nobuo was enveloped in feelings he had never experienced before.

'Nobuo. I've never seen the like of it. Go and sit down in your room. When Yoshikawa comes I will tell you straight away.' It was as though Machiko could read his thoughts. He felt vaguely ill at ease.

'No, I was wondering if he had forgotten the way . . .' Nobuo mumbled, and went back to his room. It was nearly ten years since Yoshikawa had left Tokyo, and the place had changed considerably, he tried to persuade himself. But his thoughts produced nothing but anxiety.

Not long after that, he heard Machiko call, 'Nobuo, Nobuo, someone's here.'

Flustered, Nobuo stood up, sat down again, then finally got up slowly.

'Perhaps Yoshikawa has come by himself,' he told himself doubtfully.

Nobuo caught his breath as he came into the entrance hall. Standing behind Yoshikawa's large form was a beautiful fair-complexioned girl with her hair parted in the middle.

'Come in,' he said, looking at Yoshikawa. He was unable to let himself relax and felt stiff and formal. So as not to let this show, he tried to sound at ease. 'You're late,' he said with a laugh.

'I'm terribly sorry. We're like complete strangers in these parts,' replied Yoshikawa cheerily, and glanced behind him. 'I've brought Fujiko along too,' he said.

'How are you all?' said Fujiko. She turned to Machiko with a nod and then bowed in silence to Nobuo. The Yukijima kimono with its red muslin sash was very attractive.

'It's lovely to see you. We thought you'd be sure to come along too, and we were looking forward to seeing you. Weren't we . . .?' Machiko made it sound as though Nobuo had also been very much waiting for Fujiko.

'Er, well . . . I . . .' Nobuo scratched his head, not knowing what to say, and abruptly led the way into the room where they received visitors.

Yoshikawa followed unhesitatingly, with his large strides. 'I can scarcely believe that I'm here again. This house is just the same as it was ten years ago. Isn't this the same mountain picture?' He wandered nostalgically around the room. It was still light enough for the garden to be seen through the glass doors of the verandah.

'How big the "eight fingers" tree has grown.' Yoshikawa

turned to Nobuo and gazed at him keenly. 'It's been a long time, hasn't it?'

'Yes, ten whole years.'

Machiko and Fujiko did not go straight into the sitting room, but stayed for a while in the entrance hall, laughing together as if they were old friends.

'First, will you allow me to pay my respects?' Yoshikawa glanced around to the Buddhist altar, its doors standing open.

'Ah, thank you. But I'm afraid there's no memorial tablet to my father.'

'Huh?'

'It appears that my father suddenly became a follower of Christianity.' Nobuo felt embarrassed.

'Is that so? In that case I needn't have brought any incense sticks,' Yoshikawa said unexpectedly, and opened the bundle he was carrying. 'However, since you have an altar, these might come in handy,' and he laid the incense sticks in front of Nobuo.

'And here is some dried seaweed from Hokkaido.' He produced a large paper parcel.

'That's very kind of you. But it must have been quite something for you to carry this all the way from Hokkaido.' Nobuo bowed formally, in thanks. Just then his mother came into the room with Fujiko and Machiko.

'My, how you've grown! You've turned into a fine young man,' said Kiku affectionately, and expressed her condolences over the death of his grandmother and his father, though he had been dead for a number of years. 'And your sister has grown into a beautiful young lady.'

Fujiko's bright eyes and attractively shaped, smiling lips were even more beautiful than Nobuo had ever imagined. Moreover, there was more to her beauty than mere good looks. There was a radiance about her as though the purity of her heart was shining through.

'Fujiko certainly is very beautiful,' said Machiko with

unconcealed admiration. There was nothing about the appearance of either Yoshikawa or Fujiko to suggest that they had suffered the loss of their father while they were still young children. Rather, as if having lived through long winters in the pure white snows and having learned to endure the cold of bitter experience, they were endowed with a purity and simplicity of character.

Kiku had prepared *sukiyaki*, in honour of the guests. The sliced beef and vegetables were laid out appetisingly on the table, and the skillet was bubbling, all ready for them.

Yoshikawa said hardly anything about what had happened to them from the time of his father's death up to the present. He did not say whether it had been hard, or whether he had wanted to continue his schooling. He only spoke of Hokkaido's wide open spaces, and of the cold. As they listened it seemed as though he was like a young tree on the plains of Hokkaido, its branches stretching upwards and outwards.

'Nobuo, why don't you come to Hokkaido too?' asked Yoshikawa earnestly, at the same time heartily attacking a piece of meat.

'Hokkaido? Ah, but that's too far away,' Nobuo answered, recoiling.

'Don't say such cowardly things! If you look at the atlas, why, Japan's just a tiny place. How can you say that Hokkaido is far away, when nowadays even girls go all the way to America to study?' Yoshikawa gave a loud laugh.

'Yes, but there are bears in Hokkaido, aren't there? I'd be scared!' Machiko screwed up her face as if terrified.

'No, no, I've never set eyes on a bear yet.'

'Oh, is that true?'

'Of course. If you ask me, it's the bears who are afraid of human beings. However many there may be in the mountains, there aren't any in big towns like Sapporo.'

'All the same, I'd be afraid to live in Hokkaido.'

'Not at all. A place like Edo here, all swarming with people, is far more terrifying.'

While they were talking, Nobuo became conscious that he was in Fujiko's line of vision. When his eyes met hers an indescribably strange feeling welled up in his heart. He looked away, agitatedly, but in no time Fujiko's beautiful forehead and sparkling eyes captured his glance once again.

When the meal was over, the three women went into the living room. As they went out Nobuo's eyes involuntarily followed Fujiko, dragging her leg a little as she walked. At the sight of her unsteady movements he felt as though he wanted to go and put his arm around her shoulder. Yoshikawa sat in silence watching Nobuo's face as he gazed after Fujiko.

'Nobuo, do you feel sorry for Fujiko?' His question threw Nobuo into confusion.

'No, not at all . . . I was just thinking how pretty she has become,' replied Nobuo before he could realize what he was saying.

'Well, you know that she has a bad leg. But she has never once said that she hates people to see her. She thinks nothing of going shopping every day and, as you see, even in Tokyo she wasn't too shy to come and see you.'

It was dark outside. Nobuo stood up and closed the papered sliding doors which opened on to the verandah.

'But all the same, I think she's different from other girls in some ways. She reads a lot of books. She doesn't seem to be in the least bit jealous of other people, and I've never once heard her complain about her leg and what not. You know I think I'd almost go as far as to say that she's lucky to have a bad leg. It makes her so much more aware of herself in her approach to life.'

Yoshikawa's face was shining with compassion for his young sister. Nobuo wondered if he would be capable of thinking of Machiko in such an adoring way, and realized again what a cold-hearted creature he was.

'You're an extraordinary character. Even when you were a child you were streets ahead of me.' Nobuo wondered what could have made him speak like this.

'Not a bit of it. You are the one who is a real gentleman.'

'No, I haven't any of your large-heartedness and warmth of personality. There is something indescribably warm about you!'

'I don't know about that, but if there's truth in it, it's due to Fujiko. Ever since I was small I felt deeply about her leg and wanted to help her above everything else. If I got some cakes I would want to give most of them to Fujiko. When we were walking I wanted to let her walk on the best part of the road. I got more pleasure out of seeing Fujiko receiving a gift than from receiving anything myself. Without my realizing it, this has affected my whole attitude to life. You would be the same, if by chance your sister, if Machiko I mean, were disabled in any way.'

'Do you think so?' Nobuo replied incredulously.

'Of course. In fact something has just occurred to me, Nagano. I wonder if sick and deformed people and such like are not in this world for a special purpose, to soften people's hearts.'

Yoshikawa's eyes were shining. But Nobuo looked doubtful, as though unable to take in the meaning of what he was saying.

'That's it, Nagano. Until now I've always just felt sorry for Fujiko having a bad leg. I've never wondered why she should have been born with this misfortune. I've always thought it was such a terrible shame. But when we see the sufferings of people who are ill, we feel sympathy for them, we wonder if something can't be done to ease their pain. If there were no sick, no disabled people in the world, wouldn't everyone live their lives without showing sympathy or gentleness? As far as Fujiko's leg is concerned, I feel it has had a very big influence on my development!' Yoshikawa spoke earnestly.

'I see what you mean. Perhaps you're right. But on the other hand, not all people are like you, feeling nothing but sympathy for the weak of this world. There are cases where, when a person is ill for a long time, even the members of their own family wish in their hearts that they would hurry up and die.'

'Yes, there's no disputing the fact. Take Fujiko for instance. Ever since she was small, she has been made fun of, even by little children, and even now there are lots of folk who look down on her.'

Yoshikawa folded his arms. Muscular and sun-tanned, they stood out against the navy and white of his kimono sleeves. From the direction of the living room they could hear the voices of Machiko and the others.

'Hmm, is that so?'

Yoshikawa nodded deeply.

'Well, let's put it this way. Aren't people like Fujiko a kind of touchstone for the rest of us? If all people were alike, none superior in intelligence or in looks or physique, no one would know what kind of a person he really was. But, supposing we have a person who is sick. One man looks at him and his heart is drawn out in sympathy, and another looks at him and feels callous. In this way people clearly fall into two groups. Don't you think this makes sense?'

Yoshikawa's earnest eyes scanned Nobuo's face for a reply and Nobuo nodded solemnly. As he did so he remembered the beauty of the rose which he had enjoyed that very lunch time. He could not help feeling that each and every thing on earth had a purpose.

'You've made a real point there. Do you always think deeply about things, like this?'

'No, I'm not specially aware of it.'

'I used to be fairly self-reliant, but lately I've begun to feel that my existence has no particular value. Now, listening to you, I'm beginning to think that after all I may have some mission or other to fulfil.'

'Yes, I think you're right,' Yoshikawa agreed. 'I suppose there are ways of thinking which can see no meaning in life at all. To some people, human beings and dogs and cats are all alike, nothing but animals; and then, when they die, all is just nothingness. But on the other hand there are those who live with an intense awareness that their own personality is of the utmost concern.'

The two of them sensed a pure joy that each was able to communicate his thoughts so freely to the other.

'That's right,' Nobuo said. 'If you can say that everything is meaningless, you've said all you can say, but personally I want to live life feeling the meaning of every word deeply. For instance, when we think about your father and mine, who died so suddenly, don't you agree we could say that we who are left behind experience the life of those who are dead living within us?'

For the first time Nobuo began to think of Masayuki's life as something precious, and was able to appreciate the meaning of the indissoluble bond which bound him to his father.

'Nagano, how can I express myself? You and I are people who want to live life seriously, facing up to the important questions, such as death and love. I feel quite sure about that as I sit talking to you. But in the rush of everyday life there are few friends with whom one can talk like this, and unless one is careful, one can live at a very superficial level. If you were in Hokkaido, we could have wonderful times together.'

Nobuo could not help thinking, too, that if he was able to talk with Yoshikawa like this every day, his life also would be greatly enriched.

'Rather than have me go to Hokkaido, why don't you come back to Tokyo?'

'I'm afraid that would be out of the question. You see, somehow Hokkaido suits my disposition. The winters are long enough to bore you to tears . . . Everything is blanketed in white snow, there's not a speck of green to

be seen . . . Apart from the pine trees, all the trees look
dead . . . At first, when I saw these vast wastes I thought
that this was nature shrouded in death. But when, after
about half a year of winter, the green grass appears from
beneath the snow, I know that winter is by no means a
dead season. Lately I've even come to wonder if the death
of human beings may not be just like the winter in Hokkaido, and that sometime we will come back again as large
as life. Winter in Hokkaido is terribly severe. Ah, it's
impossible for a person in Tokyo even to imagine how
severe it is. Why, it's so cold that if you don't look sharp
you get frozen to death, and when you get into one of
those snow storms where you can't see an inch in front of
you, there's no way of telling where the road ends and the
fields begin. People die in the snow storms every year. But
I reckon the severity of nature is necessary for me.'

'I see what you mean. Through the long winter,
whether it's a case of waiting or merely enduring, I suppose you inevitably acquire a certain amount of patience.'

Nobuo tried to envisage the bitterness and length of the
winters in Hokkaido, a place he had never yet seen. He
could hardly bear the thought that Yoshikawa had already
experienced almost ten of these winters of which he himself
knew nothing. It made him sad to think that so long as
he continued to live in Tokyo he would drift along,
perhaps to the end of his days, in this mild climate, never
knowing exactly when spring had come or turned into
summer, or whether it was autumn or not. He had no
inclination to live the rest of his days in Hokkaido, but he
felt it would do no harm to go there for four or five years
and see what it was like.

At that moment the sliding doors opened and Machiko
brought them some tea.

'You're having a lively discussion, aren't you? Mother
says, please, won't you stay here tonight?'

'Oh, of course you must. I was thinking about that too,

Machiko. Yoshikawa, don't just say you'll stay tonight; please stay with us as long as you are in Tokyo.'

'If you say so, I'd love to stay, but aren't we putting you to a lot of trouble?'

Yoshikawa lifted the cup in his big hands and gulped down the tea.

'Not at all. The pleasure is ours, isn't it, Nobuo?'

'Of course. Even if we were to keep talking all night long and not go to sleep, we'd still not run out of topics for conversation.'

Nobuo badly wanted them to stay.

'Very well then, we'll impose on your hospitality tonight at any rate,' answered Yoshikawa; whereupon Machiko pleaded, 'Then let us join you for a while. I wouldn't mind having a game of cards.'

'Cards!' Nobuo smiled sardonically. Machiko was still just a little girl after all. 'All right then. I suppose we could. There's no need for Fujiko to be bored.'

The four young people and Kiku sat down for a game, Machiko next to Nobuo, then Kiku and Fujiko, and Yoshikawa completed the circle. Even Nobuo, who did not usually enjoy playing cards, had an enjoyable evening.

'Ah, Mr Nagano, you had that card all the time!' Whenever Fujiko spoke to him, an irrepressible joy filled Nobuo's heart. As the game proceeded he had a feeling that this evening would be one that he would remember for the rest of his life.

That night he and Yoshikawa slept in the same room, their beds spread out side by side.

'Yoshikawa, you must be very tired after travelling all the way from Hokkaido,' Nobuo remarked. Yoshikawa seemed to be thinking about something.

'No, I'm not tired. Although I'm called a railwayman, in actual fact I'm a labourer; I hoist luggage around. I had a good sleep on the train, and slept a bit today after I visited your office.'

Yoshikawa denied that he was tired, but the tone of his

voice seemed to suggest otherwise. Nobuo was puzzled, but did not like to probe further.

'You know, Yoshikawa, I read an interesting novel recently. What's more, I received the book from the author himself.' As if he was trying to arouse Yoshikawa's interest, Nobuo talked about *The Fig Tree*, and summarized the plot.

'It certainly sounds interesting.' Yoshikawa, who was nodding and grunting his approval, raised his head from the pillow.

'It would be good if you could read it too. It really makes you sit up. I couldn't stop thinking about it for a day or two.'

Yoshikawa suddenly sprang up and sat cross-legged on his bed.

'Do you mean it? You really are a dark horse. To look at you one would think you were one of those steady types, who never even look at a novel.'

'Oh, I do sometimes,' Nobuo answered, 'but I hardly ever go to a play,' he added with a laugh and a passing blush.

'That reminds me, your letter about going to the gate of the Yoshiwara really took me by surprise.' This blunt reference made Nobuo blush all over again.

'I was relieved to learn that you have sexual problems too. You always struck me as a type who would prefer to discuss philosophical subjects. You were rather awe-inspiring.'

Drawing the tobacco box towards him, he began to fill his pipe. Those chunky rounded fingers conveyed a sense of Yoshikawa's warm personality.

'Believe me, I had problems all right,' Nobuo said. 'My head seemed so full of such thoughts that I could hardly study or anything.'

'It's the same with everybody. And that's as it's meant to be. Of course, I've had some hard experiences too. But

that's the way men are made, to lose their hearts to
women, and I'm prepared to accept the situation as it is.'

Nobuo was filled with admiration at Yoshikawa's relaxed,
matter of fact way of talking about the subject.

'You amaze me. You seem really experienced.'

'Don't make me laugh. There's nothing experienced
about me. It's just that I don't possess a highly developed
sense of sin like you.' Yoshikawa waved his massive hand
as he spoke and disturbed the cloud of smoke that was
floating beneath the light bulb.

'Stop teasing. I don't know much about a sense of sin.
But I felt it keenly when I read *The Fig Tree*.'

'Feeling something keenly, that's a remarkable thing in
itself.'

'Yes, but I hardly know anything.'

'That's exactly it. The priest who comes to our house
says that the truly wise person is the man who really knows
he doesn't know anything.'

'Are you still planning to become a priest?'

'What? What did you say? Me, become a priest?' When
he had got over his initial surprise Yoshikawa burst into
loud laughter. Nobuo had never forgotten the day when,
as boys, Yoshikawa and he had sworn to become priests.

'You're an astonishing fellow!' protested Yoshikawa,
when Nobuo reminded him of the occasion. 'That was
just a boyish dream. There's nothing wrong in having such
dreams when you're ten years old; and when you're fifteen
it's reasonable to have the aspirations of a fifteen-year-old.
But human beings are not like trees which bear only a
certain kind of flower; there's nothing predetermined in
human life.'

'I wonder why I am so naïve. I've always had at the
back of my mind the fact that I swore to you I'd become
a priest. So much so that in working in the law courts I
felt I was doing something wrong!'

At this, Yoshikawa roared with laughter for the best

part of a minute. When he became more composed he studied Nobuo's face keenly.

'Nagano, you are a good person. You are absolutely sincere. I never imagined that a person like you existed, here in the very heart of Edo,' and he laughed softly in admiration.

Nobuo was embarrassed by his own naïvety, but he was delighted by the way Yoshikawa was looking at him – as though wrapping him round with the warmth of his gaze.

'Listen, Nagano. I plan to work on the railway to the end of my days. All I want to do is to see Fujiko married to a good man, find a woman who just suits me, get married and raise five or six children, and do my duty by my mother so that she can say it has been good to be alive. I think that's just about the kind of life I seem to be cut out for.'

Nobuo gazed into Yoshikawa's eyes – they looked so wise – and nodded.

It seemed that here was the perfect example of the dignity of living an ordinary life. In this Meiji era, when anyone and everyone had dreams of self-advancement, it was a rare experience to hear anyone talk as Yoshikawa did. In this age when so many young men dreamed of graduating from university with a bachelor's degree or a doctor's degree, or becoming a cabinet minister or a millionaire, it took a certain amount of courage to speak as Yoshikawa did. Moreover it was not merely a case of Yoshikawa being resigned to his fate. Rather, having chosen nothing more ambitious than to live for the rest of his life as a railwayman, there was a positive air of self-possession about him. Nobuo would have given anything to know what had made Yoshikawa into the kind of person he was. Perhaps it was some innate gift, something which a person like himself could not hope to achieve, even if he spent the rest of his life seeking it.

'You're an extraordinary fellow, Yoshikawa. Really extraordinary.'

'What's so unusual about that?' Yoshikawa could not see anything either extraordinary or particularly ordinary in himself.

'Well, you're the same age as I am. Yet I haven't any plans for my life. But somehow, in my heart of hearts I feel a vague ambition stirring. I don't imagine I shall keep on at the law court like this for the rest of my days. Even though I don't know what it is I want to do, I can't escape from the feeling that I must do something.'

'If you ask me, that's real integrity. That is how a young man of twenty ought to think. What's more, you've done well in your studies ever since you were in junior school. It's quite natural that you should feel capable of making something of life.'

As he said this Yoshikawa threw himself down on his bed again. The distant sound of the night watchman's wooden clappers grew gradually louder and louder.

'But, Yoshikawa, there aren't many young fellows who want to live as you do, you know. You are a person who believes in living each day to the full, regarding the present as being the most precious time. That's what I call really living. People like myself, with great ideas of doing something in the future, idle away the present while we wish our lives away. What it boils down to is that we are like shaky saplings, whereas you are growing up like a sturdy tree.'

'That's another gross over-estimation.' Yoshikawa folded his arms and laughed.

'This is a different subject, but, what do you think about death? I'm ashamed to say it, but on account of my grandmother and my father both having died so suddenly, I'm excessively concerned with the question. Sometimes I wake up suddenly in the middle of the night and think to myself, "Ah, I'm alive?" Then the next moment I begin to have absurdly childish thoughts and start wondering when and where I shall die, of what illness, and surrounded by what kinds of people.'

'That goes for me too. It's terrifying to think of dying. I want to prolong my life as much as possible, even if it's only one day. But I don't make a special study of the matter, or spend all my time thinking about it. Those people who died for their country in the Sino-Japanese War, I expect they were much the same as I am.'

'Is that so? Even you are afraid of death, Yoshikawa?' Nobuo looked at him with something like relief. They stared at each other and laughed.

'It's reassuring to talk to you, Yoshikawa.'

'Is it? But remember, you are only talking about the feeling of reassurance, and that's not the same thing as real reassurance.'

'Maybe you're right.'

'Of course. How could the problem of death and so on be solved just by the two of us talking together like this? When you start thinking about the reason for your being alive, you get the bottomless feeling of there being no reason at all. If you don't understand the meaning of life, how can you understand the meaning of death? Even if you could understand it, that doesn't mean to say that you would be able to die peacefully.'

'I see what you are getting at.'

'Nagano. I guess you have always worried about questions of life and death. Why don't you simply accept, as I do, the fact that living things inevitably die?'

'I'm afraid I couldn't resign myself to the idea as simply as that. In my grandmother's case and in my father's case too, they were as large as life just before they died. Isn't it more natural to suppose that a living person should go on living for ever? I would like to discuss why death should be inevitable. Oh, well, we'd better not be too long in going to sleep, I suppose. I expect you're pretty tired too.'

'Uh.'

Nobuo switched off the light. As his eyes gradually became accustomed to the darkness, he could dimly pick out the white shapes of the paper door and window panels.

Their whiteness made him think of Fujiko's face. Fujiko's forehead and eyes, without a blemish, seemed to float in front of him. To think that Fujiko lay asleep under the very same roof. It filled him with an inexpressible sensation. He had no particular memories of Fujiko, except one thing. He could never forget the time when they played hide and seek. Why was he unable to forget that afternoon, when Fujiko came into the woodshed where he was hiding, and they stood together perfectly still, holding their breath for fear of being found? Now he could see that it was then, when he was a boy, that he had become suffocatingly aware of the opposite sex for the first time in his life. And why was it that whenever he thought of his glimpses of her withered leg, he was overwhelmed with a feeling of love for her.

'Nagano? Are you awake?' Yoshikawa turned over. Nobuo had thought he was asleep.

'Yes.'

'I don't seem to be able to get to sleep either.'

'I expect it's the different bed.'

'No, I'm usually able to sleep soundly anywhere. But today somehow, I'm feeling anxious about Fujiko.'

Nobuo was unable to reply. He felt that Yoshikawa had been able to read all that he had just been thinking.

'Well, Fujiko is sixteen now. Before long I'll have to arrange a marriage for her.'

'What, at sixteen? Isn't that rather early? Why, that's just our Machiko's age. Machiko is still going to high school.'

Nobuo felt as though the ground had been swept away beneath him all of a sudden.

'Girls who go to high school generally get married at eighteen, I suppose. But up there it's not so unusual for girls to marry at sixteen. With her leg being as it is, I was afraid no one would want her, but there are some negotiations under way.'

'Oh, congratulations.' Nobuo had no alternative but to express himself in the usual manner.

'Not at all, nothing has been decided. It's just in the air as yet. The man works in the same place as I do. He's not a bad fellow, but somehow I can't bring myself to entrust Fujiko to him for life. I don't know what to do for the best.'

At last Nobuo was able to see the reason for Yoshikawa's solemn expression earlier in the evening.

'In that case, wouldn't it be better if you turned him down?'

'If it was as simple as that there would be no problem. But you see, she's not blessed with a completely sound body, like your sister. There's no guarantee that she'd ever have another offer of marriage if we turned this one down.'

Nobuo was silent. He focused his eyes on the pale glow of the paper window panels shining in the darkness. He could see what Yoshikawa meant. To lose their only chance could blight the rest of Fujiko's life. Nobuo felt himself strangely attached to Fujiko, even in the short time she had been in his house. Perhaps it was what is called love at first sight. At any rate, as soon as a betrothal was mentioned he realized that he did not want Fujiko to belong to anyone else. Yoshikawa went on.

'If she doesn't get married at sixteen or seventeen, she'll be eighteen before we know where we are. If there is a suitable proposal when she's eighteen that's all well and good, but once she turns nineteen there's no hope of marrying or giving her away, because everyone says that's an unlucky age for a woman. By the time she reaches twenty she'll be past her best, as they say, and with her bad leg there won't be much chance at all. On the whole I'm satisfied with things as they are, but when it comes to the question of Fujiko I can't make up my mind what's for the best.' Yoshikawa laughed in self-deprecation.

Once again Nobuo felt himself to be no match for Yoshikawa. He could not imagine himself losing any sleep with worry over Machiko. He wondered if the reason lay solely in the fact that Fujiko was lame. Even if Machiko suffered from the same affliction, he was sure he would take a far more detached attitude than Yoshikawa.

'You're a wonderful person.' Nobuo found himself expressing the feeling yet again.

'There's nothing remarkable about that. My trouble is self-interest. I care more for myself than for Fujiko. It's just that I want to spare myself the unpleasantness of seeing her miserably married to some worthless fellow.'

After a short silence he continued, 'Very well, I've made up my mind. As soon as I get back I'll get Fujiko's marriage arranged. Yes, that's settled. Goodnight.' He did not disclose his thoughts further, but chuckled cheerfully and in a few moments was fast asleep.

But sleep would not come to Nobuo. It seemed that Yoshikawa, while genuinely concerned for Fujiko's happiness, had entertained some motive of self-interest, and in order to be rid of this he had quickly made up his mind to go ahead with the marriage negotiations. And, as soon as he saw that Yoshikawa's mind was made up, Nobuo realized how precious Fujiko had become to him. He had not reached the point of asking to marry Fujiko himself. He could only feel very lonely.

It was almost July before Yoshikawa's letter came, on a hot, humid day after they had returned to Hokkaido.

'*Coming from the uncomfortable rainy season in Tokyo to endless days of completely blue skies in Hokkaido, I feel almost as if I have returned to a different world altogether. Thank you for all you did for us during our stay in Tokyo. Apart from anything else it was good to share the experience of being twenty-year-old young men. Even the trees in the grounds of our old school have grown so big, they made me feel the passage of those ten years. Thank you for everything; for the time when we were ten and talked about ghost-hunting under the cherry tree; for the times this spring when we strolled round the Ginza and Asakusa; for all the times we spent together.*

'Silly Fujiko can't get the time when you had your palm read in Asakusa out of her mind. You remember, that bearded old fogey said that you would have a short life. Well, I suppose I should have said the same at a guess. That fellow took one look at your pale face and thin body and guessed that you must be suffering from consumption. But I've discovered that you're really unusually tough and my mind has been put at ease.

'Since I've been back I've been very busy and somehow or other I don't seem to be able to put this letter together very well. In the midst of all my busyness there has been the question of Fujiko's engagement. I'm glad to be able to tell you that it has been agreed that she will get married this autumn. Her prospective husband is a solid fellow by the name of Sagawa. There hasn't been a formal exchange of engagement presents yet, but at least the matter is settled and I can breathe again. Both my mother and Fujiko seem to be relieved too. I hope to write a more leisurely letter later on, but please accept this letter of thanks.

'Please give my greetings to your honourable mother and to Machiko.

Yoshikawa.'

When he returned to work, Nobuo stood blankly in his office and read the letter again and again. The sweat gathered at the base of his neck.

'It's terribly sticky today,' he muttered to himself.

As he thought about the fact that this autumn, Fujiko, as pure as the driven snow, would become somebody's wife, he felt unbearably desolate. Apart from her bad leg, she was as near perfect a person as existed, and Nobuo felt a sense of irretrievable loss. During the two or three days he had shown her round Tokyo, Fujiko had become an unforgettable person to him.

In particular he was unable to forget the look on her face in the fortune teller's booth in Asakusa. Yoshikawa had spread out his enormous palm and had been told that he would rise to a position of considerable importance, and he had stretched out his own hand and been told, 'You have only another two or three years to live, but if you follow my advice and chew your food carefully and sleep in a sunny room, you may perhaps live to be fifty.'

When she heard this, Fujiko had gazed up at Nobuo with her big eyes and said softly in his ear, 'Promise me you'll live a long time.'

That gentle breath which had caressed his ear seemed to Nobuo like a treasure he would give anything to obtain.

12 The Ferry Boat

NOBUO was now twenty-three years old. It was July, three years since the Yoshikawas visited Tokyo. He was standing on the deck of the ferry boat that plied between the mainland and Hokkaido. The sea was calm and he could still clearly see the figures of people standing on the shore of Aomori Bay. Suddenly he was seized with an urge to jump into the sea and swim back. But he told himself, 'You mustn't let the image of Mother and Machiko, back in Tokyo, haunt you.'

'Machiko will be getting on well with Kishimoto, no doubt about that,' he thought. She had married Dr Kishimoto, a graduate of the Imperial University, the previous autumn. He was a Christian who had been introduced to them by Harusame Nakamura. Like Nakamura, he came from Osaka, but was now working in a hospital in Tokyo. He was nine years older than Machiko and five years older than Nobuo. Kishimoto was a warm-hearted man who gave the impression of wanting to be kind to everyone. When Nobuo had once said that he would like to go and see Hokkaido, Kishimoto had promptly encouraged him, suggesting that he ought to try living there for two or three years.

'Nobuo, before I got married I wanted to go to Hokkaido. That's where Kanzo Uchimura, the great Christian leader, studied at agricultural college.'

Kishimoto thought about Hokkaido from a Christian standpoint. Kiku also thought it a pity that Nobuo had had to give up going to university and become the family breadwinner. She had even reached the point of saying,

155

'If Nobuo wants to go to Hokkaido, I'll go with him.' But just about then Machiko became pregnant and they both came to live in the Nagano home. So Nobuo decided he would be justified in going to Hokkaido for two or three years and leaving Kiku in Kishimoto's care.

Nobuo had failed to qualify for compulsory military service, and had therefore gone on working at the law courts. He had already been promoted to the rank of junior official, but did not want to spend all his working life there. In the evenings he studied in law school, thinking that there might come a time when he could launch out on his own, before he was thirty. Now, however, Nobuo was turning his back on the mountains of Honshu, as if to shake off all that. Before he thought it possible, the mountains of Hokkaido came into view. He was caught by surprise.

'Hokkaido.'

He had imagined it would take several hours on the boat before he saw them, but with the mountains ahead of him, Nobuo felt encouraged.

'Fujiko,' he murmured.

Nobuo called to mind the memories he kept secret in the depths of his heart. It was three years ago, in the autumn, that Fujiko had become engaged to Sagawa. And then, from Yoshikawa's letters, Nobuo had learned that Fujiko had fallen ill.

'The good things in life don't automatically follow one after the other, it seems. Recently, when Fujiko's engagement present had only just arrived, she suddenly became ill. Yet, come to think of it, maybe it was not all that sudden. When we got back from Tokyo she had no appetite. We thought she was just tired from the long journey; and then the hot summer weather came. We all rather carelessly thought that with the cooler weather her appetite would get back to normal but,

when autumn came and she had a cold which dragged on and on, we began to think it strange and discovered that her chest was affected. Poor thing, just when all the plans were being made for the wedding, it looks as if they are going to come to nothing. Sagawa really likes Fujiko, and when we took his engagement present back he would not accept it. But we can't take advantage of someone's goodwill for ever.'

After this letter there was no news from Yoshikawa for quite a time. Nobuo, in his usual fashion, wanted to send off a letter of sympathy immediately, but somehow never got it done. He would not have been able to deny it was because of a fear of Fujiko's illness. It was an age when the sufferers from tuberculosis were so hated and feared that they were even persecuted and forced to leave the neighbourhood.

When New Year came, Nobuo sent a postcard. As his father Masayuki had died during the year, they could not send the usual New Year congratulation cards. *'I hope this severe weather is not affecting Fujiko's health. I can guess that you were expecting a get-well card by return, but I couldn't write anything . . .'*

Nobuo re-read his postcard with an uncomfortable feeling. The real reason why he had not sent a get-well card was that at heart he had been selfish and callous. What he had written was all lies. His card crossed with one from Yoshikawa.

'It must have been a lonely New Year for you. A New Year without a father is a bitter experience. Fujiko is very bright. She still has a slight temperature all the time but she feels well. At least, she puts on the appearance of feeling well. My mother tries to match her mood, but it is hardest for her.'

He mentioned nothing about Fujiko's engagement to

Sagawa. As Nobuo read the postcard, he wondered whether the engagement had already been called off. Spring came soon and Nobuo pressed some cherry blossoms and sent them to Hokkaido where the spring came later. He received a thick letter by return post.

'*Those pressed cherry blossoms you sent us, you don't know what joy they brought. Fujiko was even happier than I was. The day they came we had a snow storm and the windows were plastered white with snow. To see the pressed cherry blossoms in the middle of a snow storm, cheered Fujiko more than you could ever imagine.*

'*Recently Fujiko has been in bed all the time. Her chest is not so bad now, but it seems that her spine is affected. When she does walk she is very wobbly, so she just stays in bed all the time. Sagawa sometimes comes to comfort her, but he seems to have given up the idea of marriage.*'

There was another letter, from Fujiko, in the envelope :

'*Dear Mr Nagano,*

'*Thank you so much for the pressed cherry blossoms. I look at them so often, my mother laughs at me. Until I saw the flowers I did not think that I could go on living. When I saw them I was filled with joy and I feel that I shall be able to live for another year now.*'

Fujiko had written that, to Nobuo. Whenever he saw a flower after that, he could not resist pressing it. Tulips, peonies, broom, little flowers and big, he pressed them and sent them to Fujiko. Each time Fujiko sent a letter, brief but expressing her gratitude. Nobuo folded each one up in thin rice paper and put them in his desk. Even when he was at work and saw a flower, he saw it in the image of Fujiko's pale face. He felt a deep pity for her, struck down with tuberculosis, the disease everyone hated. When he looked at a flower he caught something of her feelings, fearing she would not live to see the next year. He could imagine the rose and the peony he had sent her, wet with tears.

When he saw Machiko, talking happily with her mother, Nobuo thought of Fujiko. Machiko would probably live in good health for many years. But Fujiko might well end her life at seventeen. When these thoughts came to him he felt a strong urge to sit down at his desk and get out his writing paper. Just to write a few words to her, might prolong Fujiko's life a little, he hoped.

In time Fujiko's letters became even shorter, and Nobuo had a foreboding that she did not have long to live. Worrying daily over her, he thought more and more seriously about the problem of life. Even when he saw small children as he was going along the road, he would think of how even they would die eventually.

Taking leave of his mother in the morning, formally, his hands flat on the floor, he would wonder as he raised his head whether he would return home that day; there was no guarantee of it. His father Masayuki had left from that gate in a rickshaw, and in no time at all had lost consciousness on his way to work, never to return home. Having experienced this, Nobuo could not think of life just as a matter for speculation. When his father had met with sudden death, he had been afraid of death and had squarely faced the fact that all men must die. Now his way of thinking about death had changed a little. As some-one who would surely die some day he began to consider what was the best way to live.

One day, he asked his mother, 'When people die, it's the end of everything, isn't it, Mother?'

Nobuo was thinking about Fujiko. Kiku, looking at his enquiring expression, was silent for a while. 'Nobuo, I don't think death is the end of everything.'

'Well, Mother, do you mean to say something else begins after death? Are you saying that dead people have a future?' Nobuo asked excitedly. Kiku nodded quietly, her nod filled with assurance.

'What sort of a future is it?' Nobuo pressed his questions almost sceptically.

'Listen, Nobuo. If I tell you that death is a sleep and that we awaken again, you won't believe me, will you? If you enquire seriously about something, you must treat the answer seriously too. It's the kind of thing people humbly consult a minister or a Buddhist priest about,' Kiku replied.

Somehow Nobuo did not feel satisfied. His mother seemed to be in another world, believing so easily in a life after death. Whoever he asked, he began to think, he would not be able to believe them. But even as he thought this he remembered something Fujiko had said as she faced death : 'Death is not the end for anybody.' If only he could believe that, it would be a great comfort to him. But although he did not believe what his mother had said, he wanted to pass it on to Fujiko.

This teaching, could it really give a power and meaning to life? 'What *is* the power to live?' he wondered. He wished he could find out both for Fujiko's sake and his own.

It was while he was mulling over this that another letter came from Yoshikawa. Fujiko's fiancé, Sagawa, had called off the engagement and was already married to someone else. By the standards of the time, when people used to cover their mouths with their hands and run past the home of a tuberculosis patient, Sagawa was a rare and worthy person. He had continued to visit the stricken Fujiko for over a year. Nobuo thought he would never be able to do that. From far away Tokyo he was writing letters, but if he were closer, would he have the courage to call on her . . .? He had to consider this.

Nobuo loved Fujiko but, as he admitted to himself, his love was rather irresponsible. He had never actually said that he loved her, he had made no promises, nor even promised to visit her. It was an unrealistic love, like love for a star in the sky. But worse still, it was a self-satisfying sort of love, for in thinking about Fujiko, he found satisfaction. On the other hand, Fujiko had never written anything to him about Sagawa, so he had been led to think that she did not care for him. And when he remembered her voice that night in Asakusa, when she had whispered in his ear, 'Live a long time, won't you?' his heart was flooded with bliss; he believed that Fujiko loved him.

'But then, maybe Fujiko does love Sagawa, and now she has lost him she must be really unhappy.' For the first time this thought startled him, and a feeling akin to jealousy made him depressed.

After that Nobuo did not write to the Yoshikawas for a while, nor did he receive anything from them.

'Fujiko is probably broken-hearted over the way the wedding planned for her and Sagawa came to nothing, and this autumn will probably be her last,' he concluded.

One fine Sunday, Nobuo lay on the verandah looking up at the sky. In the bright autumn sunlight many white clouds were drifting, passing out of sight behind the eaves of the house.

'Where do the clouds come from, where do they go?' A cloud shaped like a dog's head floated past, continually changing in the autumn wind. It was never the same for a moment. One thing was certain, they vanished without trace in no time at all. 'It's all so transient!' Nobuo muttered, involuntarily comparing himself with the clouds. 'People change too much, in all sorts of ways.'

His thoughts towards Fujiko had not changed, but there had been changes in Nobuo himself. On his way to and from work he felt his gaze more and more drawn towards the women he met. The white arms of a young woman as she brushed down a lattice door, her kimono sleeves tucked right up, or the sight of a girl in a bright yellow kimono, clacking along on her low wooden clogs, these had an allurement for Nobuo. The groups of cheerfully chattering schoolgirls with the bands of their pleated skirts fastened high above their waists, even they were interesting. Yet this was the same Nobuo who had not been able to speak face to face with a woman even of his mother's age.

Wondering when and where this change had taken place, he began to feel uneasy. The proverb, 'A man's heart is never settled,' came to his mind. His own heart was still bent on going ways he had never dreamed of. In its depths he still thought about Fujiko but, he chided himself, rather than Fujiko herself, he was loving a young woman through the medium of Fujiko. That Fujiko had to be the object of his love was not a strong conviction. As he gazed at the drifting clouds, he was all the more astonished at the instability of the human heart. 'I don't know where I came from, and I don't know where I'm going—just like that cloud,' he muttered in despair.

When Yoshikawa had visited Tokyo and they chatted together, he had remarked, 'Men exist for various reasons; sick people for some reasons, and we for others.' At the time Nobuo had thought this was true, but now he could only think of life as purposeless.

From that autumn day onwards, when he noticed that there was nothing permanent in his heart at all, Nobuo began to feel a chafing loneliness, like living in an empty house. One night, alone, he gave himself up to his sexual desires, a thing he had long denied himself. When this storm had passed Nobuo felt even more lonely and wretched. With a sense of self-hatred and emptiness, he clearly saw the image of his other self – not the diligent, self-controlled aspiring person, but the shameless individual willing to go to any length in dissipation and ruin.

This was the dark side of himself he had scarcely discerned before. As he became aware of it Nobuo threw off his coverlet and jumped up from his bed. Quietly he opened the verandah shutters and went out to the well. Feeling that the bucket might have the answer to his problems, he drew a pailful of water and poured it over his naked body. It was cold, for it was the end of November. With his teeth biting into his lip he poured three buckets of water over himself, one after the other, and felt that at last he had returned to his right mind.

'That was two years ago,' Nobuo thought, gazing from the ferry at Hakodate Mountain drawing nearer and nearer.

Early the previous morning, Machiko's husband had come to see him off and had given him a Bible. On the fly leaf Kishimoto had written with a brush 'God is love', but Nobuo had inward misgivings about this. 'Is God really love?'

He could not meekly accept the fact that Fujiko, who had done no wrong, should have a bad leg, and then, on top of that, lung and spinal tuberculosis. Since the time two years ago when he had poured water on himself, Nobuo had come to regard his will and reason as the things which controlled him. From that night he had battled fiercely with his sexual desires, and had overcome them. He did not think of himself as a weak person who needed to depend upon God.

13   The Streets of Sapporo

NOBUO's train was running across the Ishikari Plain, under
the bright July sun, with not a human being in sight.
'What wide open spaces,' he thought.

At the edge of the wild plain the white flowers of potato
fields caught his eye. Very soon the train would be stopping
in Sapporo. He kept thinking about the decision he had
made. 'Why did I throw up my job in the law courts and
leave my mother and sister in Tokyo, and come to Hokkaido?' But he did not know the answer.

His reasons for wanting to live in Sapporo where Yoshikawa lived, were only very flimsy, he realized. To say that
he had come because he loved Yoshikawa's sister, Fujiko,
was not really true. It was a fact that he felt sympathy for
Fujiko, who had suffered through three cold Hokkaido
winters of illness. In Tokyo he had pictured a pitiful yet
lovely Fujiko and thought of going to visit her immediately,
yet, he told himself, he did not love Fujiko enough to come
all the way to Hokkaido just for her. She had quietly
found a place in his heart, but that could have been because
at twenty-three he was sentimental. 'It's just because I'm
still young!'

He felt an urge to see new lands, to feel the adventure
of a new life unfolding before him, and at the same time
he happened to have memories of Fujiko, surely that was
it.

Suddenly, the number of houses increased and the train
slowed down, swayed hugely and entered Sapporo station.
Nobuo lowered his two cases from the rack and picked
them up. He heard a sharp knocking on the carriage

164

window and saw the familiar face of Yoshikawa outside, smiling so that his white teeth showed. When Nobuo alighted on the platform Yoshikawa almost collided with him and grasped his shoulders.

'I'm so glad you've come, I really am.' Yoshikawa wiped an eye with his sleeve.

'Yes, I've come. I've come at last.' Nobuo felt his heart warming. For the first time since their parting the two studied each other's faces, then smiled.

'You've not changed, you're still scrawny!'

'Yes, I wasn't accepted for military service. Not like you; you were classed Grade 1, weren't you, even though you were not picked in the draft lottery. You seem to be bigger than ever.'

'Maybe I'm still growing.' The two laughed. Yoshikawa's voice was so loud it completely drowned Nobuo's. He picked up the two cases as if there was nothing in them.

'I'll take one.'

'What? I handle baggage every day here at the station. Don't worry.' And Yoshikawa started off with big strides.

'It's a big station, isn't it?'

'You said you'd like to work here, didn't you? You were a law court official, so that should be quite easy. But I'm glad you decided to come. For a Nagano, you've shown a surprising ability to decide for yourself!'

'I'm young.'

Nobuo told Yoshikawa casually about the conclusions he had reached on his train journey.

'Hmm, I see. We're both still young, aren't we?'

That made Nobuo wonder what 'young' really meant.

When they left the station he saw a green avenue of acacia trees stretching into the distance and with a light clopping of horses' hooves a horse-tram was running on rails down the centre. Opposite the station stood a large hotel, the Yamagataya.

'Look over there, those are the law courts.' Still carrying the cases, Yoshikawa pointed to a big building two or three blocks away. Nobuo remembered nostalgically his desk in the law offices in Tokyo. But the ache in his heart soon vanished.

In front of the station, hotel porters were out in force seeking guests for their hotels, but they seemed to know that Yoshikawa worked at the station and did not approach them.

'There are a lot of hotels, aren't there?'

'Huh, there are plenty of big hotels like the Yamagataya and the Maruso.'

'I used to think that Hokkaido was just mountains and wild plains, but I guess I didn't know enough about it.'

The two of them walked up the wide avenue.

'I think it was at Nopporo that I saw a brick factory from the train window. And a linen company and a brewery in Sapporo. I'd never have imagined it.'

'If anyone from Sapporo heard you they'd burst out laughing. But compared with Tokyo this is still just the country.'

'Not a bit of it. That Western-style limestone building among the elms there, and these broad, straight streets, they are really modern and stylish, aren't they?'

Nobuo failed to ask after Fujiko's health. But he had heard that the Yoshikawa's house was about five or six blocks away from the station and the nearer they got, the more silent he became. It was almost as if he could already see Fujiko's pale, emaciated face. After three years in bed any words of comfort he could give would seem empty to her, and he did not know what to say to encourage her.

Even when people were in bed for one or two days with a cold they were invalids. To lie in bed every day for three years must be intolerable. To make it worse, she was a young woman. The thought that at the same age Machiko had a good husband and would soon become a mother, rose chokingly inside him.

A woman carrying a load wrapped in a large cloth on her back, leading a child . . . an old man in a straw hat, his summer kimono tucked up behind . . . a young man pulling a heavy cart, his face covered in sweat . . . they all seemed calm and deliberate. Just gazing at the peaceful avenue and thinking about Fujiko, made Nobuo feel sad. When they had walked for a while, they turned left.

'It's the third house from here,' said Yoshikawa, pointing with his chin. It was a house with two doors, and a large shingled roof which seemed to half hide it. Nobuo had imagined it as being like the small house the Yoshikawas had lived in in Tokyo and he found it much bigger than he had expected. However, inside there were only about four rooms.

'I'm so glad you've come. You're tired, I suppose,' Yoshikawa's mother greeted him, and the three of them sat formally on the *tatami*. 'You came round by Muroran and Iwamizawa, didn't you? When we came, we sailed from Hakodate to Otaru, but I don't like sailing and I was very sick. Did the boat from Hakodate to Muroran rock much?' She seemed to be at a loss for appropriate conversation.

'Even though it's Hokkaido, the weather's very hot, isn't it? I'm quite relieved.'

'Yes, Mr Nagano, they say it's hot enough to grow rice. Some days are as hot as Tokyo.'

Nobody was saying anything about Fujiko, and Nobuo began to be uneasy. Maybe she was not even in the house. Thinking that she might have gone into hospital, he became increasingly unsettled.

'Well, and how is she?' Without mentioning Fujiko's name, Nobuo asked the question at last.

'Oh, Fujiko? Will you take him to her, dear?' Yoshikawa's mother said. 'With a disease like that you can't talk about it, can you?'

As Yoshikawa got up he said, 'They say it's tuberculosis, but her lungs are hardly affected at all now.' Even so, there was a note of concern in his voice. Because there was a tuberculosis patient in their home they had to be very careful about their contacts with the outside world. Nobuo felt that he had come into direct contact with Yoshikawa's daily life, having to be very careful to hide this fact from other people.

'Whatever words of sympathy can I say?' he wondered.

Stiffening a little, Nobuo followed Yoshikawa. They passed through one room and without ceremony Yoshikawa opened the sliding doors of the next.

'Fujiko, Nagano's come.' Yoshikawa's voice was very gentle, and Nobuo's heart leaped.

'Welcome, I'm so glad you've come.'

It was a bright voice, and Nobuo stopped abruptly.

Fujiko's wasted form lay by the window of a small four and a half mat room. But her face was shining with a radiance that Nobuo had never seen before.

'Fujiko.' That was all he said as he sat down beside her.

She had spent all her days in bed and become so thin, yet in this miserable existence she had such a serene expression that it struck Nobuo to the heart and he could say nothing more.

'I suppose you're tired. It's a long way from Tokyo.'

Her sweet voice was as artless as a child's. A picture of Machiko as a bride flashed across Nobuo's mind. He suddenly noticed that the wall near where Fujiko was lying was covered with pressed flowers. They were the ones he had sent. The cherry, violet and plum blossoms were pasted on the wall with the date they were received written in small letters beside them. Nobuo's heart warmed.

'These are the flowers you sent. There are lots of them now.'

They were alone, for Yoshikawa had already got up and left. Nobuo looked steadily at Fujiko's face again with overwhelming emotion. Fujiko calmly looked back at him. Her eyes were frighteningly clear. Suddenly they began to brim with tears. But the next moment she had a bright smile.

'The pressed flowers made me really happy.' Tears were

falling from her smiling face. 'It's strange, isn't it, even when we are happy the tears come too,' she said brushing them away with her thin fingers. She was a little embarrassed. As he gazed at her Nobuo began to fall in love with her again. He felt he would be prepared to do anything for poor Fujiko. To make Fujiko happy he would not begrudge any effort possible. He was moved by her brightness, a feeling so completely different from what he had long imagined when he was in Tokyo. This was not like the sympathy of a healthy person for a sick one, but rather of admiration. Nobuo looked at Fujiko's hand which seemed about to come into his own. He resisted the impulse to grasp it strongly.

'Fujiko, I'll be coming again. I'll be in Sapporo all the time from now on, so instead of pressed flowers I'll bring you all sorts of real ones.'

Fujiko's eyes brimmed visibly with tears which glistened on her long eyelashes. The little bell in the window tinkled in the wind.

Nobuo got a job with the mining railway company, as he had planned, and started work in Sapporo Station. Yoshikawa was in charge of the parcels department, and Nobuo was responsible for the accounts. He had lodgings about two blocks away from the Yoshikawas and called on them once a week. He would have liked to call every day but he was too shy to do so, and visited Fujiko on the pretence of calling on the whole family.

A month after he arrived in Sapporo, one evening in Obon, the Festival of the Dead, Nobuo was invited to the home of Reinosuke Wakura, a senior official.

Obon was held in August in Hokkaido. Here and there on the roads the musicians' platforms had been set up, and the sound of the drumming for the Obon dances was carried on the light breeze. Reinosuke Wakura was a great drinker of *sake*.

'What's this, a fine young man like you getting red in the

face after only two or three cups of *sake*, it's disgraceful!'

Wakura was dressed in a light kimono with one shoulder bare, showing his well-muscled chest. He was a large man reputed to be skilled at archery.

Misa, his daughter, sitting beside him, smiled. Like her father, Misa was of a large build, about seventeen or eighteen, a determined young woman. She wore white make-up on her face and neck, but it looked a little too thick.

'Now then, Nagano. You're very thin, but there seems to be nothing wrong with you.'

Nobuo noticed that Wakura had become a little more formal.

'Yes, I'm like a willow tree, which bends but never breaks. I hardly ever catch cold.'

'Hmm, but Hokkaido's different from the mainland you know. The winter cold freezes you to the bone. But let's not talk about unpleasant things now, let's get some practice in drinking *sake*. Misa, you think a man who drinks *sake* is a reliable person, don't you?'

Wakura gave a great laugh. Misa blushed and hung her head, repeatedly stroking her hands over her broad thighs, swelling as if to burst her kimono.

Nobuo, sensing what sort of occasion this was, felt flustered and looked up at the lantern on the verandah.

'Nagano, I've had a lot of junior workers under me, but I've never had anyone like you. To tell the truth I was somewhat suspicious of the fact that you gave up a job in the Tokyo law courts and came up here. It just doesn't happen that someone becomes a law official and then drifts as far as Hokkaido.'

Wakura drank several cups of *sake*. He didn't worry that his nose was red and shining. Occasionally Misa would get up and go to her mother in the kitchen and get another bottle. When she moved, the scent of her make-up wafted across and Nobuo could not help noticing it. She had charming features with dark eyes, but that make-up was too thick. Nobuo was tempted to liken her to a poisonous flower.

'However, from what I've heard, Nagano, you haven't any vices; indeed you came up to Hokkaido in spite of attempts to detain you. I disliked you at first, with your face like a doll on a Girls' Day display stand. I thought you were a spineless jellyfish. However, when I gave you some work to try you out, you showed yourself to be extremely bright and learned quickly. You have a strong sense of responsibility, and your work is dependable. I've been very taken with you recently and I think I've got a good man. In fact you're not a March girls' festival doll, you're a May boys' festival warrior!'

Nobuo prepared himself for what would come next. 'Not at all,' he said. 'I've only just started this job and I'm being careful, but it will not take long for plenty of my shortcomings to appear.'

'I don't believe you. I may be a rough sort of fellow, but I'm not a bad judge of men. To come to the point, she's not exactly a beauty but I would like you to consider marrying my daughter. I don't want your answer immediately. I wanted to strike while the iron was hot, and let you see her. That's why I asked you in this evening.'

He was slightly drunk, but his tone was serious.

Misa had not come back from the kitchen. Nobuo was relieved about this but he faced a real problem.

'I'm very grateful. It is a great honour,' was all he said. And he bowed.

'I'd just like to ask you, but . . . have you decided on someone already?'

'No. There's no one.'

After he had answered, Nobuo thought of Fujiko. Nobuo had not thought of marrying her, for it seemed unlikely that she would ever get better. So of course there was no need to say anything about her. But now he had been formally introduced to Wakura's daughter, Nobuo began to feel that he could not just leave Fujiko and marry some other woman. For instance, if, instead of being asked if he had already decided on someone, he had been asked if there was someone he liked, Nobuo himself would have unashamedly admitted that there was.

'Let me ask you something else. Do you intend to live permanently in Sapporo? Or, if the chance of making money came to you, would you pull out completely and go back to the mainland?'

'I'm an only son, and I have a house and land in Tokyo. I have to look after my mother, and I don't know what would happen if she came to live in Hokkaido. But, speaking for myself alone, I mean to persevere with this job.'

Nobuo could not say that he would be returning to Tokyo two or three years after taking the job. But in a short time the railways in Japan would be coming under government management, and to get a transfer to Tokyo would not be out of the question.

Nobuo walked back to his lodgings, feeling the cool evening breeze and remembering the expression on Misa's face when he left their house. In the coquetry of the upturned eyes as she looked at him, he sensed her womanly charm. He certainly did not find it unpleasant, but he resisted the effect it had on him.

'It's because I'm still young, I suppose. Youth is incredibly complicated,' he said to himself, and his expression revealed his perplexity. 'We have so much energy and want so many things. We get all mixed up.'

Like the earth when it was young, a turbulent fiery mass, in Nobuo's heart, physical desires and youthful idealism were in confused conflict.

'No, youth is just the developing of energy,' he suddenly thought. 'If this is so, which direction ought I to take as I develop?'

Nobuo stopped and gazed up at the summer night sky. The Great Bear shone in its ordered pattern above his head.

14 Autumn Rains

ONE Sunday afternoon, Nobuo was looking out of his second-floor room in the lodging house, over the ten-foot high corn stalks in the little back garden. The patch was only about twenty yards square but, watching the leaves of the corn being beaten by the autumn rain, Nobuo had the lonely feeling that they stretched on endlessly over a wide plain.

'What's the matter with me?' he thought. 'I want to talk with someone.'

The day before, Reinosuke Wakura had stopped Nobuo on his way home from work.

'Well now, could you please tell me how you feel about Misa? It's up to you.'

Ever since he had called at the Wakura home some six weeks before, even without Reinosuke urging him, he had been thinking about Misa constantly. After that, he had met her once at the street corner. Misa had seen Nobuo and bowed, but she had turned scarlet right down to her neck and had left him in a hurry, clutching a cloth-wrapped bundle to her almost as if she was running away. She seemed a lot more charming than when Nobuo had seen her at the Wakura's. There was nothing particular that he disliked about her. If anything, her charming upward glance and the shape of her lips had something definitely attractive about them. But that was all. Nobuo had never considered that the first thing he should do when he arrived in Hokkaido would be to get married. This was the first time he had had a formal meeting with a prospective bride and, living alone, the thought of her

173

was stimulating, something he could not get out of his mind.

Not having seen Misa at all since then, he felt lonely, but he did not want to get married yet. Nor had he forgotten Fujiko. He sometimes went to visit her but they only talked for five or six minutes. He lacked the gift of conversation and could only talk about the weather and how Fujiko felt. Although he always said the same things, whenever he was there Fujiko looked bright. And when he looked at her face, somehow Nobuo's own heart became peaceful. He preferred the times he spent with Fujiko to anything else. He wondered how she would feel if he married Misa now. He thought she would probably be a little disturbed and go on living brightly in her own quiet way. But as for himself, he felt he would really be missing something if he were not able to call on Fujiko from time to time.

The stairs creaked outside his room and Osamu Yoshikawa came in.

'What's up, you look depressed. Are you homesick for Tokyo?'

Yoshikawa sat down cross-legged with a heavy thump. He was wearing a kimono with a splashed dye pattern.

'Is it your day off? It's coincided well with mine, hasn't it?'

Nobuo turned over the cushion he had been sitting on and offered it to Yoshikawa. Yoshikawa looked round the room in an appraising sort of way although he had been there many times before.

'You're lonely, I suppose. Especially on a rainy day like this,' Yoshikawa said rather hesitantly. Nobuo smiled ruefully.

'It's nearly three months since you came. They say that at about three months one gets very homesick, you know. It's about that time that everyone loses their first sense of excitement.'

Nobuo passed some salted crackers, still wrapped in their

paper bag, and fetched some tea from downstairs.

'Lonely? Not really. It's not that I'm homesick for Tokyo, but I must tell you—there's talk of a marriage for me.'

'Fancy, that's just like you. Has someone got their eye on you already?' Yoshikawa stopped drinking his tea and put his cup on the floor. Nobuo briefly told him the details of the evening during Obon which had turned into a discussion about marriage.

'What do you think I should do?'

'That's for you to decide.'

'I don't really know about that.' Nobuo told him what he felt about Misa.

'I see . . . Nagano . . . How shall I put it? You haven't had any experience with women have you?'

Yoshikawa came straight to the point. Nobuo winced.

'Nagano, to tell you the truth, I don't know anything about women either, and whenever I meet them they seem strange and mysterious and hard to win. Therefore, if I had the opportunity of getting to know some woman, I wouldn't want to forego the chance. The same goes for you.'

Nobuo nodded.

'But, Nagano, I find it painful to think about Fujiko's marriage plans that fell through. Whenever I hear the words "marriage discussion" I feel depressed. Don't hurt this girl – Misa, did you say? – get married as soon as possible. That may seem to be uncalled for advice, but if you think it's good, take it.'

It was just like Yoshikawa to be large-hearted like this. But with every word he spoke Nobuo felt his own feelings towards Fujiko welling up inside him. To raise the matter of Misa had been rather heartless. But Yoshikawa's remark about not hurting a woman penetrated his conscience painfully and he experienced a surge of feeling such as he had never before thought possible.

'As I guessed, I really do love Fujiko,' he realized clearly.

From now on, if a proposal of marriage came up, even if the delay was perplexing and his affections were swayed a little, it was impossible to believe that he could desert Fujiko and marry another woman.

'Well, then,' he thought, 'I'll decide now that Fujiko is going to be my wife, and live with that in mind – even if I have to wait for my whole lifetime.'

For a short while the rain beat fiercely on the roof and then passed.

'Yoshikawa." Nobuo sat up formally.

'What is it? Why do you have to sit up formally?' Yoshikawa, who had been patiently nibbling a salt cracker, looked startled.

'Yoshikawa, will you let me have Fujiko?' Nobuo pressed his two hands on the floor and bowed deeply.

'What do you mean, "let me have Fujiko"?'

Even Yoshikawa's equanimity was broken, and he raised one knee from its cross-legged position.

'I'm asking you if you will let me have Fujiko.'

'Do you know what you are saying, Nagano? Fujiko's an invalid, and I don't know when she'll get better. You shouldn't make a joke of it like that.'

'But it's obvious I'm not joking! I suppose it's because I said it so suddenly that you think I'm being flippant. You know I'm usually discreet and think well before I speak, but, to tell you the truth, up till this very moment I had not thought of Fujiko as my life partner! Even after thinking things over for a long time, it's not always easy to understand your own feelings, is it? It has just dawned on me on the spur of the moment. But don't think I was being frivolous or false.'

'Hmm!' Yoshikawa nodded, looking at a break in the clouds outside.

'I'll not hide anything from you. When I met Fujiko in Tokyo three years ago, when she had grown up, it was a case of love at first sight. Then when I heard about her engagement I felt very lonely. And when she became ill and we exchanged so many letters, as you might have guessed, I thought about Fujiko a good deal. Come to think of it, one of my main reasons for coming to Hokkaido was Fujiko.'

'Nagano, I'm very grateful for your kind feelings. As Fujiko's elder brother, I can't think of adequate words of thanks. But, to face facts, Fujiko's an invalid. The doctor won't say she'll recover. I don't think she will recover, either. It's hardly reasonable for you to ask me if you can marry her.'

'Of course, I'm not saying I want her at once. But I do want to do something to help her to get back to her former health. I somehow think she could get better. Now you know what sort of feelings I have about her, I'd like you to let me continue seeing her.'

The sun came out from between the clouds.

'That's very kind of you, but I must refuse, first for your sake and secondly for Fujiko's.'

'For my sake?' Nobuo looked puzzled. Two flies walked across the sun-browned *tatami*.

'Yes. If you had to keep your word, if you wanted to marry someone else in the future, you would not be able to. Remember that to an honest-to-goodness person like you the promise you made when you were ten, to become a priest, still weighed on your mind when you were over twenty.'

What Yoshikawa said was quite logical, but Nobuo could no longer even imagine himself leaving Fujiko and marrying someone else. His obstinate trait became evident. Yoshikawa went on.

'Well, we'll leave your feelings out of it for the moment, but Fujiko, when Sagawa got married, never said one word of complaint. It was hard enough for me, her older brother. Just the fact that she did not grumble was hard to bear. Now you have appeared on the scene, she may be comforted for a little, but she'll be inconsolable when you marry someone else.'

The sky had cleared rapidly, completely free of clouds.

'A woman's heart, like the autumn sky, changing all the time.' Nobuo pondered the proverb. 'But a man's heart is even more changeable.'

Yet there was nothing false in what he had just said. He had simply become conscious of something in his own heart that he had not noticed until now.

'Nobuo, I'll just forget what you've been saying.'

'No, please don't. I want Fujiko.'

'Nagano, you've got very sentimental since you came to Hokkaido.'

'No, that's not true.'

'Well, when you settle down in Hokkaido you won't say such things.'

'But that's not so . . . Yoshikawa, do you really think I'm such a fickle fellow?' said Nobuo, edging closer to him.

'No . . . this "civilized and enlightened era of Meiji" you are still remarkably honest, I must confess.'

'Then why don't you believe me?'

'But, Nagano, no matter how fine a man you may be, you're still only a man. You're not God or Buddha. I'll tell you something – Fujiko's an *invalid*!'

'I know.'

'Yes, I suppose you know that. But you don't know the real truth about Fujiko.' Yoshikawa fixed his eyes on Nobuo.

'Maybe, but I think I know a little about what sort of person she is. She's always bright and smiling and that in itself shows what a fine person she is, if you ask me.'

'Is that all? Well, you've overlooked the most important thing about her.' Yoshikawa remained staring fixedly at Nobuo.

'Something important?'

'Nobuo . . . Fujiko's . . . a *Christian*!'

'What!' Nobuo was startled and words failed him.

'You didn't know. Fujiko's a Christian – one of your pet aversions.'

Nobuo remembered Fujiko's face, always lovely, whenever he visited her. Now he knew the reason.

'But Yoshikawa, I haven't a blind dislike for Christianity. My mother, my sister and her husband are all Christians.'

'But . . . from quite a while back you gave me the impression that you were having problems about Christianity,' Yoshikawa said quietly.

Clouds began to scud across the sky again, their shapes changing rapidly. The leaves of corn began rustling.

'Yoshikawa, just how did Fujiko become a Christian? She couldn't go to church when she was in bed.'

'No, but before she became ill my mother had a lot of young girls coming to the house to learn dressmaking. There was a Christian among them who used to go to the Independent church. This girl often came to visit Fujiko.'

'I see.'

'Of course, nobody would think of going near a person with lung tuberculosis, so my mother stopped teaching dressmaking. But this one girl kept calling. She didn't seem to bother at all. She was extremely kind to Fujiko. When she left to get married, she was in tears when she took Fujiko's hands in hers and said goodbye. Since then Fujiko has read the Bible the girl gave her, and in course of time became a Christian.'

'In the course of time?'

'Yes. Because Fujiko is lame, I suppose she has thought about things a lot. On top of that, she fell ill just at the time she got engaged, and must have wondered why it should be she who met with all these misfortunes. Of course, she never once spoke to us about it. In her heart she loves God and it makes her very happy. She often says God is love.'

Nobuo was all attention. He remembered the Bible Machiko's husband had given him and the words 'God is love' which he had written on the title page. That Yoshikawa should repeat them and in the same breath describe Fujiko's happiness was no coincidence, it seemed to him.

Already he believed that something higher than human beings existed in this world. From his earliest childhood he had continued to pray before the Buddhist altar and the shrine shelf without any misgivings, because he believed vaguely in some great supernatural being. However, for Nobuo this had always been a typically Japanese way of thinking about God. There were myriads of gods, people who lived in far off mythical times, and Buddha, who was something like his ancestors. They were all men who had died, whose desires and defilement had passed away, and who now enjoyed an exalted existence. This was the limit of his conception of superhuman existence. Therefore, when he saw this coincidence as something more than blind chance, he was thinking of it as a thing brought about by the Buddha. Whatever the explanation, Nobuo felt strongly that something was binding Fujiko and himself together.

'But . . . Yoshikawa, your family are Buddhists. What were you and your mother doing, letting Fujiko become a Christian?'

'Nagano, it sounds as if you are assuming that Buddhism is right and better than Christianity. But you can't go as far as that. Even I sometimes read a little of Fujiko's Bible by her bedside.'

'Do you read the Bible too?' Nobuo asked in amazement.

'Yes, I do. Since Fujiko began reading the Bible, her way of thinking about things has changed a lot. I thought it must be an extraordinary book. In it there are some interesting . . . No, interesting is the wrong word . . . For me, the most painful things . . .' As he said this Yoshikawa looked earnestly at Nobuo.

'What sort of things?' asked Nobuo, overwhelmed by Yoshikawa's mood of sincerity.

'I've learnt some by heart, so I can tell you. They are these, "You have heard that it was said, 'You shall not commit adultery', but I say to you that every one who looks at a woman lustfully has already committed adultery with her in his heart".'

'Hmm, please say that once more.'

Yoshikawa repeated it.

'It's amazing.' Nobuo gazed down at his knees, pondering the meaning of the words.

'I thought you'd find them startling.'

'Yes, that's a very high-minded way of thinking. Just to think things is bad, is it? In that case I don't know how many hundred times I've committed adultery.'

'That's it, and it's the same with me.'

'If that's the case, and you commit adultery by just thinking, there's no one in the world who hasn't, I suppose.'

'That's true. Therefore it says in the Bible, "There is no one righteous; no, not one".'

'Wait. I know that bit too. I read it three years ago in Harusame Nakamura's novel.' Nobuo rested his elbow on the little writing table beside him, his chin in his hand. When he had read it before, it had not penetrated so deeply. But now, to his surprise, this sentence claimed a place in his heart and he could not get rid of it. He suddenly realized that he understood in his deepest consciousness what the words meant. Nobuo suddenly wanted to read the Bible, every word of it. He had the feeling that it was filled with wonderful teaching that he had not yet discovered.

'What's the matter? You seem completely lost in thought,' said Yoshikawa. Nobuo was staring at him, longing to start reading.

As soon as Yoshikawa had gone, Nobuo took the Bible that Machiko's husband had given him, close to the lamp. He was carried away with a desire to read it right through. However, he braced himself and opened it at the New Testament – but it was not in the least interesting.

In the first chapter almost the only thing he could see was a lot of names and of foreigners at that. What had any of this to do with him? If anything, a recitation of the names of the emperors of Japan would have been more interesting.

'Why do they put such dull things right at the beginning?' Nobuo thought. 'If, instead of these names, there was something like what I heard from Yoshikawa, "Everyone who looks on a woman lustfully . . ." it would be much easier to grasp.'

With this thought in mind, the punctilious Nobuo proceeded to read through the names, without skipping a word. But the story that came after the names perplexed him even more. This was the story of how Jesus was born of the Virgin Mary.

'That's stupid. How can a child be born from a virgin?'

Nobuo felt that he had been made a fool of and raised his eyes from the Bible. His room, with only the low writing table in it, looked cold and cheerless. Apart from his clothes and a towel hanging on the wall, there was nothing. He looked down and read through the story of Mary once more. However one approached it, it was strange. At any rate this book was not written to make money.

'That long, boring list! A story of how a virgin had a child! It just makes me want to throw the book away. But that would be the end of it. If I persevere, however, maybe I'll come to the better parts further on.'

Thinking he was over the major hurdle, Nobuo read on, until in the fifth chapter he found the words Yoshikawa had quoted. At once he began to learn them by heart. 'You have heard that it was said, "you shall not commit adultery", but I say to you that everyone who looks at a woman lustfully has already committed adultery with her in his heart.'

The more he repeated it the more frightening Nobuo felt the words to be. 'This Yaso, the man who preached such things, what sort of man was he, I wonder?' Thinking how strange these words were, he tried repeating them to him-

self. When he had memorized that portion he felt that the
Bible had become part of his personal experience. Nobuo
moved on to the next paragraph, looking for another good
passage to memorize.

'Do not resist one who is evil but if anyone strikes you
on the right cheek, turn to him the other also. And if
anyone would sue you and take your coat, let him have
your cloak as well.' These words caught Nobuo's attention.
They were truly startling. When he was small he had often
heard his grandmother Tose say, 'Nobuo, you are a man.
If you are hit once, you must hit back twice. If three times,
you must reply with six blows. If you do not do that you
cannot be a real man.'

If anything could be different from the Bible's words
it was that attitude. Nobuo was surprised. 'Is it more
manly, then, not to return a blow than to return it?'

Nobuo shut his eyes and thought about it. Supposing
someone hit him on the head once, would he strike back
twice without further ado? Or would his other self just
smile composedly and turn the other cheek to the aggressor?

'Which do I want to become?' Nobuo asked himself. As
he searched his heart Nobuo realized that the training he
had received from his grandmother, and its influence on
his thinking, was relatively slight.

'Even so, not hitting back when one is hit, and giving
your cloak as well, when your coat is taken, doesn't that
mean treating evil rather too kindly?' It seemed like deep
teaching, but he could not understand this part of it. Soon
he was forced to accept that there were in the Bible many
ways of thinking that were completely different from his
own.

As he read on Nobuo came immediately to the words,
'Love your enemies and pray for them that despitefully
use you.' This teaching was completely incompatible with
Japanese feeling. Japanese liked stories of formal revenge.
Nobuo earnestly considered what the forty-seven *samurai*
retainers of Ako would have done if they had lived by this

teaching of the Bible. Asano Takumi-no-kami would not have been avenged if Kira had not been beheaded. If they had forgiven Kira Kozuke-no-suke, shown him love, and prayed for his security, the public of that day would never have forgiven them. For in the world of the *samurai*, taking revenge on an enemy was an honourable deed. If his father, if his feudal lord had been killed, would this man Jesus have avenged them? Was it possible to love such an enemy? 'He must have been a very remarkable man,' Nobuo thought.

' "Do not hate". Is that such an important thing? To hate someone who deserves hate, isn't that what people should do?' Nobuo thought so, but without conviction. He had to admit that it was rather a shallow philosophy.

15   Mount Moiwa

WHILE he was eating his supper in his landlady's living room, Nobuo thought about what he had said to Yoshikawa. With his hands on the floor in a formal bow, he had asked Yoshikawa for Fujiko; nothing could be more definite. And once uttered, words could bring about great things. How he would love to make it possible for Fujiko, who always had her meals in bed, to take them sitting up like himself. Until now he had not felt Fujiko's hardships as an invalid in such a closely personal way. He was surprised that he had not been aware of this before.

'Please let me marry Fujiko.' These words had awakened something that had been dormant in him.

'Can you tell me, ma'am, who is the most successful doctor in Sapporo?' Nobuo asked, sipping his tea after supper. His landlady was a widow of over fifty and had a son who was a junior school teacher. That night he was doing night watchman duty at the school.

'What's the matter, Mr Nagano? Is something wrong with you?'

'No, there's nothing wrong with me . . .' Nobuo hesitated.

'Well, that's a relief. In Sapporo there are more than thirty doctors, but there's no doubt about it, Dr Sekiba, of the Hokushin Hospital, has the highest reputation,' his landlady replied promptly. 'Why, there's hardly anyone who hasn't heard of Dr Fujihiko Sekiba. They say some people get better when he just takes their pulse.'

When Nobuo heard this he decided to go and see him the very next day.

185

'But . . . no matter how good a doctor he is, he can't cure lung and spinal tuberculosis, can he?'

When she heard the word 'tuberculosis,' his landlady became agitated and covered her mouth with her hand.

'Mr Nagano, even if you only mention the name of that dreadful disease it makes your lungs rot. Even the gods . . . even Buddha can't cure such a terrible plague. Do you know someone who has the disease?'

'No . . . certainly not. But you know the novel *Hototokisu* – it's very popular just now. I was thinking about the woman Nami in the novel, she never did get better, so . . .'

If by some chance he let it out that Yoshikawa's sister had the illness, the landlady would not let Yoshikawa into the house, he reminded himself.

'What's that, a novel? You young people, there's no telling what you'll be up to next.' The landlady laughed and took away the tray.

Nobuo went up to his room and decided to take half a day off, the next day. The only medicine Fujiko was taking was anti-febrile infusions, and the doctor was not coming to see her now. One had come and charged a high fee, but it was not the sort of illness that could be cured quickly. Simply to leave her as she was, confined to bed, however, made him anxious. If at all possible, he would like the best doctor in Sapporo to see Fujiko. With a really good doctor, even if the disease was incurable, there might be some chance of an improvement.

He wondered if he should discuss it with Yoshikawa before going to see the doctor. But then he realized that Yoshikawa's income and the money his mother got from dressmaking were not enough to pay the fee. Anyway, if he consulted the famous Dr Sekiba first, some way of treating Fujiko would surely open up.

The next morning, as soon as he reached the office, Nobuo made a formal request to Reinosuke Wakura, to leave work early.

'What's the matter with you, why do you want to see a

doctor?' Wakura's face showed concern. He looked rough and formidable, but at heart he was a kindly man. To Nobuo, however, as he thought of how he would have to refuse his daughter Misa in the near future, this kindness was embarrassing.

'It's nothing much,' Nobuo mumbled.

'Nagano, if you're feeling bad, don't overdo things, don't come to work at all. You are new to Hokkaido and in the autumn you can catch colds easily.'

Wakura put his big hand on Nobuo's forehead.

'Hmm, you've got a bit of a temperature. Take care of yourself.'

Nobuo returned to his desk feeling almost like a fugitive. He must turn down Misa's proposal as soon as possible, but thinking how disappointed Wakura would be, he found it very difficult to tell him. Moreover, he had the feeling that no one would understand him if he rejected the vivacious Misa because he had in mind Fujiko, whose prospects of recovery were uncertain.

Nobuo left the office at noon. He had a bowl of thick, pot-boiled noodles at a restaurant on the main street. Perhaps because he was worried about meeting Dr Sekiba, or because he felt he was treating Reinosuke Wakura badly, the noodles seemed to stick in his throat.

The hospital was full of patients, even in the corridors. Everyone seemed completely occupied with their own troubles. Nobuo was amazed that there should be so many sick people in Sapporo, for it only had a population of forty thousand. There were people with dry yellow skin, people with discharging red eyes, and a continual low coughing could be heard. Whoever he looked at had the gloomy expression of someone peering into a dark hole. Nobuo could not but think of Fujiko's bright face; Fujiko who had been lying in that room for three years. These patients were at least able to get themselves to hospital, but Fujiko could not even do that. There was no one here with as bright a face as Fujiko, he reflected, and not only

so, Fujiko was more cheerful than anyone in his office too.
Nobuo had the feeling he would like to boast about Fujiko
in front of everyone.

The patients were called one by one into the consulting
room and some of them showed relief on their faces when
they came out. They all put their medicine, brown and
clear liquids or medicinal powders, carefully into their
bundles, and left. Nobuo became more and more tense.
'There seems to be no lack of medicines, but is there something to help Fujiko?' he wondered. At last his name was
called.

Nobuo walked rapidly along the Sapporo streets bathed
in the bright autumn sun. When he realized where he was,
he was striding down the middle of a broad street. Many
carts and rickshaws were passing him. Thinking that things
seemed busier than usual, he looked around. Half a block
ahead of him the flags of all the nations of the world
were draped on a building wherever they could be fixed.
Going closer, Nobuo saw a busy scene like a festival in
front of the Marui department store, with paper lanterns
advertising a bargain sale. To him, this cheerful prosperity
was a good omen. He stopped and gazed at the shop
windows for a while, and then hurried on again. At the
hospital Dr Sekiba had said that without seeing Fujiko
he could not say much, but he had explained about spinal
tuberculosis.

'Briefly, it is caused by germs which make the bones
decay. Once you catch it you usually waste away and die
after ten or twenty years. Of those who get better, many
become deformed hunchbacks. It is a terrible disease,' Dr
Sekiba had said sympathetically. 'But it is not incurable.
The secret is to keep the patient's strength up. The most
important thing is for her to rest quietly, and the next is
to eat plenty of little fish and vegetables, chewing them
very thoroughly. Then, every two days she should have a
blanket bath. The patient and others must persevere with

the treatment. And it is vital that both she and members of the family should keep cheerful, and feel confident that she will recover.'

Nobuo thought over and over again of what Dr Sekiba had said to him, as if to digest its meaning. On the way he bought some sardines and a large white radish and some carrots, in a side street. Anyway, Dr Sekiba had not said she would not recover. This alone was enough to make Nobuo more optimistic.

'The most difficult thing is to keep the patient's spirits up,' Dr Sekiba had said. Nobuo was thinking about this and imagining Fujiko fully recovered when he looked up by chance and saw Miss Wakura standing about five yards away. She was carrying a cloth bundle, as usual.

'Surely, when I met her before it was at this same corner,' he thought, and gave a flustered bow. This time Misa did not hurry away, but returned his greeting.

'Have you been shopping?' Nobuo said. He could not very well go past her; she was standing in the way.

'No, I'm just returning from my sewing lesson,' Misa said, and did not move. Nobuo was nonplussed. He felt shy of talking to a young woman in broad daylight. But he could not simply disregard her.

'Er . . . Was there something you wanted to say?' Nobuo was lost for the right words.

'No.' Misa stood smiling. He did not know what to do. Her eyes were downcast, flicking up a glance at him now and again.

'Well . . . I'll be saying goodbye.'

Nobuo hung his head and set off.

'Oh! . . .' Misa gave a little cry of surprise.

Nobuo looked round and caught a glimpse of the red muslin sash about her waist. She drew her sewing bundle closer to her and the sash was hidden. Their eyes met and they bowed again and parted.

Nobuo's depression returned. He certainly did not dislike Misa as he had just seen her. Even that brief conversation with her had been enjoyable in a way. If there had been no Fujiko, he would probably have married Misa, he was inclined to think. But this attitude was unforgivable, considering the vow he had made concerning Fujiko. As if to tear himself away from these thoughts he turned towards the Yoshikawas' house with quickened steps.

But the fact that his heart had warmed for an instant when he met Misa now weighed on his conscience. He decided not to go straight to the Yoshikawas', and lingered beside the Sosei river that ran through Sapporo from south to north. The sky was cloudless and he could see Mount Moiwa very clearly. The autumn colours were beginning to show here and there, and the summit wore a purplish mantle. A feeling of desolation overcame him as he gazed at it. The mountain would not change, however long he looked at it, but his affections had been swayed. Why was he so fickle?

'That mountain was there when Sapporo was virgin forest. Nature is completely indifferent to man,' he thought, and envied its detachment.

A long white leek was carried past him on the water, bobbing up and down. Its paleness touched a chord in Nobuo's mind. He pictured Fujiko's white face as she lay bedridden, and smiled ruefully.

'I'll never attain to such detachment,' he told himself, and started walking again.

A month had elapsed since Nobuo visited Dr Sekiba at the Hokushin Hospital. Fujiko had meekly accepted Nobuo's recommendations and kept to them. When he told her to chew her food very well, she chewed each mouthful fifty or sixty times. Maybe it was just imagination, but Nobuo fancied that her cheeks had become a little plumper. Fujiko's mother, who up till now had been afraid to do anything for fear of making the patient worse, bathed her every other day. A fresh wind of change, of activity, was blowing in the Yoshikawas' home.

Up till that time the snow had been falling and quickly melting again, but it had showed no sign of melting for two or three days now. Nobuo was on his way to Reinosuke Wakura's home to decline the offer of marriage to Misa. He walked along streets bright with light reflected from the snow, feeling as wretched as might be expected. Some students from the fencing school passed in the other direction, singing a martial song.

When it came to opening the Wakura's front door, Nobuo wanted to turn and run away. But it would not do to go on another day without giving an answer. He opened the outer door determinedly and Misa drew open the sliding inside door. They could not see each other's face in the darkness.

'Good evening, it's Nagano,' he said.

'Oh!' Misa raised her voice a little and formally invited Nobuo inside.

'Ah . . . It's good of you to come, on such a cold night.' Reinosuke Wakura threw some wood into the stove and called Misa.

'Misa, go and buy some *sake*.'

'Oh, no . . . no . . . there's no need for *sake*.'

When Nobuo protested, Wakura laughed. 'I didn't tell you you had to drink.'

When Misa had gone out, Wakura moved over towards Nobuo, and slapped him on the shoulder.

'This isn't the time for so much formality. It's not as if I don't know what you have come for. I shouldn't think there is anything harder to refuse than a proposition of marriage to the daughter of one of your superiors. So if there is any embarrassment it's the fault of the one who suggested it.'

Nobuo looked at him in surprise. Although he knew Reinosuke Wakura was a good-natured man, he had steeled himself to hear the inevitable hard comments when he announced his decision. But Wakura had seen things from Nobuo's point of view, and understood his feelings. Quite apart from what he thought of Misa, Nobuo felt like replying affectionately, as if to his father-in-law.

He bowed deeply, his hands pressed on the *tatami* matting.

'I'm very sorry . . .'

'There's someone else, I suppose. As Misa's father I'd very much like to know why you turned down this proposal. Surely you said you had decided on no one else.'

'Yes . . . but . . .' And Nobuo told him quite freely about Fujiko, how that, when Misa had been suggested as his bride, Fujiko had become more dear to him, and how he had made the decision to wait until Fujiko was cured.

'I see. The proposal about Misa served to deepen and clarify your love for this girl,' said Wakura and looked steadily at Nobuo.

'But what do you plan to do if your girl does not get better even after many years?'

'I plan to wait, even if it takes many years.'

'Well! . . . You're a fool, a big, high-minded fool. Over the centuries people have been growing a little wiser, I used to think, but there are still great fools like you left!' In order to hide his emotions Reinosuke laughed loudly. Nobuo looked down, without speaking.

'You can have your laugh too, at the doting father. As a matter of fact I could not bear to tell Misa that the proposal had been turned down. I wanted her to think it came from my side, so I sent her out. But I've given that idea up. I've a feeling I want her to know that there are still people like you in the world. Well, anyway, take great care of that girl of yours.'

Nobuo gave a deep bow.

'Well, that's that. Even if you have this girl, there are other fish in the sea for Misa. But for a young lady with an illness such as yours has, someone like you only appears once in a blue moon. I'm a parent too.'

With this Reinosuke Wakura became silent and stared fixedly at the glowing stove. From the kitchen came the sound of his wife chopping food on a board.

16   Street Corner in the Snow

EVEN at the office, Reinosuke Wakura's attitude toward Nobuo did not change.

As the day's work was coming to an end, one of Nobuo's colleagues, Minekichi Mihori, was the cause of an unpleasant incident. It was pay day, and a man in the office lost his pay packet almost immediately after receiving it. He had carelessly left it on his desk when he went to another office. He was away only fifteen minutes. When he returned and saw that his pay packet was not there, he raised the alarm.

Reinosuke Wakura called him and told him not to make a disturbance. If the pay packet had really been on his desk, it must have been stolen by someone else in the room. So close to leaving time, many people had been moving about, and it was not easy to pick out the person responsible. Wakura made all his subordinates sit down at their desks.

'I don't like to have to involve you all, but one of the pay packets has been lost. Today no one else has been in the office so, unpleasant though it is, the suspicion must lie with someone in this room. I want everyone to shut their eyes tightly and put their pay packets back in their desks. Please do not open your eyes on any account until I give the word. If someone has made a mistake and taken two packets, kindly put both into your desk.'

Everyone did as they were told. Then Wakura remained in the room while everybody else went out into the corridor. When he searched the desks there was one pay packet in each. However, the one in Mihori's desk was not his own. On it was written the name of the man who had lost his. Mihori had carelessly confused the stolen packet with his own. Reinosuke Wakura called them all back into the office and ordered them to take their own pay packet and go home.

'But one packet is still missing,' he said. 'I wanted to appeal to your consciences, gentlemen, but somehow it has not worked out as I hoped. If the stolen packet is handed over at my home today I will overlook this; if not, I want you all to realize that someone is not worthy to be an employee of the railway office.'

Mihori noticed that he had made a mistake in putting the wrong packet into his desk but, thinking that Wakura had not discovered anything, he left with the others.

The next morning Mihori was still in bed when he received Reinosuke Wakura's surprise attack. When he was woken by his mother and saw Wakura's face, his colour changed.

'Why didn't you come to my house last night?' Wakura said no more so that the other members of the household might not know what it was all about.

'Bring it to me immediately. As from today you need not come to the office. You'll receive your instructions presently.'

Mihori, deathly pale, nodded abstractedly. When Wakura had been handed the pay packet he returned home.

As the day went past Mihori's absence attracted everyone's attention. Wakura was in a bad mood. The next day, and the day following, Mihori was still absent.

Nobuo guessed that Minekichi Mihori was the offender, but it distressed him that someone like Mihori should lose his job like that. He had a reputation for being a reckless man, and Nobuo had heard him boast many times about his exploits in Susukino, the red light district. Maybe he had been short of money for his diversions and although he knew it was wrong, had taken a chance. Moreover,

Nobuo remembered that when he himself had arrived in Sapporo and started work, no one had been kinder to him than Mihori. 'He's not completely bad by any means,' he said to himself.

He was sure he had heard that Mihori lived alone with his mother, and now, he thought, 'How hard it will be for his mother when she knows that her son has lost his job.' But to say anything to Wakura would be too presumptuous. If he visited Mihori's home, that would not be very good either. So, he thought, 'If Mihori makes a genuine apology, the large-hearted Wakura will surely accept it.' He hesitated as to what to do, but at last decided to call on Mihori.

It was a Sunday afternoon and the disconsolate Mihori had shut himself up in his room. When he heard Nobuo's urging, Mihori shook his head. 'If I did that I don't know whether he would forgive me or not. That boss is a tough one and no mistake.'

However many times Nobuo urged him, Mihori would not agree even to go and see what would happen.

'I know I'm in the wrong, but that stupid fool who left his pay packet on his desk, he is in the wrong too.'

He was a more stubborn man than he looked. If the man whose pay he had stolen did not admit his fault too, no one was going to take him to Wakura's house! Nobuo went out into the snow. It creaked under his feet as he made his way along the road past the station.

New Year was approaching and there were more people about than usual. Several horse sleighs passed, their bells jingling. When he got as far as the famous red brick Agricultural Development Office, he heard someone shouting in a loud voice. Looking up, he saw a man without any overcoat, shouting something for all he was worth. Not a soul was listening to him. But Nobuo, attracted by something he heard, stood still.

'Listen everybody, what sort of creatures do you think

we men are? Isn't it true that all men like themselves
better than anything else?'

It was cold even for late December. The man was thirty,
maybe older, thirty-three or thirty-four. When he opened
his mouth to speak, his breath became a white mist. Seeing
Nobuo standing there he raised his voice a little.

'Now then, what does it mean to love ourselves more
than anything else? It means that we hate to admit we
are wrong. We all know it's wrong to embezzle money, but
when we do it, we justify ourselves. We know it's wrong
to speak evil of others, but when we do it we say we are
promoting right and condemning wrongdoing. There's a
saying, "Even a thief is three parts virtue". Yes, even a
thief can find some sort of excuse for himself.'

Nobuo gazed at the man in surprise. A woman with a
big red shawl over her head, a shop assistant carrying a
big load on his back and others passed him, but Nobuo
had forgotten where he was now, drawn by the man's
words.

'But listen, everyone, I know the biggest fool in all the
world. That man is Jesus Christ.' The man jerked forward
one step towards Nobuo. 'Jesus never did a single thing
that was wrong. He healed people that had been blind
from birth, men who had been lame from birth, and he
taught men what true love was. Do you know . . . all of
you . . . what true love really is?' His voice was urgent
and sonorous, but the only one who stayed to listen was
Nobuo.

'Ladies and gentlemen, to love is to give your most
precious thing to somebody else. And what is our most
precious thing, do you suppose? It is our life, isn't it? This
Jesus Christ gave His life to us. It is quite certain that He
did not commit a crime. Ordinary people, even when they
do something wrong, try to claim that they are innocent;
but Jesus Christ, who never did anything wrong, shoul-
dered the sins of the whole world and was nailed to a
cross. He probably could have claimed that He was

innocent and escaped, but He did not do that. The good
Man bore the sins of bad men.

'Bad men claim they are innocent and escape. This
clearly shows the difference between the Son of God and
sinful men. Now listen, when Jesus was nailed to the cross,
He prayed like this—nailed to the cross, remember. Are
you listening, everyone? When He was on the cross Jesus
prayed for the people who nailed Him there, like this:
"Father, forgive them, for they know not what they do.
Father, forgive them, for they know not what they do".

'Did you hear that, everybody? This Man who could
pray for forgiveness for the men who nailed Him to the
cross, I believe this Man possessed the very character of
God.'

Suddenly from the young preacher's clear eyes tears
began to fall. Nobuo was rooted to the spot.

'In order to tell you about this man Jesus Christ, I came
from Tokyo. For ten days I have shouted it out from here
and no one has listened to me.'

He put his hands together on his chest and began to
pray. 'Heavenly Father, thank you for your great grace.
You have seen this sheep for your flock standing before
me. Take him, Lord, and make him your own. Where my
words have been inadequate, please make things clear to
him. I offer up this prayer before you in the precious name
of your Son, Jesus. Amen.'

When he said 'Amen' in a loud voice, several people
passing by laughed.

'A Yaso!'

'A Yaso priest.'

One man threw these words over his shoulder loud
enough to be heard, but the preacher took no notice and
looked at Nobuo. Then he dropped his head. At that
moment a snowball grazed Nobuo's ear. As he gave a start,
another struck him on the shoulder. Nobuo turned round
fiercely.

'That must have hurt,' the preacher said. Knitting his brow, he put his hand on Nobuo's shoulder.

'They're a public menace!' Nobuo looked around angrily. Very soon he caught sight of some children running down a side street.

That night Nobuo could not sleep for excitement. He had brought the preacher home to his own lodgings. His name was Kazuma Iki. Once there he had said, 'Teacher, after hearing your preaching, I have come to think very seriously that Jesus is God. Indeed if Jesus is not God, I do not know who could be.' Moreover Nobuo really believed this.

When the snowball struck him hard on the shoulder, he looked round, filled with unthinking anger. Then suddenly the words of Jesus from the cross, 'Father, forgive them, for they know not what they do', had pierced him painfully. It was the same sort of situation. The children who threw the snowballs did not know what they were doing; they had acted half in fun. However, if he had been within reach of them, would he have forgiven them, Nobuo wondered? If he had caught them he would certainly have given them a piece of his mind or more likely cuffed their heads. But Jesus, at the moment when He was suffering the pains of death, had loved the people who were killing him. If this were not God's true character, what could be? Nobuo was painfully moved.

As he had read in Matthew's Gospel, this Jesus said, 'Love your enemies'. Now, thinking of Jesus who could love His enemies enough to die for them just as He had taught, Nobuo had a poignant longing to live in accordance with the teachings of Jesus – even if the whole thing were a deception.

'Well, Mr Nagano, you believe that Jesus is the Son of God?'

'I believe that.' Nobuo nodded decisively.

'Then do you intend to spend your life following Christ and His teaching?'

'Yes, that is what I want to do.'

'But do you think you will be able to say in front of others that you are Christ's disciple?' Kazuma Iki asked gently.

'I think I could.'

'But you have only just heard about Christ, do you think you can go on believing in Him?'

'My father and mother, my sister and her husband, and . . . the girl I hope to marry, they are all Christians. I have had an interest in Christianity for a long time.'

A few days before, Fujiko had said, 'I don't think reverence for our ancestors need be shown by praying before the Buddhist altar. If we can live each day in a way that our ancestors would approve, that surely is a true act of respect.' Her words had remained in Nobuo's mind. Now he repeated them and many other things to Kazuma Iki.

'It seems that you have been seeking for Christ for a long time, haven't you?' Kazuma at last seemed content with Nobuo's confessions. Inside the stove the fire crackled sharply.

'Well then, I'd like to ask you some more questions. Mr Nagano, you have said that you believe that Jesus is the Son of God and that you want to follow His teachings. And you say that you could confess in front of people that you are a disciple of Christ?'

Nobuo gave a clear nod of agreement.

'But you have forgotten one thing. Do you know why Jesus was nailed to the cross?'

'Well, you said that Jesus bore the sins of the whole world on the cross, but . . .'

'That's right. Quite right. But, Nagano, do you understand that He was nailed to the cross for your sake; in fact that you were the one who nailed Him to the cross?' And Kazuma Iki's glance became penetrating.

'That's impossible! I have no recollection of ever nailing Christ to the cross,' Nobuo protested. Seeing him waving his hands, Kazuma Iki smiled broadly. 'Well, if that's the case, you have no relationship to Christ.'

Nobuo could not understand this.

'But, Teacher, I'm a man of the Meiji era and Christ was crucified well over a thousand years ago, wasn't He? How can I, born in the reign of Meiji, have nailed Christ to the cross?'

'That's it, yours is the usual way of thinking. But I'm different; I know I nailed Christ to the cross. You see, Mr Nagano, if you do not realize that the problem of sin is your own problem, you cannot understand. Do you see yourself as a great sinner?'

As Nobuo had confessed to Yoshikawa, he considered himself a respectable sort of person. If at the times when he gave way to sexual thoughts he did think of himself as sinful, when someone else questioned him he would not admit that he was as bad as all that.

'I'm not very sure,' he said to Kazuma Iki. 'I don't think I'm specially bad, but when I read in the Bible where it says, "He who looks at a woman lustfully has already committed adultery with her in his heart", I find it a very lofty ethic, beyond my reach. As for the passage, "There is no one righteous; no, not one", I can understand that, but I don't think I'm so conscious of sin as to admit that I am a great sinner.'

Kazuma Iki listened, giving several large nods to show he understood, and then pulled out a Bible.

'I understand. Mr Nagano, I tried this myself and I would like you to try it too. I would like you to take any passage of Scripture you like and try to obey it absolutely. It must be perfectly, thoroughly followed. If you do that you will see how far short you fall from being the person you ought to be. I took the passage, "Give to him who begs from you and do not refuse him who would borrow from you", to follow, and on the tenth day I had to call it off. You'll find yourself a passage to follow, won't you?'

Kazuma Iki had supper and left. Before going to bed,

Nobuo read his Bible very earnestly and found a passage that attracted him.

'And behold, a lawyer stood up and put him to the test, saying, "Teacher, what shall I do to inherit eternal life?" He said to him, "What is written in the law? How do you read?" And he answered, "You shall love the Lord your God with all your heart, and with all your soul, and with all your strength, and with all your mind; and your neighbour as yourself." And he said to him, "You have answered right; do this, and you will live."

'But he, desiring to justify himself, said to Jesus, "And who is my neighbour?" Jesus replied, "A man was going down from Jerusalem to Jericho, and he fell among robbers, who stripped him and beat him, and departed, leaving him half dead. Now by chance a priest was going down that road; and when he saw him he passed by on the other side. So likewise a Levite, when he came to the place and saw him, passed by on the other side. But a Samaritan, as he journeyed, came to where he was; and when he saw him he had compassion, and went to him and bound up his wounds, pouring on oil and wine; then he set him on his own beast and brought him to an inn, and took care of him. And the next day he took out two *denarii* and gave them to the innkeeper, saying, "Take care of him; and whatever more you spend, I will repay you when I come back." "Which of these three, do you think, proved neighbour to the man who fell among the robbers."

'He said, "The one who showed mercy on him." And Jesus said to him, "Go and do likewise".'

When he first read this, Nobuo wondered if such a story of human cold-heartedness could be true. Surely it would be impossible for anyone not to help someone who had been attacked by robbers, and left wounded and half dead. 'I would certainly have helped, if it had been me,' he thought, as he read the story again.

Then suddenly he remembered Mihori. As he considered it, Mihori reminded him of the man left wounded and half dead. All his colleagues were unsympathetic towards him.

'Anybody who steals money is a worthless wretch.' Who wouldn't think that? Even if the amount were small, for a member of the railway company to steal his colleague's pay packet was shameful even to speak of. No wonder they were all angry.

'Since the Imperial Restoration people seem to have lost their integrity. They have put on Western dress, and the true spirit of Japan has been left behind and forgotten,' one of them had said, indirectly criticizing Mihori. Nobuo himself agreed that thieving was a crime which was hard to forgive. Nonetheless he had felt a sense of obligation towards Mihori.

When Nobuo had joined the company his employers had given him an unusually warm welcome for a young man of his age. This was because of his good record in the Tokyo law courts, but all the same, many people were jealous and had cold-shouldered him. Only Mihori, with no thought of being repaid, had kindly showed him all the workings of the office. 'Even if you are given a single sheet of paper, you have an obligation. To forget your obligations lowers you to the level of cats and dogs,' Tose, his grandmother, had told Nobuo often enough. Maybe because of this he could not be hard on Mihori, like his other colleagues.

So Nobuo came to think of Mihori as the wounded man by the roadside.

'Can I really be a good neighbour to him? In the Bible, the Samaritan became a neighbour to someone he had never seen before, and helped him. Well then, in my case Mihori is a colleague and I have an obligation to him. I'll carry out what the Scripture says, and be a really good neighbour whatever it costs,' he decided, and settled down for the night.

Nobuo was hardly able to sleep at all, thinking of Kazuma Iki's teaching.

The following morning he called at Minekichi Mihori's house. Mihori got up with a glum face, rubbing his sleepy eyes. But Nobuo ignored this, came unbidden into the guest room, and began to speak to Mihori and his mother.

'Won't you go to Wakura's house now, at once?'

This was a different Nobuo, speaking authoritatively. He was sitting in a strictly formal posture.

'Going there won't do any good,' Mihori answered sullenly.

'Maybe it won't, just as you say, but even if it doesn't do any good, if you act like a man and admit your fault, at least that will be something, won't it? That's what's needed now, isn't it?'

His words gave the impression that there was no alternative. The mother chimed in, 'Whether you will be forgiven or not, I don't know, but to admit one's fault humbly is the proper thing to do. You go, Minekichi. Mr Nagano has come specially to say this. I'll go with you and apologise.'

Mihori's mother seemed to have grasped the situation already. Without any further resistance, he reluctantly agreed to go to Mr Wakura's home.

It was still too early for office workers to be astir. A white haze drifted down the snowy road. Sometimes, as they hurried silently along, they passed people going in the other direction, looking like silhouettes. As they approached the house Mihori said, 'Nagano, why are you coming with us?'

'I'll tell you why. When I started at the office you were always kinder to me than the others. If you left now, I would be lonely.'

That was not a lie. But Nobuo could not reveal a more powerful motive.

'Even if someone like me leaves, you would feel lonely, Nagano?' Mihori seemed moved.

When he came to the door Reinosuke Wakura looked at them with distaste. At the sight of his face, Mihori was speechless. But his mother spoke timidly, her head bowed.

'It's true that Minekichi has done wrong, but . . . can't we ask you to forgive him?'

'Mother, I've been a bad son, how sad it must be for you,' said Mihori.

But Wakura neither spoke nor invited them into the house. They just stood there with bowed heads. Then, 'Mihori, there are noodle shops and the like in Sapporo. There are plenty of places if you want work.'

This sarcasm had the tone of finality. Nobuo gave Wakura a look of entreaty.

'Mr Wakura, could you not forgive Mihori, just this once? There's no question that he was guilty, but surely he would never do such a thing again. Please! His mother has come with him to apologise too. Please forgive him.'

'You're a little late in coming to apologise. If he was really prepared to admit his guilt, he would have come to my house the next day. There are plenty of places where you can get a job, Mihori. You had better give up now and go home.'

Wakura put his hand on the door to shut it. Nobuo became desperate.

'Mr Wakura!' Nobuo suddenly knelt and placed his hands on the porch step, his head bowed. Mihori and his mother joined him, kneeling on the step.

'Mr Wakura, it really is despicable to steal someone's money. It's something to be ashamed of, a wicked thing. Mihori wanted to come and apologise but was too ashamed to come alone, I believe. As his colleague I should have realized this sooner. I didn't care about him enough. Mr Wakura, it is true there are other jobs in Sapporo. But they will never stop saying about Mihori, "That man stole some money and was dismissed." When he gets married someone will say it. If he has children someone will tell them. Mr Wakura, if Mihori can't be forgiven dismiss me with him. But won't you help him, just this time?'

Nobuo bowed till his forehead met the cold step, and did not move.

17 Orders to Move

THE year drew to a close. No instructions came from Wakura. Anxiously, Nobuo spent his first New Year in Sapporo but could not enjoy himself with Mihori's problem on his mind.

'If there really is a God, He should have answered my prayers, but . . .' Many times this thought passed through his mind.

The New Year holiday ended. Wakura did not change at all and said nothing. Nobuo became increasingly uneasy. More days passed, and he began to think that his going with Mihori might have been a mistake. Maybe his calling at Wakura's home not so long after he had refused Misa had been tactless. He had gone knowing full well that it would be a difficult visit to make, but how Wakura had received it he did not know. He had pressed on and included himself in the apology with Mihori and his mother, he now thought regretfully, but perhaps it would have been better for the two of them to have gone alone.

About two weeks later, when he came to work in the morning, the men in the office seemed strangely unsettled. They were all whispering together. For an instant Nobuo thought that Mihori had been forgiven and his heart leaped.

'They've promoted the chief to Asahikawa. It's a pity, isn't it?' the man next to him whispered to Nobuo.

'What! Mr Wakura's going . . .'

Nobuo could not believe his ears. It was not that he did not expect Wakura to be promoted some day, and move elsewhere. Such a man, so popular with his superiors and juniors alike, could not possibly remain always in Sapporo. So it was not the fact that he was being moved that startled Nobuo. But if Wakura left Sapporo, what hope was there of Mihori regaining his position? It was a disappointing shock.

'Look, you'd better stop bowing and scraping and get off home. It will be worse for you if you don't.' Surely those had been Wakura's words that morning? But had he simply been evading the issue? Nobuo wondered, looking absent-mindedly out of the window. Big flakes of snow were falling without a sound. He felt desolate. That such a man as Wakura should fight shy of a decision made Nobuo feel wretched.

'Our prayers are not answered as easily as that,' he concluded sadly, and left his work untouched.

Reinosuke Wakura seemed very busy and spent no time at his desk that day. The morning's snow had ceased falling and Nobuo was preparing to go home when Wakura tapped him on the shoulder. With a look he indicated that Nobuo should follow him into the conference room.

'Well, they've decided on Asahikawa, at last,' said Wakura as he sat down on a chair.

'Congratulations!' Nobuo bowed a little stiffly.

'A sinecure for an old man who's finished, they might say. Asahikawa is cold and not a very welcoming place, but that can't be helped.'

Having said this, Wakura said no more. Nobuo did not speak either. Wakura's silence continued. Nobuo fancied he knew what Wakura was thinking about. He was going to say that there was not time to do anything about Mihori, and there was no more that could be done. Nobuo also remained silent.

'Sit down. This is your first winter, isn't it?' Wakura spoke casually. So he was thinking of Nobuo, after all.

'Yes.'

'You find it cold?'

'No, it has not been as cold as I thought it would be, yet.'

'Hmm.' For the second time Wakura's speech tailed off. 'Do you have something for me to do?'

'Yes, I have, two big jobs.' Wakura smiled broadly. 'What are they?'

'Nagano, you are an amazing person. First of all you turn down my daughter Misa, who is a strong girl and would probably bear you I don't know how many children, to wait for some girl who may never recover. That's surprising enough in itself, but then you go and surprise me again. You, a man of *samurai* stock, prostrating yourself on my front step, pleading for that half-baked Mihori, and on top of that saying that you would leave your job if he did, you completely astonish me.'

Wakura gazed intently at him and Nobuo looked down.

'Just to look at your face, you seem mild enough. I've known a lot of men but it's the first time I've met anyone like you. I've never thought of anyone as frightening before but, you know, deep down I think I'm scared of you. And to answer the request of such a frightening man, I've been busying myself a little. Nagano, Mihori is going with me to Asahikawa.'

'What, to Asahikawa?'

'Yes, it would be hard on the fellow to have to work here, wouldn't it? I'll take him to Asahikawa and straighten him out there. The order for him to move has been issued.'

Wakura took a rolled-up document from his pocket, and thumped it down on the table. Nobuo instinctively rose to his feet and made a deep bow. 'Thank you . . . Thank you very much.' He bowed deeply again.

'Wait a bit. It's too early to start thanking me yet. As a matter of fact I'm generally a good loser, but this time things are going to be different. It would be a pity to leave you behind. One doesn't meet a junior like you more

than once in a lifetime. I'd like you to come with me to
Asahikawa. What about it?'

Nobuo could not reply.

'You know, you have a responsibility for Mihori. I don't
like to remind you, but after what you have said I have a
feeling you yourself ought to keep an eye on him. Think
about it, will you?'

Nobuo nodded.

'Dear Mother,

*'I am sorry not to have written for so long. I hope
you and Machiko and her husband are still well. I am
writing this letter at the upstairs window of my lodging
house, looking out over roofs piled with snow. The roof
of this house is piled high with it too.*

*'Mother, the daffodils will be blooming in the garden
in Tokyo now. I think how amazing that is when I gaze
at the streets of Sapporo, all white with snow. But, of
course, it is just the normal thing for the people of
Tokyo to spend their winter without snow, while the
people of Hokkaido have to bear the cold. I can't help
pitying them. Up here, when it gets really cold things
are frozen up. The edges of your quilt get stiff with
frost, and the glass in the windows is frozen over with
beautiful white patterns, like fern leaves or peacock
feathers; and sometimes there are spiral patterns, an
endless variety which I don't know how to describe,
they are so beautiful. Maybe it's because I'm young, but
I enjoy even really cold days and snow storms. Walking
about bent double in a raging snow storm really gives
you a sense of being alive. On days when the cold stings
like a knife I feel a sort of heightened pleasure.*

*'Mother, now I've come to Hokkaido and faced the
winter here I'm glad I came. There may be pleasure in
looking at cherry blossoms under a beautiful blue sky,
but when all one's body and spirit are nerved to face the
fierce cold, maybe there is an even greater pleasure.*

Perhaps next winter I shall have gone to an even colder place still, Asahikawa.'

At this point Nobuo laid down his pen and put some logs in the stove. He could hear the high-pitched ringing of the sleigh bells as a horse-drawn sledge passed by the house. For a little while he worked out how he would announce the news about Mihori.

When Reinosuke Wakura had urged him, Nobuo had acquiesced immediately.

'Mr Nagano, you are a really surprising person,' Wakura said with a note of admiration and amazement in his voice. Regardless of what it may cost you, you are going as far as Asahikawa, just for the sake of Mihori.'

Nobuo sat for a little, looking at the thick icicles which hung in front of his window, and then took up his pen again.

'Mother, I've changed since I came to Hokkaido. Every day I think about Christ. For some reason I could not help hating the fact that you were a Christian, Mother. But, in spite of that, I have decided to go to cold Asahikawa in order to help a man in obedience to Christ's teaching. Yet as the days pass, the resolve that I have made seems to be in danger of wavering. Mother, please pray that I may become a good Christian.

'I ask you earnestly to take care of yourself, and give my best regards to Kishimoto and Machiko.'

When he re-read his letter and put it into the envelope Nobuo had a sudden wish that he could get in with it and return to Tokyo. In a few days the letter would be taken through the gate of his own home in his own city, and find its way into his mother's kind hands. The thought gave him a longing to be there. The mental image of her, opening the letter with scissors and running her eyes over what he had written, flashed through his mind. Nobuo blew a puff of breath into the envelope and sealed it.

By April the snow had melted, and soon May, the month of cherry blossoms, had passed. It was now June, the season of lilac and acacia, but for some reason or other there was no further word of Nobuo's move to Asahikawa. Maybe Mr Wakura, thinking sympathetically about Fujiko, had postponed the move, Nobuo thought thankfully, but it was strange that no order for his transfer had been issued. Meanwhile he was very thankful that he had not had to go. Each week without fail he visited Fujiko and they would read the Bible and pray together. Even though Nobuo did not express his feelings towards her, they soon found a deep mutual understanding. Nobuo thought of the times he spent with Fujiko as the most satisfying he had known. He would talk to her about the scenery outside, or things that had happened in the streets, and Fujiko always listened with genuine happiness. And when he visited her, whatever he brought as a present, even if it were a single dandelion plucked from the roadside, Fujiko's whole face would light up with joy.

'Mr Nagano, I can imagine quite clearly the place where you picked that dandelion. It was in a quiet street in front of a big Western-style building, and near it there was a willow tree and a little girl playing with some red jack-stones. That was where you picked it, wasn't it, Mr Nagano? And you picked it for me.'

Even a single very ordinary dandelion could bring a variety of scenes to Fujiko's mind, though she had not left her bed for several years. But more than that, she always brought a peculiar delight to Nobuo, who had done it to please her. He valued her sweetness and kindness more and more. Fujiko had a gift for receiving other people's courtesies so graciously. However small the gift, with her inexhaustible imagination she created a child's story or a poem about it.

When he brought her apples and tangerines, Fujiko would take them in her hands and gaze raptly at them.

'Look, Mr Nagano. It's God who has created such beautiful colours. I would love to see God's paint box,' she would say with innocent happiness. 'I wonder how many different colours He has?' She was so joyful that the people who came to see her became cheerful too.

Nobuo found himself wanting to show everything he saw to Fujiko, especially the evening sun, sinking behind the mountains and the rows of acacia trees. Just from imagining how happy she would be to see them, Nobuo had the feeling that she was with him. In this way, visiting Fujiko and telling her about everything became a great joy and comfort to him. Only one thing distressed him more and more, the question of when he would be moved to Asahikawa.

The order for his transfer finally came at the beginning of September. It was a morning when the cosmos flowers were tossing in the wind that he first got the news. Although he had been prepared for it, he was depressed and even annoyed. Wakura knew about Fujiko's illness, and had a daughter himself, so he must have been able to understand something of Fujiko's sad position. Moreover, Nobuo suspected that if he left Fujiko and went to Asahikawa, Wakura would try to bring him and Misa together again.

Nobuo had not forgotten the verses of Scripture that he had read, nor his decision to be a true friend and neighbour to Mihori. But, if the truth were known, he felt that rather than go to Asahikawa for the sake of Mihori who was well, there was a greater need to be a good neighbour to Fujiko who was ill. Because he had apologised for him, Mihori had escaped losing his job, and Nobuo felt that he had done enough. That same day, with his mind still unsettled, Nobuo went straight to Fujiko's house.

Seeing Yoshikawa, who had a day off, Nobuo gave way to his feelings.

'Yoshikawa, I've been transferred,' he said as soon as he entered the guest room.

'Transferred? Where?' Yoshikawa's face stiffened immediately, and he looked behind him in the direction of Fujiko's room.

'It's Asahikawa.'

'Asahikawa? But you've only been a year in the company.'

'Yes, but . . . well, it can't be helped.' Nobuo thought of telling Yoshikawa about Mihori, but felt that it would not be right to reveal everything to him.

'Fancy . . . Asahikawa,' Yoshikawa murmured, pressing down with his big hands on the knees of his crossed legs. Yoshikawa's mother, who had put her head out from the kitchen when she heard that Nobuo was moving, began to sob, 'Well, what shall we do, what shall we do now?'

Seeing the agitation of both Yoshikawa and his mother, Nobuo himself became uneasy. If the two of them could be so sad about it, what would Fujiko be like? he thought dejectedly.

For a year Fujiko had been making steady progress, and he was afraid that to announce his transfer to someone in her state would not only be very cruel but might affect her health.

'Well, it can't be helped,' Yoshikawa said. 'Meeting and parting, it's all part of life. We can't ignore the strict rules of the railroad. But, Nobuo, you tell Fujiko, please. I'll stay in here.'

Yoshikawa seemed lacking in resolution, unlike his usual self. His mother also sank to the floor and sat without moving. There was nothing else he could do. Nobuo went to Fujiko's room.

'Come in! You're welcome. Do you know what happened today? A dragonfly flew into the room. It made me very happy.'

Seeing Fujiko's face so bright that it almost shone, Nobuo became even more downcast. How many times had he visited her, flat on her back in this room, he wondered? But no matter how often, he had never found Fujiko out of sorts. Probably it would be safe after all to tell her everything. Pulling himself together with an effort, Nobuo sat down by her bedside.

'Fujiko.'

At the sound of his formal tone she turned her frank eyes on him with a questioning look. When he saw them, Nobuo found himself unable to speak. He searched for words which somehow would not startle or sadden her.

'What's happened? You look as if you've got a difficult problem.'

'Yes, it's a very difficult one.'

'Fujiko.' Without thinking, he took her hand. The hand was so soft that it almost seemed to melt as he grasped it. He felt he could sense Fujiko's weakly flickering life and almost choked with emotion. If he told her about his transfer, it could well be that that hand would lose all power to live, he thought as he held it tenderly.

'What's the matter? There's something different about you today.'

'Fujiko . . . It's like this.' Nobuo summoned up his courage and spoke. 'I've been transferred to Asahikawa. Asahikawa is close and I'll be able to visit you once or twice a month.'

Nobuo looked steadily at Fujiko's widely opened eyes as she realized what was happening. Quickly they filled with tears which rolled down to her ears. She did not say a word, but softly pulled up the quilt as far as her chest, then until it hid her neck and finally covered her face. The quilt moved slightly as if Fujiko was weeping silently beneath it. The slender hand was hidden now. The thought of it brushing away her tears, was like a great weight crushing Nobuo's chest. Minutes passed, they did not know how long. At last Fujiko put her head out from under the quilt. Her eyes were still red with weeping, but she looked at Nobuo and broke into a smile.

'That's strange. I didn't think I had any tears; I wonder where they were hidden.' From her smiling eyes, tears began to fall again.

'I must not forget to offer you my congratulations.' After she had said this her lips began to tremble uncontrollably and she started to weep again. Nobuo wiped away his tears too.

'I always pray that God's will may be done, but sometimes when things happen according to His will, they are hard to bear, aren't they,' said Fujiko after some time.

'But, Fujiko. It's not as if we were parting for life. I'll be able to see you every Sunday. Don't take it so hard.'

'Thank you, but sooner or later you will forget all about me, Mr Nagano. As far as you are concerned, that will be a good thing.'

'Fujiko, don't say such a thing. I have not said what I feel in actual words, but I thought you understood.'

'But . . . Mr Nagano, you are well and strong.'

'Well, this is a good opportunity, I'll tell you clearly. This is the truth, Fujiko. Almost as soon as I came to Sapporo there was talk of my marrying the daughter of my superior, but I refused. I did that because of you.'

Fujiko looked at Nobuo in surprise and he went on.

'I'm sure you are going to get better and then marry me. It may take a long time, but even if you never do, all my life I'll never marry anyone else.'

This was the first time Nobuo had been able to declare his love and intentions to Fujiko. As he did so he renewed the vow in his heart not to marry anyone except this sweet but pitiful Fujiko.

'But . . . I'm not worthy of such a . . .'

'What do you mean, you're not worthy? I am unworthy of you, with your beautiful nature!'

Nobuo sat up in a straight and formal position.

'Fujiko, will you be my life partner?'

Tears welled up in Fujiko's eyes again.

'I will not allow it. Mr Nagano, you should marry someone who is strong. There's no need to feel sorry for me.'

Nobuo edged closer to Fujiko. As he wiped away her tears with his handkerchief he spoke. 'Fujiko, do you think the most important part of a person is their body? I don't. I think the spirit is more important than the body.'

'Thank you . . . but . . .'

'I don't understand it,' Nobuo said passionately, 'but it seems to me that the personality is the chief thing about anyone. Even if someone had no hands or eyes, if his spirit were a fine one you could say he was a fine person. Don't reproach yourself for being ill. No one could imitate your sweet gentleness and sincerity.'

'You make me very happy when you say things like that, but . . .'

'What is it now, why are you saying "but" again? Don't say "but" any more.'

'But . . .'

This time Nobuo leaned right over her and pressed his lips to her quivering ones. In a panic Fujiko tried to push Nobuo off with both her hands.

After a moment Nobuo raised his head. Fujiko was pale and trembling. Her chest rose and fell as she gasped for breath.

'Fujiko.' Nobuo spoke her name softly. Fujiko covered her face with both hands and said, 'Mr Nagano! I have the lung disease! If it should pass to you . . .'

Fujiko's concern for his health was even greater than the happiness of being kissed.

'Don't worry. The sickness has almost left your lungs, hasn't it, Fujiko? If it were infectious it would have reached Yoshikawa and me long ago,' Nobuo smiled.

The room had grown a little dark. Nobuo lit the lamp by her bed. The oil sputtered a little and the flame flickered. They gazed at each other silently. The window panes rattled in the wind.

'It's been a year, hasn't it?' Fujiko broke the silence.

'You mean since I came to Sapporo?'

'Yes, a year and two months, isn't it?' Fujiko was thinking about something.

'What is it?'

'Nothing. I was just thinking that all the happiness that I've had in the last ten years is nothing to compare with the happiness of the last year and two months.' And a smile lit up her face.

18   My Neighbour

NOBUO had been in Asahikawa for about ten days. He had been told that Asahikawa was like a smaller version of Sapporo, and certainly the straight streets laid out in a chequer-board pattern gave a pleasant feeling of space. Although it was smaller than Sapporo, the presence of an army division quartered there lent the streets an air of activity and bustle.

What gave Nobuo the greatest pleasure was to see the Daisetsu and Tokachi mountain ranges standing clear against the September sky. Snow had already come to them. Those white peaks hinted what life would be like in Asahikawa. He found the sight of them invigorating. The little house he rented was near the station, as it had been in Sapporo. It was a very ordinary one-storey house with just three rooms, but in the wide street in front stood a large straight elm tree which took his fancy.

In the evening when he prepared his supper he could hear the voices of children playing under the tree until it grew dark. When he came to Asahikawa Nobuo decided that he would do his own cooking. He felt that some day, when he married Fujiko, he might have to do the cooking himself.

One evening, as he was clearing up after supper, Minekichi Mihori arrived.

'Ah, hello . . . Welcome!' Nobuo was glad to see him. However, Mihori was well under the influence of *sake* and had a fixed stare.

'Is it all right to come in?'

'Of course, I'm by myself, make yourself at home.'

Mihori stumbled over the threshold as he slipped off his clogs and went into the sitting room.

'You've drunk quite a lot, haven't you, Mihori?'

Mihori sat down heavily by the fireplace in the middle of the room and crossed his legs.

'Whether I'm drunk or not, that's my business. I bought the drink with my own money, not stolen money, Nagano.'

Nobuo looked blankly at Mihori.

'Nagano, do you know what sort of *sake* I've been drinking today?'

'No . . . I've no idea.'

'You don't know? I wouldn't expect you not to know.' Suspicion and resentment seethed in his drink-fuddled mind.

Mihori jerked a pair of tongs from the ashes in the fireplace. Nobuo was sitting some distance away.

'Don't beat about the bush. I was just asking you how I got this *sake* to drink.'

'You've got me puzzled. I haven't a clue what you are talking about.'

Nobuo recalled Mihori's expression when he came to meet him at Asahikawa station. He had looked so happy that Reinosuke Wakura, who had come with him to meet Nobuo, had slapped him on the shoulder and said, 'You look disgustingly cheerful.'

Now the same Mihori sat cross-legged before him, hands on knees, tongs in hand and his shoulders raised threateningly.

'Well, you've put me in an awkward spot!' he said.

'An awkward spot. Has something happened?'

'Yes, you can be sure of that. It's you, Nagano. What have you come to Asahikawa for?'

'What do you mean, Mihori? Has my coming to Asahikawa put you in a spot?'

'Of course it has. There used to be no one in Asahikawa who knew my past record, only the boss, Wakura. And now you have to come.'

Nobuo felt he understood Mihori's feelings.

'Nagano, you've come all the way to Asahikawa to keep a close eye on what I do.'

'Keep an eye on you, what a thing to say . . .'

'No, that's what you came for, and no mistake. You came to see that I don't steal anybody's pay packet again.' You're making a fool of me. Even if you weren't watching me I wouldn't lay hands on anybody's pay packet again.'

Those words, 'You're making a fool of me' struck home to Nobuo.

'Mihori, don't say such unpleasant things.'

'Unpleasant? Yes, it's unpleasant all right. The things I say and do are unpleasant to you, I don't doubt. I know what you are really thinking. I know all right. I know what you said to the boss. You said that in the event of this wretched fellow doing anything bad again, you would leave the railway company with him. Please, please forgive him, you said. You're a very fine person, Nagano. But this is what you are really thinking. You came here to keep an eye on me, so that you would be able to take care of yourself and keep your job.' Mihori's speech was becoming thicker and thicker.

'What are you talking about, Mihori? I came to Asahikawa because my transfer was ordered. If you are ordered to move you can't do anything about it.'

'Huh . . . An order to move. As far as that's concerned, if you asked the boss you could get any number of them. When I was whisked off to Asahikawa it was at your instigation, I don't doubt.' Mihori spoke as if he had forgotten how he had been reinstated, on the point of being dismissed.

'Mihori . . . is that all you want to say?' Nobuo was thinking how he had left Fujiko in Sapporo and come all the way to Asahikawa. His plans of becoming a true friend to Mihori and really helping him had been over-ambitious, he reflected gloomily. He did not know how many times he had longed to be with Fujiko. The thought that he was more necessary to her than to Mihori troubled him. But he had really wanted to do as the Bible taught. Now, however, the most important thing for him was Fujiko. To leave her, the dearest thing he had, and come to Asahikawa, was being true to Mihori, but his faithfulness was completely lost on him, it seemed.

'No, I've plenty to say. Mr Nagano, you've come to Asahikawa to spread bad stories about me.'

'But look here, Mihori. Just now you said it was at my instigation that you were transferred to Asahikawa. I want to be your true friend. There's no reason why I should spread stories about you.'

'You a friend! Don't make me laugh. You're a most dangerous fellow to me, even if you never announce that I stole a colleague's pay packet.' Mihori was not listening to Nobuo.

'Mihori!' Nobuo could stand it no longer and became severe. 'Mihori, stop suspecting such things. And you had better stop drinking. It's disgusting to go drinking and pick quarrels with people. If you'd just stop drinking you'd be a decent person.'

'A-ah, now you've shown your true colours. You're scared that I'll get drunk and make a big mistake and there'll be a row. But, Nagano, I'm going to drink; yes, I'm going to drink. I've been whisked off to cold Asahikawa; do you think I can carry on living without drinking?'

Mihori swayed on his feet. 'Nagano, I've got one more thing to say. You want to win my gratitude, but I don't want anyone doing me any favours.'

He sat down on the step in the porch and searched for his shoes. Nobuo gave him a lamp. Mihori thrust his feet into his worn clogs, bumped into the door with a crash so that it jammed and he had to struggle to open it, and went out.

'Ah, just a minute, I've forgotten something. Perhaps

you have designs on Wakura's daughter? No—I'm sorry,
I shouldn't have mentioned that.'

Mihori went off laughing loudly, leaving the door about
six inches open.

It was a fine Sunday in October. Nobuo had heard that
there was a church nearby and plucked up courage to go
and visit it. In Sapporo he had been to church once or
twice, but although there was a friendly spirit among
people of the same interests as himself, they gave the
impression of being cold towards newcomers. Or was it
that Nobuo was not used to the way they did things?

The one Nobuo was now directed to, although it was
called a church, was really a deserted Buddhist temple, re-
paired and put to use as both pastor's residence and meeting
place. He was surprised to see the fine lattice work in the
windows. Looking inside, he saw twenty or thirty children
singing a hymn. When they saw Nobuo their faces lit up
– a strange reaction, he could not help thinking.

At the end, a young man in Japanese dress and short
cropped hair, who had been teaching the hymn, came up
to Nobuo, followed by his pupils.

'Are you going to become our teacher now, sir?' a lively
looking boy asked Nobuo.

'No . . . no. I'm not yet . . . er . . . It's the first time I've
come to this church.'

'That's all right, that makes no difference. Please be our
teacher. What is your name, sir?'

Nobuo introduced himself to the Sunday school teacher,
who was about the same age as himself.

'My name is Nobuo Nagano. I'm a railway employee,
and I live about two blocks away.'

'Teacher Nagano, Teacher Nagano.' For some reason
the children seemed to have decided on Nobuo as their
teacher.

Later, in the church records, this was written of him.
'When he stood to speak, it was with a fierce earnestness,

and his pale face became flushed. From his slim, five-foot frame a message from Heaven sounded forth. However, when he came down from the pulpit, he had a kind and mild expression, which no one could help but love and admire.' Probably the children recognized his kindness at a glance, and accepted him. Nobuo must have been the only person, before or since, to be accepted as a Sunday school teacher on his very first appearance inside a church.

And so it was that Nobuo became one of them. He had already decided to be baptised, and the congregation accepted him as a believer like themselves. With his new life in the church, Nobuo found every day very satisfying. At work, however, Minekichi Mihori kept looking at him in a servile, obsequious way that weighed on his mind. At first Mihori's drunken words had made him angry and Nobuo had hated him, but, discovering to his shame that he was not capable of living up to the commands of Scripture, he felt humbled and grateful, in a way, for what Mihori had said. Certainly he had no thought of getting his own back on him. In fact, he had to admit that there had been an element of selfishness in his desire to help Mihori. So now he tried his best to be a true friend.

Nobuo's baptism and public confession of faith were to be held at Christmas that year. The evening before the Christmas service, Nobuo was sitting by the lamp, totally absorbed in writing out his confession of faith, when Minekichi Mihori called again. And he had been drinking, as he usually did in the evening.

'What's this? Are you writing a love letter, Nagano?' Seeing the ink stone and paper, Mihori gave a mocking laugh.

'A love letter . . . I see, well you could call it that,' laughed Nobuo. As he laughed the lamp threw a huge shadow of his head on the paper screen.

'I thought it might be. Who are you writing to? Wakura's daughter, I suppose.' Mihori seemed to have Wakura's daughter on his mind a good deal.

'No, it's not to her.'

'Well, then, who is it to?'

'It's to the Lord.' And Nobuo used an expression which Mihori took to mean the 'landlady'.

'Some landlady! Where does she live? You'll get in great trouble with the police if you molest someone like that. That's worse than stealing someone's pay packet.'

Nobuo said nothing, but laid the confession of faith he had written in front of Mihori.

'Is it all right to read it?' Mihori shrank back a little.

'Yes, it's all right if you read it out to me.'

'Well, I'll have a look. What you write in a love letter to a landlady will be a fine topic for conversation.' He opened the rolled-up letter.

'What's this? "Before God and men I humbly confess my faith . . ." What is it? It's a strange sort of love letter.' He was on the point of throwing the letter down, but took it up and continued.

' *"Before God and men I humbly confess my faith. My mother was driven out of the house by my grandmother because she was a Christian. My grandmother was a great hater of Christianity and I was brought up largely under her influence. When my grandmother died, my mother came to live with my father again, but I found it very hard to feel affectionate toward a Christian mother. I was unable to forgive her for being prepared to desert me, her own child, in obedience to her faith. But because my grandmother and then my father died very suddenly, I began to think about death and then sin. And, especially during my adolescent years I learned from my struggles with physical longings that I was a sinful person.*

"Then, by chance, in the winter of the year I came to Sapporo, in the cold streets I listened to the preaching of Teacher Iki, an open-air evangelist. I was greatly moved and wanted to become a Christian. Previously I

had reached my own conclusions about Buddhism, and no longer felt any resistance to being a Christian.

"However, Teacher Iki asked me if I admitted that it was my sins that caused Christ to be nailed to the cross, and I did not think that I had committed a great enough sin for that. This was because I prided myself that I was a more earnest person than others. But the teacher immediately told me to take a passage out of the Bible, just one, and see if I could carry it out perfectly.

"I read the story of the Good Samaritan, and thought I could never be as cold-hearted as the men in the story. I flattered myself that I would be like the good Samaritan. So I decided to become a true neighbour to one of my friends, no matter what it cost.

"In order to be a good neighbour to him, I came to Asahikawa, where he lived, although I knew I would be the loser in several ways by doing so. And I thought that, seeing I had loved him from the heart and been a good friend to him, naturally he would be glad. But he did not accept my efforts, and I built up a great hatred towards him.

"I was like the Samaritan, putting all his efforts into helping an injured, half-dead man on a mountain road, and I could not understand why he should shout at me. I was trying to help him, but he roughly pushed off my helping hands. When he did that, I hated and cursed him in my heart. I became more and more filled with hatred toward him, until at last I realized what was happening.

"I realized that, right from the beginning I had looked down on him. Every day I was unhappy, and prayed to God. Then I heard God's voice, 'You yourself are the wounded traveller, fallen on the mountain road. The fact that you are continually crying out to Me for help proves it.' I was the sinner who needed help. Then it *came to me that it was really Jesus Christ, the Son of God, who was the Good Samaritan.*

"This was all so true; in my pride I had taken the place of God and looked down on my friend. I realized what a great sin it was, not to give God His rightful place. And then I knew that it was my sin that had nailed Christ to the cross. Now I believe in Christ's atonement on the cross for my sin. I believe in His resurrection, and in the eternal life that He has promised. When I think about Christ who was crucified for us, I want to offer my life to God and very genuinely to become His disciple. Here I humbly close my confession of faith. In the name of Jesus Christ. Amen."'

Minekichi Mihori, who had read avidly to the end, rolled up the paper in silence.

' "Amen" . . . Is that what you say?' As he spoke he put down the document heavily in front of Nobuo. But he showed no sign of moving from his place beside the stove. Nobuo prayed that in some way his friend might come to know that God really loved him.

'Mihori, it was very impertinent of me. I was conceited and thought that somehow or other I could elevate and change your character. When you first came to this house and angrily told me not to make a fool of you, I had no intention of doing so. But I see now that I was really looking down on you. Please forgive me.'

Nobuo bowed his head low. The only sound to be heard was the stove burning. Mihori sat without moving.

Two months had elapsed since Nobuo's baptism. It was a warm evening, for March was drawing near and the drips from the roof could be heard even at night. Nobuo sat warming himself by the stove, reading a manual of railway regulations. The front door slid open noisily. He went out to see, thinking that Mihori had called again but, to his surprise, it was the large form of Reinosuke Wakura filling his small porch.

'This is a snug little house,' said Wakura, wheeling round and looking at the living room, as in his Sapporo lodgings devoid of any furniture except for a desk.

'Nagano . . . I've got a problem,' he went on, taking a great gulp of the tea which Nobuo had set before him.

'I see.' Nobuo had a premonition that this sudden visit from Wakura was to talk about something difficult.

'The lamp is bright, isn't it? You're a methodical person; you take good care of things.' Wakura characteristically changed the subject.

'As a matter of fact, it's about Misa . . .'

He looked searchingly at Nobuo's face. Nobuo frowned, thinking that this matter of Misa had been settled long ago.

'Don't worry, I'm not asking you to consider her again,' Wakura laughed, seeing Nobuo's dismay.

'To be frank with you, Misa's husband has been decided.'

'Well, well, congratulations.' Nobuo remembered Misa's plump form. For a moment he had a feeling as if he had lost something.

'No, it's not a matter for congratulations . . . her partner is Mihori.'

For a moment Nobuo could not reply.

'You're surprised?'

'Yes, I am,' Nobuo replied frankly.

'Young lovers, there's no stopping them, I just didn't realize it. As a matter of fact, Mihori stayed with us for a month after he came to Asahikawa from Sapporo.'

Nobuo had heard about this. He had heard that for some reason, maybe his mother's neuralgia, Mihori had come to take up his appointment alone. But he had thought that Mihori had stayed at the Wakuras' home only a few days.

'He stayed a month, did he?'

'I'm just a silly, doting father. I thought Misa had more sense than most girls. I never thought she'd fall in love with a fellow like Mihori.'

Wakura had never told his wife or Misa what Mihori had done in Sapporo. They knew that he had come to the house early one morning with Nobuo to apologise, but they had no reason to know why. They simply knew it was enough to make Wakura angry.

'A girl like Misa, she's not like Mihori's mother, always hovering half-hidden in the background. Seeing Mihori acting so deferentially, and yet so depressed, in my house, she felt sorry for him, it seems. She was kinder to him than she need have been. Whether Mihori misunderstood this and interpreted it as love, and whether Misa was glad to be misunderstood ... I don't know exactly.'

'I see, that's what happened.'

'When you think of it, if two young people like them live together under the same roof for a month, there's nothing strange about their coming to feel deeply for one another. Thinking about it now, it was just my carelessness that I did not notice it. After that, they used to meet now and again secretly. Anyway, it seems she's going to have a baby.'

Even Wakura, usually so large-hearted and stable, appeared shaken. Nobuo felt there was nothing he could do but listen in silence. He could not very well say that it was a terrible thing to happen, nor could he repeat his congratulations. But, knowing the situation now, he knew why Mihori wanted to pick a quarrel with him when he was drunk. Just the fact that Wakura was well disposed toward Nobuo could make Mihori think that Misa might be taken away from him.

'Mr Wakura, don't you think Mihori will settle down when he gets married? He's not a bad person at heart.'

Nobuo really believed this. He did not think Mihori would get into trouble again. He thought that when the child was born he would become a kindly, devoted father.

'Hmm. Maybe that's true. He's a timid man. He would not be able to do anything really bad,' said Wakura, striking his knees lightly with his hands. 'But you know,

Nagano. I really wanted someone like you for Misa. There's too much of a difference between you and Mihori!' Wakura laughed regretfully.

Nobuo raised his head and spoke.

'Mr Wakura, that's not true. In church I've learned that all men are the same. Don't think of someone like me as anything special. In the eyes of God, Mihori may be a better person that me,' he said eagerly.

Undoubtedly Mihori had been quarrelsome because he considered himself inferior to Nobuo. And Nobuo was ashamed that he had unconsciously come to think of himself as superior to Mihori.

Wakura looked at Nobuo, a little surprised, and then, waving his big hands, he said, 'Not at all. You and Mihori, you're as different as the moon and a snapping turtle.'

'No, that's not true. It says in the Bible, "There is no one righteous, no not one". It's stated clearly.'

'No. Whatever the Bible may say, what I see with my eyes is true. And not only me. No matter who looks at you, a fine person is a fine person, and a fool is a fool . . .' Wakura cracked a salted biscuit with a loud snap.

'You don't understand.'

'Well, listen to me. You're saying that Mihori and *I* are the same. Don't joke with me. I think I'm a little bit cleverer than Mihori!' Wakura munched his biscuit loudly.

'Mr Wakura, won't you please read the Bible, once. With our human judgement we see one as a fine man and another as a fool, but if we had to stand before God, it would be a different matter. Would we be able to stand up straight before God and claim to be great men?' Nobuo was deeply in earnest.

'Well . . . if it's a question of an affair with a woman, I've had about five. In this Meiji age, most men play around with women, and it doesn't particularly matter. I've not stolen anybody's things, and of course I've not killed anyone. I would not have so much to be ashamed

of before the devil or God.' Wakura laughed loudly. Then
he talked a little about their work and left.

As he was pulling on his long boots, Wakura said,
'Nagano, I know he's a good-for-nothing fool . . . but, will
you look after Mihori? Ah, I've got it, that talk you just
gave me about Yaso, let him hear it too. I don't need that
sort of talk so much.' Wakura put out his big hand and
grasped Nobuo's lightly.

In July, the month after Misa and Mihori were married,
they had a pretty little girl. Mihori stopped his heavy
drinking and became a diligent worker. They were a happy
couple and the times when he took even a little *sake*
became few.

Nobuo had intended to visit Fujiko once a week, but his
plans came to nothing. Because he was a Sunday school
teacher, he was hardly ever able to return to Sapporo. If
anything, it was Yoshikawa who took to calling sometimes
on Nobuo in Asahikawa.

One day Nobuo was telling his pupils a story about
Jesus, when, unexpectedly, Yoshikawa came shambling into
the church. Nobuo gave him a glance of recognition, and
was about to go on with the lesson. However, another man
came in behind Yoshikawa.

'Ah . . . Cousin Takashi!' Nobuo called out in a loud
voice without thinking, and as one, the thirty or forty
pupils turned round to look. Nobuo resumed his lesson in
a fluster, and the pupils were soon drawn again to his
story.

'Jesus was walking on the waves, gently stretching out
his hands to the disciples as he walked towards them.' The
children all nodded approval. Nobuo's story-telling had an
unconscious earnestness which absorbed the children's
attention. They were intent, almost as if gazing at Jesus
walking over the dark waves.

When Sunday school ended, the pupils all rushed around
Nobuo and when he had touched them or laid his hand on
their shoulders, they went home looking very satisfied.

'The lad's really grown up, hasn't he?' Takashi's voice was as loud as usual.

'Cousin Takashi, it's very good of you to come as far as here. Yoshikawa, how did you meet him . . .?"

'Your mother in Tokyo told him to call on me, and she sent a present.'

'I see; and then you went out of your way to show him how to find me. You shouldn't have gone to so much trouble.'

Seeing that they had come right to the church, Nobuo urged them to stay for the adults' worship service.

'Remarkable, isn't it; being made to listen to a talk we don't understand?' said Takashi on the way home. But in spite of that he seemed cheerful.

'Well, I've something good to tell your mother. When she hears that I specially came all the way to Asahikawa and went to hear some Yaso preaching, she'll be moved to tears of joy. And on top of that I don't know how glad she will be to hear that her dear lad has been teaching Yaso stories with an earnest face.'

Nobuo and Yoshikawa laughed together. The August sun was hot in Asahikawa. The three walked the two blocks to Nobuo's house, and as they ate the noodles they had ordered to be delivered, on the way back, Nobuo listened to Takashi's news. In his colourful manner Takashi told him how Machiko's child was growing up and running around the garden, how her husband Kishimoto took great care of his mother Kiku, and how Kiku would like to see him. Nobuo had a sudden longing to join Takashi and return to Tokyo.

'Takashi, I'm beginning to want to go back and see everyone.'

Takashi smiled.

'Well, if you want to, there's no one to stop you. My boy, two years in Hokkaido is enough. It's time for you to be pulling out.'

'You can call it work if you like, but I had the idea of

taking you back to Tokyo, so I made the excuse of coming to see whether Sapporo would be a good place for business.'

Nobuo looked at Yoshikawa, who interposed no words of his own but listened, smiling, to the conversation of the other two.

'Cousin Takashi, thank you for coming up specially, but I plan to be in Hokkaido for a little longer.' Nobuo spoke with decision. He had written about Fujiko in detail when he had announced his baptism and his mother had written several times to say that she was praying for them both. Nobuo felt a little uneasy, wondering why Takashi had not been told about this.

'You may say that, but, Nobuo, you're the eldest son. For the eldest son in the family to reach twenty-four or twenty-five and not get married, and not look after his parents, is that the way to go about things?'

'Well, just wait another four or five years,' said Nobuo quietly.

'So . . . if you think anywhere in the wilds is all right, and intend to stay for another four or five years – if that's what you want, that's all right. But I'll bring you a nice bride from Tokyo.'

For a second time Nobuo looked at Yoshikawa. He was eating a white bean-paste bun, holding it in his stubby fingers, and appeared not to be listening.

'Cousin Takashi. I've decided who I want to marry.' Nobuo sat up formally.

'Whew, it's hot. Asahikawa's a strange place. Look here . . . at New Year it was forty-one below zero or something shockingly cold, they say. Even in summer I was scared about how cold it would be when I came. But today, it's hardly any different from Tokyo.' With his handkerchief Takashi wiped away the sweat running down his thick neck.

'Cousin Takashi. I've decided on someone to marry.' Nobuo was determined not to let the conversation drift away from the subject.

'Huh, I know, I know. The sister of Mr Yoshikawa here. But, look here, I met her in Sapporo and she's got lung TB, and on top of that, spinal TB. It's sad, but she won't recover. Mr Yoshikawa isn't a person not to understand such things. Surely you are not intending to wait for a woman who will never get better?'

'Don't speak so wildly.'

'It's you who's being reckless, saying you want to make this bed-ridden invalid your wife. That's wild talk if anything is. Just to look at her; she's thin and so fragile, she might go any time.'

'Cousin Takashi, Fujiko is certain to get better. I'm sure she is going to become strong.'

'Huh, the God of Yaso must really answer your prayers!'

'Christianity is not a religion for personal advantage. But she will surely recover. And she doesn't have to get better. If she never recovers, I'll just not marry.'

'You fool, that's no way to talk,' said Takashi without restraint.

'Yes, I'm a fool. Truly, I want to be a fool for Christ.'

'That may be so, but you are the eldest son of the Nagano family. You have a duty to leave some heirs.'

'Is my family such an important thing?'

'Of course. Good family and continuous lineage are more important than anything in this world. Don't you understand that? Since you came to Hokkaido you have become a little strange in the head. Forty-one below zero must have frozen into the middle of your brain.'

Yoshikawa had been listening quietly, but now he spoke deliberately.

'Nagano, this is a good opportunity to tell you something, as Fujiko's brother. I'm very grateful to you for your feelings towards her. But as your friend, I can't just leave it at that. I feel sorry for Fujiko, yes, but I want you to be really happy.'

'Don't suggest anything so despicable; it upsets me,' said Nobuo sharply.

'That's not despicable at all. Men have only one life to live, you know. I don't think you should spend your youthful years waiting for someone like Fujiko. I would like you to think this over again, thoroughly.'

'Yoshikawa, my life is more important to me than it is to anybody else. This is the way I have chosen, because I think it is best. Thank you for your kind words of warning, but I'm going to wait until Fujiko gets better.'

'But . . .'

When Yoshikawa started to speak, Takashi silenced him with a big wave of his hand.

'Yoshikawa, it's no good talking. This fellow's mother left even her child and her home for the sake of Yaso. He inherits his mother's stubbornness. Mere words will not do any good.' After this Takashi looked long and fixedly at Nobuo's face.

'Well, Mr Yoshikawa, let's leave it at that. He's a remarkable person.' Takashi fanned himself calmly with a big fan, but his eyes were moist.

Five years passed after this incident. During that time Nobuo became the Sunday school principal of the young Asahikawa Church, and was hardly ever absent from service. At work he won the greatest trust from his superiors and juniors. Already he had been promoted general manager of the Asahikawa transport office, but apart from this, requests for him to give Bible expositions came from railway employees, not only in Asahikawa but Sapporo and places at a distance. Using holidays and business trips, Nobuo did his best to make time for Bible study with those who wanted it. Young men who went through the Russo-Japanese war in the thirty-seventh and thirty-eighth years of Meiji, as well as those who applauded the victory, had been made to think seriously about life and death. Some of them had returned from the war, and some had lost friends and brothers. Mihori was one who survived. He became a regular attender at the Asahikawa

Bible study, but for some reason or other he always had a scornful, mocking expression on his face.

Increasingly many people in different places became attached to Nobuo, and there were those who said that though the Bible was hard to understand, if they could only see his face, they would come to the meeting, for it seemed to glow with light. It became the custom, if his superiors had an intractable employee, for them to get him transferred to Nobuo. Nobuo Nagano was becoming indispensable to both the railway authorities and the Sixth Avenue Church in Asahikawa.

Whenever he had business in Sapporo, Nobuo went straight to Fujiko's bedside. But as the five years progressed, Fijuko's health improved surprisingly. It was hard to imagine her as having been a bed-ridden invalid; her colour was good and she could get about the house without trouble. Yoshikawa had married meanwhile, and had brought his wife to join them in the family home. In another year, Nobuo thought happily, he might be able to marry Fujiko, and take her to Asahikawa.

19   The Ornamental Hair Pin

THE Asahikawa Young Railwaymen's Bible Study Group were holding their regular monthly get-together in the men's hostel, and as usual the speaker was Nobuo Nagano. Among the fifteen or sixteen men was Mihori, sitting in a corner and looking, as might be expected, as cynical as ever. Nobuo had finished expounding the Bible passage and everyone was deep in conversation, but Mihori sat alone. His kimono had parted, exposing his knees, and he was hugging them in silence, just watching. Nobuo had no idea what was the cause of Mihori's mood.

At last the meeting broke up and the men went home. But Mihori remained sitting fixedly in his place.

'You always come; you're a keen attender.' Nobuo turned to Mihori with a smile.

'Huh, I come for the fun of the thing,' said Mihori as if to sidetrack the conversation.

'Even if it's just for fun, you'll sooner or later find it really interesting if you never miss a meeting.'

'Hmm, I don't know what to think. There's no denying that you are a good speaker, Mr Nagano, but do you really believe in the existence of God?'

Mihori stretched out his feet on the frayed brown *tatami* mats. It was a hot and humid evening in July.

'Do you think I talk to everyone about God but don't believe in Him?'

'Excuse me for saying this, but whenever I come to listen I think the whole thing is a fake.'

'Well . . . faith is something you either have or don't have. There's nothing I can say in reply to a comment

237

like that,' Nobuo answered gently. He wondered why Mihori was perplexed about the existence of God. There could be no doubt that his coming to the meeting showed that he wanted to believe in Him.

Mihori had become the father of a son and a daughter, one born before the war and one after.

'This is a different matter, Mr Nagano, but they say that when I went to the war, you used to look in at Misa's home now and again.'

When Mihori left for the front, Misa and her child went to live with Mihori's mother. After he had been away about a month his mother had collapsed with a stroke and died four days later, in spite of Misa's devoted nursing. After that, Misa and her child had moved back to her old home, Reinosuke Wakura's house. Mihori was one of Nobuo Nagano's subordinates, and it was natural that in the course of time Nobuo should call there. But it was exactly the same as his visits to the homes of other men who had gone to the war. He went in his position as a senior member of his office, and he never went alone. He always took one of his juniors as a companion. Quite apart from that, he had called several times at the invitation of Reinosuke Wakura.

'I didn't go more than a few times, not even to offer my respects.'

But Mihori laughed mockingly. 'No, you used to drop in from time to time. In spite of the fact that I'm a returned war veteran, Misa seems to look down on me. And in the same breath she says what a fine person you are. She often praises you.'

'Is that so? But I'm quite unworthy.' Nobuo bowed informally. Now he thought he understood Mihori's feelings. The reason why he had started attending the meetings was that Misa's remarks had made him jealous.

Mihori left quietly, but his parting words were disturbing. Nobuo recalled how long ago, when Mihori was drunk he had often called on him and tried to pick a quarrel.

Now, thought Nobuo with a twinge of sadness, even without drinking *sake* he was being quarrelsome.

After his marriage Mihori had been a happy man. It was when he returned from the war that he had become strangely gloomy. Nobuo assumed that this was because he had seen so many deaths in the fierce fighting. The fact that he never missed a Bible study surely showed that deep down he was searching for something. But this was not really what was the matter with him. The real trouble was that his mother had died while he was away fighting, and he thought angrily that Misa was responsible in some way. If he had been there, somehow or other his mother would still be alive, he could not help thinking. Then, alas, while he was away Misa had moved back to her old home and he had an overriding revulsion against becoming a sort of adopted son of the Wakura family. But the third reason for his distress was that Misa spoke too much about Nobuo Nagano. It was not that Mihori did not respect Nobuo in his heart of hearts, but it angered him that Wakura never spoke of Nobuo except to praise him. And as for Misa, when she chimed in she became strangely hateful to him. Neither of them was trying to disparage Mihori, but he felt that by praising Nagano they were indirectly doing so.

Then, involuntarily, Mihori began to suspect that Misa had a fondness for Nobuo. His attendance at the Bible class was certainly not out of any desire to hear about Christ. The two things he had in mind were that he might be able to speak as well as Nobuo could, and to find out how genuine Nobuo's faith really was.

Nobuo was eloquent. When he listened, even Mihori found himself drawn along by his speaking. Sometimes as he went back from the class he wondered seriously whether God did exist or not. It worried him.

Once, on a day when Nobuo had been on a business trip and was away from the office, the lunch-time conversation turned to him.

'Hey, why doesn't Mr Nagano get married?'

'That fellow, he's not like us ordinary mortals, he doesn't need a woman.'

'That's not possible, there must be something wrong with him, there's no other reason why he doesn't need a woman.'

Then Mihori remembered that he had overheard Wakura and Misa talking about Fujiko. But he had not been able to believe that anyone would wait for so many years to marry a person with spinal tuberculosis. Maybe this was just an excuse to turn down Misa, he thought, and maybe, however unlikely, there was something wrong with Nobuo.

'No, a healthy mind lives in a healthy body. There's nothing wrong with the manager.' Kenichi Hara, who had been transferred from Sapporo two months before, came up with a counter-argument immediately. Hara had a fierce nature, and soon got into arguments with his colleagues and superiors. He was a kind-hearted and earnest fellow, but too excitable, and no one in the Sapporo office could handle him. It was generally accepted that Mr Nagano in Asahikawa could handle anybody – so here he was.

He was immediately attracted by Nobuo's personality. However busy they might be with work, Nobuo always dismissed his juniors promptly at five o'clock. Any work that was left, Nobuo did himself, no matter how late he stayed. Just this one thing deeply moved Hara. If anyone made a mistake, Nobuo took all the blame. He did not scold people. But in spite of this he was a good leader. He was gentle but he had a firmness which was hard to go against. As far as Hara was concerned, everything Nobuo Nagano did was absolutely right.

'It's going too far, saying there's something wrong with the manager!'

This was the first time that Hara, who had been peaceful since moving to the Asahikawa office, had revealed his fiery temperament.

'Well then, Hara, why doesn't Mr Nagano get married? Soon he'll be thirty, I guess. Nowadays if someone is still single at nearly thirty, it's natural to think it a bit strange,' Mihori chaffed him.

Hara's face flushed as if he was being strangled. 'What's that? If you speak badly of the manager I won't just do nothing about it.' Hara got up from his seat and closed in on Mihori.

'Mr Mihori, do you have proof? What proof have you that there is something wrong with the manager?'

'The fact that he has reached this age and hasn't married, that's proof enough.'

'Is that what you call proof? A person who is fit to be the manager's wife doesn't just turn up anywhere. You wait and see. It's certain that he'll marry someone like an angel even you'd feel like worshipping.'

His words had a strangely persuasive power. Someone who felt the same way chimed in. 'Yes, that's it. Mr Nagano's going to marry a stunner.' At this Hara became a little calmer.

From that time on, Mihori imagined that Nobuo was probably sexually abnormal. He could not believe that a normal healthy man could live just for this world of business and the church, without even having a woman now and again. A man has a man's desires, he thought. They are just the same as his appetite for food. Since he ate food, it would be natural that Nobuo had sexual desires too. To say, like the dedicated Buddhist priest, that he had finished with them, seemed to him to be a great hypocrisy. Nagano had never told a dirty story. Whenever he opened his mouth it was to speak about the Faith.

'There must be something false somewhere. He'll show himself in his true colours one day,' thought Mihori, and kept a spiteful eye on Nobuo.

One day when Nobuo returned from church, a letter from his mother was waiting for him. It was a letter of thanks for the money he had recently been in the habit of sending home each month. Taking off his suit, he changed into a summer kimono. He had only one suit for going out, his railwayman's uniform. Whether at work or in church, this single faded suit served all his needs. It was so faded that simply by noting its colour you could tell it was Nobuo.

Sitting up formally in his cool kimono, he carefully opened the letter with scissors. Kiku's writing was beautiful, as always.

On the paper of the rolled letter, the contrast of the light and dark tones was fresh, and the characters were written flowingly.

'It continues to be hot every day, and at this time of year it will be as hot where you are, as in Tokyo, so do be careful to avoid heat stroke and bad water. I want to thank you for sending so much of your precious salary this month.

'Kishimoto, Machiko and both their children are standing up to the heat and keep well, so please don't worry about them. We are all very glad to hear from you that Fujiko is so much better and that you hope to get married next spring. You have waited a long time for her, because of her serious illness. Even though you are my own child, without any prejudice I think it is splendid of you.

'I hope you will not think badly of my suggestion, but when you get married, if it is God's will, I long and wait for you to come back to Tokyo together. One reason is that Fujiko was born in Tokyo, and I'm sure that she would find living in Tokyo more tolerable than in Asahikawa where the cold is so severe. I understand your feelings when you say that you will do the cooking and the washing, but a man has a man's work to do. If you lived here, I could help, even a little.

'Also in the near future, Kishimoto is setting up a practice in Osaka, and I shall be alone in this house. . . .'

Nobuo remembered that Kishimoto had mentioned two or three years as a suitable length of time for him to live in Hokkaido, and he himself had had the same idea, but had not acted on it. The previous year, Kishimoto had gained his doctor's degree, but he had been unable to leave the home in Hongo.

'Maybe I have put him to some trouble,' thought Nobuo regretfully. Now he too considered that, just as his mother Kiku had said, it would be better for Fujiko's health if they returned to Tokyo. To leave the Sunday school, which was flourishing, would be hard. However, it would be unkind to ask his mother to come up to Hokkaido. It would be difficult for him to get a transfer to Tokyo, but in the circumstances it would be better if he left his present job.

Nobuo was hoping that, if possible, he might enter a theological college. It would be hard to train as a minister and to support both his mother and Fujiko, but, being who they were, he believed they would be equal to the hardship and give him whole-hearted support. If they should find it impossible to make ends meet, Nobuo would think of something when that time came.

'Therefore do not be anxious, saying "What shall we eat?" or "What shall we drink?" or "What shall we wear?" For the Gentiles seek all these things; and your heavenly Father knows that you need them all. But seek first His kingdom and His righteousness, and all these things shall be yours as well. Therefore do not be anxious about tomorrow, for tomorrow will be anxious for itself. Let the day's own trouble be sufficient for the day.'

Nobuo had spoken these words of Christ many times to others, and could not tell how often he had weighed their importance.

The last time he had been to Sapporo, Fujiko had said to him, 'Nobuo, do you think the work you are doing now is your true work? Isn't it true that you are thinking about a different way of life?' She had asked it with her round bright eyes shining.

'That's just like Fujiko,' Nobuo had thought at the time.
'Can you understand it too, Fujiko?'

'Yes, I understand. You have feelings about a life worth
living, living for God and dying for Him. Nobuo, the thing
you want most is not money, nor a high place in society,
is it? You just want to live a life of faith. Living a life of
faith doesn't necessarily mean becoming a minister, but I
have a feeling you were born to be a minister.'

Nobuo had been thinking about this continually, and with
the coming of his mother's letter he made up his mind. He
would ask Wakura and see if it was possible to get a transfer to Tokyo next spring. All the railways had already come
under national control, and Asahikawa's had changed from
being a private railway company to a national one.

'Anyway, next April I'll return with Fujiko to Tokyo,'
Nobuo decided.

Meanwhile there was the matter of an engagement
present for Fujiko. He did not like taking her the betrothal
money, for to him the custom smacked of buying and
selling women. However, it would be too bad if her family,
who were not wealthy, were saddled with the expenses of
the wedding. Not only that, but the Yoshikawas had a
child now and it would be very difficult for them. So
Nobuo resolved to give his year-end bonus as an engagement present. That would mean that the engagement
would be finally settled as the New Year began. It was still
six months away, but he would like Mr and Mrs Wakura
to be the official go-betweens.

At the end of November Nobuo went to Wakura's house
with Osamu Yoshikawa. They walked together shoulder to
shoulder through the streets covered with the snow which
would lie there till the spring. Yoshikawa was taller and
stouter and in every way looked older than Nobuo.

'I have a very strange feeling,' said Yoshikawa.

'What do you mean?'

'Mm . . . Well, it's a feeling that we are somehow blood
relations. A little while ago I remembered the time when

we were fourth formers in the junior school, ghost hunting.'

'Yes, that was real ghost hunting. They said you could hear someone crying in the senior girls' cloakrooms and everyone was scared it was a ghost or something! That was a black rainy night, wasn't it?'

Nobuo remembered how only Yoshikawa and himself had kept their promise to go; in his case because his father had scolded him and he had had no alternative. Yoshikawa had been different, he had kept his promise and come, but he had never bragged about it. But for his father's scolding that night, he and Yoshikawa would never have become such good friends.

'Yoshikawa, it was because of you that I came to Hokkaido. And here I found my faith, and Fujiko.' His tone of voice expressed his gratitude.

'Fujiko's a lucky girl . . .' Yoshikawa was smitten to the heart when he thought again about Nobuo's faithfulness in waiting so long for Fujiko.

'I'm lucky too. With you as a brother and Fujiko as a wife there could not be anything better.'

'Do you really think that?' said Yoshikawa with emotion.

They had told Wakura beforehand that they would be calling. Nobuo did the introductions.

'I see . . . It's his young sister, is it? Well, I can understand Nagano's feelings.' It seemed that Wakura approved of Yoshikawa at first sight.

'I'm sorry to trouble you, but I would like the wedding to be next spring, and we would like you to be the go-between.' Yoshikawa and Nobuo bowed respectfully.

'Well, well . . . Is she so much better already?' Wakura glanced back at his wife, who was coming in with the tea, with a look of surprise.

'Hey, did you hear that? The girl Nagano has been waiting for, she's cured. That's wonderful, just wonderful!' Wakura was really amazed. 'But it must have seemed a long time to wait. Your name is Nagano, and it's been a

long story.[1] You've waited seven years, haven't you?'
Jovially Wakura counted off the years on his big fingers.

'When our Misa hears this she'll be really glad,' Mrs
Wakura said. At that time Misa was living in one of the
railway company houses about a block away.

'Misa? Misa, she's . . . Well, we'll not talk about that
now. Anyway, congratulations.'

Wakura seated himself in a formal posture and bowed.

On January the third, in the New Year, Nobuo visited
Fujiko's home in Sapporo. It was a relatively warm and
calm afternoon with snow gently falling. Yoshikawa's wife
and his mother, sitting in the living room, diffused the
genial mood of the New Year. But Nobuo could not see
Fujiko, the most important person.

'She's just gone to buy something, she'll be back in a
moment.'

Nobuo smiled at the friendly insight of Yoshikawa's
wife. He was happy. Although it could be said to be a
warm day, it was the middle of winter, and it seemed like
a dream – just to think that Fujiko was able to go out in
the depths of winter. At last she came back, wearing a
deep red shawl. Her white face was pink from the cold air
outside. Surely this was a sign that she was well again, and
Nobuo became unbearably happy.

When Fujiko had concluded her formal New Year's
greeting she showed the soft shawl to Nobuo and said, 'It's
a lovely shawl, isn't it, Nobuo? Osamu and his wife bought
it for me at the end of last year. This is the first time I've
worn a shawl.'

Fujiko had a silver ornamental pin in the front of her
hair which was done in the divided peach style.

'Won't you catch a cold, going outside?'

'I'm all right. This winter I haven't had a single cold.
The next time you come to Sapporo, Nobuo, I'll meet you
at the station.' As she said this Fujiko became shy and

[1] One of the Japanese characters in the name Nagano means
'long'.

blushed. The artless expression on her face was charming.

'Is that true, Fujiko?' Yoshikawa said teasingly. Nobuo imagined what Fujiko would look like, standing in her red shawl by the ticket barrier. When he thought of her as she had lain in bed for so many years, she seemed to be unbelievably fortunate.

The conversation turned to fixing the date for the engagement ceremony. Nobuo would have liked to have it in the middle of January if possible. But Yoshikawa's wife was expecting another baby then. Once into February, because of Sunday school and work commitments, Nobuo could not take a day off easily. Looking at the brand new calendar, they finally decided on the evening of the twenty-eighth day of February.

'It's a bit late in the month, isn't it? There'll be all sorts of things to get ready.' Nobuo looked thoughtful.

'What do you mean? The shops here only send out their bills at Obon and the New Year, so we could do something on credit even if we didn't have the money to hand,' said Yoshikawa casually.

Nobuo felt relieved. 'Well then, I understand. We'll leave the engagement ceremony until then. But on the twenty-seventh of February, a branch of the Young Railwaymen's Christian Association is being formed in Nayoro. I simply have to be at that.'

Nobuo decided that he would set out from Nayoro on the morning of the twenty-eighth, join Wakura and his wife, the go-betweens, in Asahikawa, and proceed to Sapporo.

'Mr Nagano. The fact that you are marrying a girl like Fujiko . . .' Yoshikawa's mother was moved to tears. Fujiko's recovery had removed the strain she had been living under, but now she seemed to have grown old quite suddenly. Looking at her, Nobuo could not help feeling that his mother, Kiku, must have aged too. But then, in April he was going to Tokyo with Fujiko. Fujiko and he, the two of them, would take the greatest care of his mother.

'I've got a hankering to go back to Tokyo too,' Yoshikawa's mother said as if reading his thoughts. She sounded disgruntled, a rare thing for her.

'You'll soon be in Tokyo all right. About this time next year Fujiko will be sending you a letter asking you to come and help with the first baby.' Yoshikawa was teasing again.

'You horrid brother!' Fujiko flushed scarlet and hid her face. The ornamental pin trembled in her hair. Yoshikawa's mother and his wife laughed together. It was a happy time.

When Nobuo said he must be leaving, Fujiko said she would go with him to the station.

'Thanks very much, Fujiko, but I'll just look forward to when you come to meet me next time.'

'But that's in the future. I want to see you off. Big brother, can I?'

'Hmm . . . Well.'

Yoshikawa looked at Nobuo. It was not like Fujiko to be so insistent.

'Thank you very much, but you've already been out once today. It's cold by now, and you ought to take proper care of yourself, especially since you have come all this way to recovery.'

Fujiko at last nodded meekly. She had always immediately done everything Nobuo told her.

'Why do you always do what I say, Fujiko?' Whenever Nobuo had asked that she would reply self-consciously, 'It's in Ephesians, chapter five.'

'I see . . . now you've set me a poser.'

'But in Ephesians, chapter 5, there's something for you. "Wives be subject to your husbands, as to the Lord . . . Even so husbands should love their wives as their own bodies." '

So Nobuo found it very strange that Fujiko should have insisted on going with him to the station.

Even after he had returned to Asahikawa, he kept wondering whether Fujiko had caught a cold, and if her old illness had broken out again. Perhaps she had even contracted pneumonia, and would die suddenly.

20   The Pass

'WELL, Mr Nagano, tomorrow's your engagement ceremony.'

Nobuo and Mihori were having supper, facing each
other across the table. The clock showed that it was already
nine. They were in the railwaymen's hostel in Nayoro.
Since they had left Asahikawa that morning on business,
Mihori had been in unusually low spirits. Any subject Nobuo
raised had been futile, for Mihori had not replied. Now it
was he who started the conversation. Nobuo replied with
a sense of relief.

'Yes. Thanks to you.'

'Thanks to me! I've had nothing to do with it.' Mihori,
who was drinking alone, poured himself some *sake* and
answered spitefully. Feeling cornered as a son-in-law in the
Wakura household, he still seized every opportunity to pick
on Nobuo.

'No, for everything that happens, we are indebted to
God and men,' Nobuo replied calmly, unruffled by Mihori's
attitude. He had the cheerful feeling that he would like to
thank everybody for his engagement to Fujiko.

Mihori had noticed that Misa had been out of sorts for
a week now, and guessed that Nobuo's engagement must
be the cause. She had been especially bad the previous
night. Wakura had come to Mihori's house and asked,
'Your mother and I will be staying the night of the 28th in
Sapporo. We have to go to Nagano's engagement ceremony. There'll be no one in the house, so could you send
Misa over to sleep the night there?'

'I don't want to do that.' Before Mihori could reply, Misa had refused point blank.

'If Misa won't go, Mihori, will you?'

Thinking that he had made an untimely entry on a family row, Wakura decided not to be put off by Misa's attitude.

'Anyway, Nagano's a fine man. In this Meiji era everyone is frivolous and self-seeking, but as for him . . .'

Misa interrupted her father as he began to speak. 'If he's such a good person you should have got him for me.'

'Don't be a fool.' Wakura laughed.

'Yes, I'm a fool. You all know I'm a fool,' and disregarding Japanese custom, Misa burst into loud sobs in her father's and husband's presence. She was by nature a woman of spirit, and not without ability. She took good care of Mihori and managed her household well. Moreover, she was a cheerful person and hardly ever grumbled. But for a whole week she had been at rock bottom. Mihori thought he understood what was going on in her heart and it offended him. Up till now Misa had comforted herself with the fact that Nobuo was still single, and now, just before the engagement, her feelings had inadvertently expressed themselves. So Mihori was exasperated. Constantly recalling the events of the previous evening, he could only think how disagreeable Nobuo was.

'Mr Nagano, the person you are going to marry has lung TB and spinal TB and on top of that is lame, isn't she?'

'That's right.'

Clearly Mihori was a little drunk and becoming bold. Nobuo was used to his rudeness, but when he spoke about Fujiko so contemptuously, even Nobuo became angry.

Mihori went on, 'A fine person like you, if you had your choice you wouldn't marry a person like that, would you? There was something about my wife Misa you didn't like, wasn't there?'

Nobuo silently plied his chopsticks.

'Hey, Mr Nagano, what has this woman got about her

that's better than my wife? Yes, I heard there was something about my Misa that you didn't like. There's nothing to complain about in Misa, as far as health and beauty are concerned. It's an insult to prefer a cripple to Misa. It stands to reason that Misa should be annoyed.'

As he spoke, Mihori became a little more cheerful. The thought that it was not that Misa had any attachment to Nobuo, but was mortified by having a sick woman preferred to her, was a new idea. If there was anything else, she would not have wept so much in front of him, her husband.

'Anyway, she's a Christian, isn't she?' Mihori suddenly felt much better.

'Yes, she's a fine Christian.'

Nobuo felt sorry for Mihori, spending his days with such miserable thoughts. How strangely irritable he had been ever since stealing his colleague's pay packet years ago. If it had not been for that, he might have been known as an upright man. Nobuo longed to help and encourage Mihori.

'A fine Christian, eh? I couldn't take that. A fine Christian and the noble Nobuo getting married, "Amen, Amen" from morning till night. Not much fun in that.'

Nobuo laughed. 'I suppose so.'

'But if you are a Christian, you still have children, don't you? Are you going to have any children, Mr Nagano? Ha, ha, ha . . .' Mihori laughed loudly and choked over his *sake*. Nobuo flushed a little.

'You're very inexperienced, aren't you? Mr Nagano, I've been longing to ask you something for a long time. If I ask you, you won't be angry, will you?'

'Ask me anything you like.' Nobuo had finished his rice and was enjoying his tea.

'Mr Nagano, why don't you play around with women?' Mihori fixed his drunken eyes on him. Nobuo considered his reply. To argue that it was because he was a Christian would not be the honest truth. Even before he became a believer he had never got himself a woman.

'Mr Nagano, listen. Haven't you ever got yourself a woman yet?'

'No. Not once.'

'What, not even once?' Mihori looked at Nobuo with an air of disgust.

'Well then, when you look at a woman, don't you get the feeling you want her?'

'Yes, I feel that constantly.' Nobuo answered frankly.

'In a head like yours, you constantly have thoughts like that . . .?' Mihori gazed steadily at Nobuo's serious face, then continued.

'You look as if you don't care a hang about women, that you've finished with them, but you still think about them, do you? You're a bad one, Mr Nagano.'

Nobuo smiled wryly.

'Well then, how have you managed without getting yourself a woman, not even one? I can't understand it. It's a strange story, I wouldn't have believed there could be such hypocrites.'

Mihori took the last of the many *sake* bottles he had emptied and upturned it against his lips.

'Blast—not a drop left!'

He knocked the bottle over and lay down himself.

'Don't you think you'll be sacrificing yourself for that woman in the end?' Mihori brought the conversation back to Fujiko.

'I love her, that's why I'm marrying her.'

'Is that so? I can't completely trust this man Nagano yet. Somewhere you have the smell of a swindler about you. The more fine and noble you appear to be, the less I feel I can trust you. This girl, I suppose she's rolling in money?' he laughed scornfully.

He really knew surprisingly little about Fujiko.

In a moment Mihori was asleep and snoring. Nobuo pulled out a mattress, rolled him on to it and covered him with a quilt. It did not matter what he had been saying – when he lay asleep, it was impossible not to love him.

Nobuo began to read his Bible in an undertone :

'Do not wonder, brethren, that the world hates you. We know that we have passed out of death into life, because we love the brethren. He who does not love remains in death. Anyone who hates his brother is a murderer and you know that no murderer has eternal life abiding in him. By this we know love, that he laid down his life for us. And we ought to lay down our lives for the brethren.'

Nobuo read the passage through again. Did he really have enough love for somebody else to throw away his life for them? He looked at Mihori snoring loudly with his mouth open.

When at last he himself got into bed, Nobuo thought about the engagement ceremony the next day. A picture flitted through his mind, of Fujiko in her deep red shawl and split-peach hairstyle, coming to meet him at the station. Soon she would not be able to wear that hairstyle any more. As a young wife, maybe a glossy chignon would become her.

She might have a bad leg, she might be weak and ill, but for him, Fujiko was a wife without price. Nobuo's thoughts were filled with tenderness. He imagined her pale face. He could not forget that lovable, demure expression. She was clever, charming and obedient, you could not criticize her at all. She was a perfect woman. When he thought of the day when he would be able to clasp her to him freely, he was filled with a deep happiness. As a result of his long wait, his joy was all the greater. He smiled as he realized how much Fujiko had been in his thoughts – on this, the day before his engagement.

The next morning the temperature had fallen lower than anyone would have expected for so late in the winter. At Nayoro station Nobuo bought two boxes of bean confection, a local delicacy. One box was for the Yoshikawa family and the other for the Wakuras who would join him in Asahikawa.

Mihori had not forgotten what he had said the previous evening. Now he was sober he remained silent, as if he felt conscience stricken that he had said too much.

Although it was early morning, seven or eight members of the Young Railwaymen's group came to see Nobuo off.

'Mr Nagano, thank you very much for last night. It was a very successful meeting.' The local leader spoke with youthful enthusiasm.

The previous evening's inaugural meeting had been from five till seven, and as some had come from Wassamu and Shibetsu, as well as some from the town, there had been as many as fifty people present. For a little country station to get together so many young railwaymen was almost beyond belief.

'It was a really powerful talk you gave us last night, Mr Nagano. You always say something good, but last night's talk made a special impression on me,' said another, and they all joined in together, saying how good it had been.

The previous night, Nobuo had given an impassioned address on 'You are the light of the world'.

'Together, let us take our lives, which we can never live again, and let them burn as we live. Let us proclaim the words of Christ and reflect His light. Let us not pass our days in idleness but gain the victory over ourselves. If it be necessary, let us be ready at any time to give our lives for God.'

Nobuo had spoken for an hour. His words did not cease to pierce the hearts of his hearers.

'Thank you. I will pray that this branch will keep on growing. Invite lots of the young men of this town to your meetings.'

'We understand. We'll do our best. You will come next month, won't you?' said their leader.

Nobuo suddenly remembered that he would be leaving

Hokkaido in April. He would like to come again once more and see them.

'We are waiting for you. Please, please come again.'

The whistle sounded for the train to leave. The young men ran after it, waving.

'You are the light of the world!'

Mihori, to whom no one had spoken a word, smiled scornfully.

It was the early morning train, but every seat was taken and in their carriage everyone was in a brisk early morning mood. As it ran, the train cast its shadow over the snowy expanse. The smoke from the engine made a flowing picture on the snow. Nobuo breathed on the window, frozen over white. The glass became misted, and after he had breathed two or three times, a little round patch cleared. The silver frost on the white firs and Hokkaido pines glittered in the morning sun. It was a clear blue morning, and Nobuo, thinking of his engagement ceremony in the evening, could not have been happier.

Mihori was dozing, his head propped against the back of his seat. Soon they arrived at Shibetsu. Seven or eight people boarded the train, the men with balaclava helmets, and the women with shawls, carrying big burdens on their backs. Among them was a man with a crutch, wearing a tattered military uniform.

'Look, a disabled soldier,' five or six boys in the centre of the coach cried out in unison. The man threw a sharp glance in the direction of the voices and then cautiously, with a light tapping of his crutch, went to a seat about two rows ahead of Nobuo and sat down. Then, as the train was about to start, a man came running up with a load on his back wrapped in a cloth patterned with arabesques.

'My, . . . a bit later and I'd have missed it,' he said laughingly to Nobuo, as he sat down beside Mihori. Looking at the newcomer's kind face, Nobuo gave a start of recognition.

'Excuse me, but you're from Tokyo, aren't you?'

'How did you know that?' The man looked hard at Nobuo as he spoke. 'Perhaps I've seen *you* somewhere before?' he muttered with his head on one side.

'It couldn't be that you are *Roku*, could it?' Nostalgia added a liveliness to Nobuo's voice.

'Yes, I'm Roku, . . . but who are you?'

'I'm . . . You know the Naganos of Hongo . . .? I'm . . .' The man clapped his hands on Nobuo's knees as he spoke.

'Ah, that's it. Mr Nagano's little boy. Yes, that's certainly who you are. You still have the look you had when you were small. But you've grown up to be a fine man.' Roku flushed unconsciously, excited by the chance meeting. 'It's been a long time, hasn't it, young master.'

Roku stood up and bowed politely. At the same moment the train rocked and swayed and he put his hand on Mihori's shoulder.

'Uh, I'm sorry. Pardon me.'

Mihori smiled broadly and shook his head. It both amused and jarred him that Nobuo had been brought up being called 'little master'.

'Anyway, young master, why have you come to desolate Hokkaido?'

'I have friends in Sapporo.'

'I see . . . You are employed on the railway.' He could see that at a glance, from his uniform.

'I'm working in Asahikawa.'

'Hm, in Asahikawa. Well, what's happened to your fine house in Tokyo?'

'My mother lives there with my sister and her husband.'

'Your mother? Ah, I remember. Your old grandmother died suddenly, and then I went a long way away. Is that so? They say she was a beautiful lady. But you know, your old grandmother was very kind, even to people like me.'

Nobuo remembered with affection his grandmother

standing for a long time by the back door talking to Roku.

'Young master, how many years have passed since then?'

'My grandmother died when I was ten, so it's nearly twenty years ago.'

'My goodness . . . twenty years. It seems like two ages ago. No wonder I've gone bald.' Roku slapped his forehead.

'No, you haven't changed a bit. I knew it was you, Roku, at a glance.'

In his heart Nobuo wanted to know what had happened to Torao.

'You used to play so happily with my Torao.' Before Nobuo could ask, Roku had mentioned him.

'How is young Torao?'

'Well, thank you. He went astray once. My wife, she was a bad one and he took after her, I think. Young master, I wept for Torao. But I'm glad to say he's got a job in a haberdashers in Sapporo. He's got two children and he's doing very well.'

'That's good news. I hadn't the faintest idea he was in Sapporo.' Nobuo nodded with a sigh of relief. However, he wondered whether Torao would really want to talk frankly with him. He had turned his face away in the lobby of the law courts.

'Anyway, young master, how many children have you now?'

'I haven't any, I'm still single.'

'What, you haven't got a wife yet?'

Roku stopped filling his pipe and looked at Nobuo afresh. Nobuo, thinking of the reason for his journey that day, smiled.

'But, young master, you look very like your father. You've become a very fine man.'

'Like my father?' Nobuo was surprised, for he thought that he looked only like his mother.

'Of course. Your father was a man of character. Why,

on one occasion he bowed low to us, his hands on the ground in apology, even to us.'

'Now you mention it, something like that did happen.' Nobuo scratched his head. It was something he would never forget – how Torao had pushed him off the roof of the garden shed, and he had said no slum kid could push him off! And his father had slapped him on the cheek with all his strength, and then apologized before Roku and Torao for him, because he was too stubborn to do it himself.

'Young master, please don't take it badly. You used to be a sharp, strong-willed little boy, but you've got a very friendly face now.'

Mihori smiled again and looked at Nobuo. Though only one pot-bellied stove in the carriage was lit, the glazing of frost on the windows had melted and the passengers were talking amicably in small groups.

Roku talked on for a while about how his wife had died five years ago, and how he had been at his wits end to know what to do with the impetuous Torao. Then suddenly he turned his face towards the window. 'Hey, we've gone right past Wassamu.'

The train was near the top of the Shiokari Pass, about thirty kilometres north of Asahikawa. It was a steep pass, winding through the forest-clad mountains, so usually, at Wassamu, at the foot of the pass, trains took on an extra engine at the back, and panted up to the top.

'Yes, we're near the top.'

'Hey, there's no engine at the rear,' said Roku, looking back as they went round a curve.

'Hmm, it must be because there are only a few coaches. But it's unusual to go up without one,' Nobuo chimed in.

The train was climbing slowly, threatening to come to a stop at any moment. Even while they were sitting, they could feel the thrust of the coach seats pressing them upwards.

The virgin forest of white fir and Hokkaido pine flowed slowly past.

'No matter how many times you cross over, it feels steep, doesn't it?' Roku tapped out the ash of his pipe into his palm.

'Yes, it's a steep gradient.'

Outside the window a crow flew away low, skimming the ground.

'This area is hard to develop, isn't it? Torao has never been out of Sapporo. I must show him around here sometime.'

'I'd very much like to meet him.'

The train went round a sharp curve. It seemed like a complete right angle. They had passed a number of such curves already.

'Thank you. Young master, Torao has so much . . .'

It happened just as Roku was speaking. They felt the coach stop suddenly with a jolt. Then, strangely, it began to move backwards, helplessly. The vibrations from the engine had ceased abruptly. Even as they looked out, the coach was gaining speed. The scenery they had left behind now passed them again, in the other direction. An ominous silence swept over the coach. But only for a few seconds.

'Help, a coupling has broken!' someone shouted. Fear ran through the coach.

'Heavens, we'll overturn!'

In terror everyone imagined them becoming derailed and hurtling to the bottom of the valley. Now nearly everyone was standing up, clinging to the backs of the seats. Some were speechless, their faces twisted with fear.

'Amida Buddha, Amida Buddha!' Roku had his eyes closed tight.

Knowing the seriousness of the situation, Nobuo immediately began praying. Whatever happened he must save the passengers. This was the most important thing to do. As he prayed, an exciting thought came to him. It dawned on him that on the outer platform there was an emergency brake. He stood up immediately, shouting,

'Be calm, everyone. The train will soon stop.' His voice, trained by preaching, rang through the coach.

'Mihori, take charge of the passengers.'

With tense fascination in their eyes, everyone gazed with desperate hope at Nobuo. But he was disappearing through the door. He pounced on the icy brake wheel with both hands. At that time there was a hand brake for each coach, on the conductor's platform. It stood vertically up from the floor like the brake wheel of an old tram car. Nobuo was in a frenzy to check their momentum as soon as possible. He paid no attention to the trees flying past on either side.

Exerting all his strength, he managed to move the wheel. Gradually the speed dropped. The whole episode had taken only a minute, but for Nobuo it seemed an unbearably long time. Sweat dripped from his forehead. Soon the speed slackened off considerably.

Nobuo took a deep breath of relief. 'It's nearly over,' he thought. But for some reason the brake wheel would move no further. He began to feel desperate again. He was an office worker, unfamiliar with such things. He could not judge whether it was damaged or whether he was using it wrongly. Yet it was imperative to stop the train completely. The sight of the frightened faces of the women passengers passed through his mind.

'If it goes on like this, the train will certainly run away again,' Nobuo realized. At that moment he saw a steep curve about fifty yards ahead. He threw himself on the brake again with all his strength. But whatever he did, the coach would not stop. The curve pressed closer. If they began to run away again a derailment was inevitable . . .

Nobuo came to a swift decision. Now, when they were travelling so slowly, he could stop it with his own body. For an instant the faces of Fujiko, Kiku and Machiko flashed largely before his eyes. To shake off this vision he shut them tightly. In the next second his hands had left the brake wheel and he had jumped down, aiming for the rails.

The coach lurched ominously as it rolled on to Nobuo's body and finally came to a stop.

Yoshikawa planned to take time off after lunch. This was the long awaited day of Fujiko's engagement. He had not been able to avoid breaking into a smile at odd times during the morning.

'Hey, Yoshikawa. Those smiles must be worth something,' his workmates bantered. He was expecting Nobuo, and the Wakuras as go-betweens, to arrive in Sapporo that evening. And he had promised to take Fujiko to the station to meet them.

At that time Osamu Yoshikawa was in charge of the small parcels section. As he was busy registering a passenger's parcel a friend, Yamaguchi from the freight office, came running up. He was a member of the Young Railwaymen's Christian Association.

'Yoshikawa, something dreadful has happened.'

'What's the matter? Forgotten your lunch box or something?' joked Yoshikawa.

'Yoshikawa, be prepared for a shock. You won't take it badly, will you?'

'What is it?'

Now Yoshikawa looked troubled. The passenger's parcel hung from his hand.

'Well, it's Mr Nagano. Mr Nagano's . . .'

'What? What's he done?'

'He's dead.'

'Dead?'

Almost shouting, Yoshikawa repeated the question. Yamaguchi clung to his shoulder and wept. Like the other Young Railwaymen, Yamaguchi was an admirer of Nobuo.

'What nonsense . . .!' Wasn't this the day of Nobuo's

engagement to Fujiko . . .? How could he have died? thought Yoshikawa.

'There must be some mistake!'

Yamaguchi shook his head weakly. 'There's no mistake. There was a phone call from Asahikawa. Please go to the office and ask.'

Yoshikawa threw down the parcel and ran to the freight office. On the way he bumped into someone but was hardly aware of it. He had gone but a step into the office when he knew at a glance that Nobuo was dead. Not a man was sitting at his desk. They were gathered here and there in little excited groups. Some were weeping loudly. Seeing Yoshikawa's face, three or four men came running up.

'Mr Nagano's . . .'

'What happened?'

'He died for the others,' a youth shouted.

Yoshikawa heard a description of the accident from several people. He stood aghast. He could vividly imagine Nobuo jumping down on to the railway track. He had a feeling that he himself had seen Nobuo's bright blood spattered on the pure white snow. It was a death worthy of Nobuo and somehow he had known about it for a long time. Somewhere in his heart, as well as the fierce sense of shock, there was a peace which was unshaken. Deep inside, he was completely calm. This surely was his love for the friend he knew.

'Please let me go to Asahikawa.'

'I'll go too.'

'No, let me go.'

The excited men pressed round the freight manager.

Pushing his way through them, Yoshikawa said, 'Manager, Mr Nagano always carried a copy of his will on him, in an inside pocket. Please get in touch, and ask them to find out about it.'

'Oh yes, that. I've heard about the will too. It was covered with blood but still intact.'

Osamu Yoshikawa left the freight office in a daze, his

head bowed. When he thought about Fujiko, the pain was as if his heart were literally breaking. He explained about the engagement ceremony to his superior and obtained leave off work until Nobuo's funeral.

'Welcome home, Osamu. What's happened? You're very pale.'

'Huh, I've got a headache.'

'Oh . . . Elder Sister, Osamu says he's got a headache,' Fujiko called out to her sister-in-law in the kitchen.

'That's too bad, with the celebration today,' she replied cheerily from the other side of the sliding doors.

'Did you say Osamu has a headache? It must be the first he's had in his life. He hasn't caught a cold, has he?' Yoshikawa's mother and his wife were busy with preparations for the evening's festivities and went on with their work.

'Do you want to lie down? Shall I pull out a bed for you?'

Fujiko peered at her brother's face as he slumped cross-legged by the stove.

'No, I don't need that.'

Yoshikawa was determined not to announce Nobuo's death until after lunch. When Fujiko heard about it she would probably not eat for days. At least let them have this happy meal together, he thought.

'Let me tell you something, Osamu. It was just as if a big stone fell on to the roof. There was a great crashing sound.'

'What time was that?' Yoshikawa muttered, keeping his head down and his eyes fixed on a spot between his crossed legs, so that she would not see how startled he was.

'Mother, that strange noise, when was it?'

'About ten o'clock, I think. In these days of rapid developments you never know when the next detonation is going to be.' She sounded unconcerned.

They started lunch.

'Osamu, Nobuo and his party will have left Asahikawa by now, won't they?'

Yoshikawa remained silent, busily putting rice into his mouth. He could taste nothing.

'You're certainly out of sorts, aren't you?' For the first time his mother spoke anxiously.

'Yes.'

'This evening's going to be a time of celebration. Please cheer up.'

Yoshikawa suddenly dropped his chopsticks. He could bear it no longer. His wife, his mother and Fujiko all gazed at him in surprise.

'What's the matter, why are you feeling so bad?' Yoshikawa's wife reached out and placed her hand on his forehead. 'Osamu, you're tired, aren't you?'

'If only you would just take a rest, brother Osamu.'

His mother and Fujiko spoke in anxious voices, peering at his drawn face. He was gazing at the ground, and his shoulders began to shake. He could remain silent no longer.

'Fujiko, Mother!' Yoshikawa raised his voice resolutely. 'I'm planning to go to Asahikawa on the two o'clock train.'

He had no idea how to break the news.

'To Asahikawa? What's happened?' His mother looked uneasily at him and then at Fujiko.

'Osamu, if something has happened about the engagement and Nobuo . . .' Fujiko faltered.

'That's impossible. Mr Nagano wouldn't say at this stage that he didn't want to marry Fujiko,' his mother said, to comfort Fujiko. Yoshikawa's face twisted as he bit his lower lip.

'The truth is . . . really . . .' No matter how he tried, he could not go on.

'Osamu! What's happened?'

'Well, it's this . . . There was a train accident on the Shiokari Pass. A coupling broke and the rear part of the train ran away.'

'No! Was it derailed? Was Mr Nagano on it?' His mother pressed him for the answer.

"All the passengers were saved. Nagano saved them.'

'How did he do it, Osamu?'

'Mm . . . Nagano . . . You see, Nagano . . . Fujiko, Nagano threw himself under the train and stopped it. The lives of all the passengers were saved.' Yoshikawa could not look at Fujiko's face.

'But Osamu! Is Mr Nagano dead then?' His mother was the one to cry out.

'Yes, he's dead. Fujiko, he died in a wonderful way, a truly splendid way.'

Fujiko was deathly white; even her lips were colourless. In the extreme shock her face was as expressionless as a Noh mask.

'Fujiko!'

'Fujiko!' Mother and sister-in-law both broke down and cried.

Yoshikawa looked fearfully at Fujiko. He shouted at her as she sat transfixed with wide open, vacant eyes.

'Fujiko! Pull yourself together!'

Fujiko did not even blink. She sat motionless until evening. She showed neither horror nor grief. Yoshikawa gave up the thought of going to Asahikawa that day. He stayed with Fujiko. It seemed as if her spirit had departed, leaving only her body behind. She made no reply, either by speech or movement. Deep in his heart Yoshikawa was conscious of relief that Fujiko had faith in God. She might grieve for a time, but he believed that her faith would support her. As the day progressed, however, he became anxious. Fujiko neither sighed nor wept. He wondered if she had gone out of her mind. He worried about this many times as he wiped away his tears with his big fist.

When evening came, Fujiko rose trembling to her feet.

'Fujiko, where are you going?'

Fujiko said nothing, but put on her shawl.

'Where are you going?'

'To the station.'

Her voice was faint. Yoshikawa and his mother glanced at one another. Had she gone completely mad?

'Fujiko, I'll come too.'

Slipping on his overcoat, Yoshikawa went after her. Half supporting Fujiko, he walked along the darkening streets. It was only half a mile to the station, but it seemed endless to Yoshikawa.

When Fujiko reached the station she turned toward the ticket barrier and stood there listlessly. After a little while the train pulled in promptly on time. Yoshikawa's thoughts were heart-rending.

A man carrying luggage in both hands, a woman with her hair in a chignon, an official with a thin moustache, a girl student with a pleated purple dress, passengers streamed from the train and Yoshikawa glanced at each of them, his face twisted with grief.

It seemed natural that Nobuo Nagano should be among these people, that he was now nearing the barrier. With a shout of 'Ha, thank you for coming to meet me,' he would come up to them with his usual smiling face. Then he would greet Fujiko, who had come to the station for the first time to meet him, with some kind remark. And then an hour later, wouldn't they be having the engagement party? To prevent himself from weeping Yoshikawa opened his eyes wide and looked at Fujiko.

She was standing eagerly on tip-toe, gazing at everyone coming towards the ticket barrier. She could not believe that Nobuo was dead. It was certain he would come on the train as he had promised. She had said she would come and meet him, wearing her red shawl; more than just keeping her promise, Fujiko felt that she must wait there for him. But among all the faces, Nobuo's was not to be seen. The last person passed through the barrier and left.

At that moment Fujiko saw Nobuo getting down from the train. She saw him clearly. She distinctly saw him smile in his usual kindly way.

'Ah, Nobuo!'
Fujiko smiled happily and raised her hand. But Nobuo suddenly vanished. She could not see him. The next moment she fell in a faint into Yoshikawa's arms.

Fujiko and Yoshikawa were allowed to get off at the Shiokari Pass signal halt. The engine gave a loud blast on its whistle to announce its departure, and drew away. They stood where they were until the smoke from the engine had faded away into the wild larch-scented forest.

It was the 28th of May, exactly three months after the accident. Nobuo's death had been a shock to the railwaymen, of course, but others had been shocked too. In the bath houses and the barbers' shops, talk about Nobuo flourished, and excitement bred greater excitement.

'I thought the Yaso were an evil sect, but look how splendidly one of them died. You can't say Yaso is a bad religion,' people were saying.

At a time when a man had to forfeit his inheritance if he became a Christian, Nobuo's death dispelled this ignorance. Not only that – ten railway workers, mostly from Sapporo and Asahikawa, entered the Christian faith together. Among them was Minekichi Mihori.

Mihori had seen Nobuo's death with his own eyes. When the train began to run away and Mihori involuntarily clutched the back of the seat, he happened to look up and see Nobuo praying quietly. It had only been for two or three seconds but the sight burned itself sharply into his mind. Then he heard the commanding voice which calmed the passengers so dramatically. He saw Nobuo desperately wrestling with the hand brake and thought he had suddenly turned and nodded to him, but in an instant Nobuo had jumped down, aiming for the track. Mihori, standing at the doorway of the coach, had witnessed it all clearly.

The passengers could not believe that the train had finally stopped. They were bewildered, the look on their faces showing that they had not yet emerged from their state of panic.

'It's stopped, we're saved!' somebody shouted, and a woman suddenly burst into tears. When someone announced what Nobuo had done, there was silence for a moment and then the passengers broke into rapidly mounting excitement. In twos and threes the men jumped from the high platform into the deep snow. Its pure whiteness was spattered with bright red, and Nobuo's body was drenched with blood. They leaned over it and wept. In death, he appeared to be laughing. Mihori, who, right up to the time of Nobuo's death had sneered and resisted him, could only condemn himself now. Nobuo's death changed Mihori completely.

The funeral was held in the Asahikawa church on the 2nd of March. The congregation overflowed the building and among them the weeping Sunday school children, who so admired Nobuo, were a pitiful sight. The minister leading the service read Nobuo's will. Since he became a Christian Nobuo had re-written it every New Year, and kept it on him all the time.

'My will :

'(1) I thankfully offer all to God.

'(2) My great sins have been atoned by the Lord Jesus. Brothers and sisters, all my sins, great and small, have been forgiven. My brothers and sisters, I pray that you may be able to join in giving thanks that through death I have gone to my Heavenly Father.

'(3) I wish the funeral to be within twenty-four hours without waiting for my mother or relatives to come.

'(4) I wish that my personal diary, my written notes, letters and postcards be burned. I wish to be cremated with the avoidance of all empty show and ceremony, and with the greatest economy of money and time. I do not want any eulogies.

'(5) I give thanks in the same measure for both life and death, happiness and sorrow. I would be much obliged to you if you do as I have requested. With my humble respects.

'To the beloved brothers and sisters whom it may concern,

Nobuo Nagano.'

The sound of sobbing from the whole congregation filled the church after the will had been read.

When the coffin was leaving the church, people surged forward, wanting to share in carrying it on their shoulders – all the way to the cemetery outside the town. Yoshikawa and Mihori were two of the pall-bearers, but although the grief of Nobuo's death lay heavily on them, so many others gave a hand that the coffin felt light. Among them was Torao, whose father's life had been saved.

A month later, a copy of Nobuo's will and his photograph were distributed by the Young Railwaymen's Christian Association to his friends and business associates, and again made a deep impression.

Yoshikawa, grieving, remembered what Mihori had said :

'Nobuo's sacrificial death, which I saw, was a more eloquent message to me than his will or anything else.' And the great change in Mihori's life was a realistic proof of this. Until then Reinosuke Wakura had never bought himself a Bible, but in his love for Nobuo he lagged behind no one. For a month after Nobuo's death he made a daily visit to the grave, over two miles away. He became thin and downcast like a man who had lost his only son. But Yoshikawa heard that he had begun to read the Bible. 'I'll go to Fujiko and study the Bible sometimes,' Wakura said on the Forty-ninth Day after Nobuo's death, rubbing his hollow cheeks.

On the Shiokari Pass it was now the season of young green leaves. The virgin forest pressed in on the railway line and mounted high above it. Everywhere were great colourful carpets of wild flowers. Under a hot spring sun Yoshikawa and Fujiko stood on the line and gazed into the distance, down the slope which stretched away from them. Thinking how many times he had asked about the incident, inquiring exactly where the coaches had broken off and run away, Yoshikawa said, 'Do you feel all right, Fujiko? It's quite a way to the scene of the accident.'

Fujiko smiled a little and nodded firmly. She held a bunch of pure white spiraea to her breast.

'You are like the spiraea, Fujiko, pure and bright,' Nobuo had said many times, gazing out of the window of Fujiko's room. This sprig of it was from Fujiko's garden.

She started to walk, step by step along the track. Somewhere a warbler began to sing intermittently. When she first heard of Nobuo's death Fujiko had been half-stunned by the shock. At the ticket barrier she really thought she had seen him. To Fujiko, Nobuo was still alive. When she recovered from her faint, she was amazed at how much she had returned to being her old self. The strange sound they had heard, as if a great stone had fallen on to the roof, must have been at the moment of Nobuo's death. She could only explain it, and the illusion she had had of seeing Nobuo at the ticket barrier, by thinking that Nobuo had come to her. Fujiko was deeply comforted by this.

She called to mind wise things that Nobuo had often said :

'Two sticks together burn better than one. In order that the flame of our faith may burn, we two should be together.'

'I want to live every day for God and for men. Of course I would like to keep on living, but I want to be prepared to die gladly at any time when the call comes.'

'What God does is always best for a person.'

So, as she walked, Fujiko felt each of these words of Nobuo pressing on her heart again like a great weight. Plainly this was the whole import of Nobuo's life.

Fujiko stopped. When the train had begun to trundle backwards over these rails, Nobuo had still been alive. The thought of this gave her a feeling she could not have expressed. But, in exchange for his own life, many lives had been saved. And not just people's bodies, but many souls also. In Asahikawa and Sapporo now, the beacon of faith was burning brightly and there was an intense spirit of earnestness in the churches. Her own faith had been strengthened and made new.

By the side of the track where Fujiko rested for a little, some clear water gleamed in the May sun, and some light purple violets bloomed thickly in the shade of trees on the far side.

Fujiko gently touched the precious letter that Kiku had sent her, tucked in her sash. Nobuo's mother had closed up the house in Hongo and gone to Machiko's home in Osaka, where she had been born and bred.

'*Fujiko,*

'*When I read your letter I was greatly relieved. When you said that you have inherited Nobuo's life, just as if he were alive, I was very glad and thankful. Nobuo hated Christianity from his early years. He did not know about Christ even when he left Tokyo. It was all my fault. Fujiko, your faith and honesty nurtured the fine faith in Nobuo which fulfilled my longings.*

'*Fujiko, to me as a mother, Nobuo's death is a sadness. But on the other hand nothing could be happier. Everyone must die. But in all the many deaths there are, few could be more blessed than Nobuo's. We must thank God from the heart that He led Nobuo in such a way.*'

She had read this letter so often that she almost knew it by heart. And she had brought it to read at the place where Nobuo had died.

A cuckoo called close by, flying from branch to branch. Fujiko started walking again. The leaves of giant knotweed, still young and tender, waved a little in the breeze.

'Nobuo, I'll be your wife all my life.'

Fujiko was proud to be Nobuo's wife.

Yoshikawa was walking about fifty yards behind Fujiko, following her slowly.

'The poor girl,' he thought. 'Born a cripple, and on top of that getting tuberculosis; having for a brief time the joy of anticipating marriage, and on the day of her engagement losing Nobuo completely. How cruel of fate!'

But scarcely had the thought come to him, than Yoshikawa was compelled to see that Fujiko had found much more happiness than himself.

'Unless a grain of wheat falls into the earth and dies, it remains alone.'

This verse of Scripture came into his mind.

When Fujiko stopped, Yoshikawa stopped too. 'What is she thinking?' he wondered. Fujiko started again, limping as always, her shoulders swaying up and down. He could see the snow-white spiraea, sometimes hidden, sometimes peeping over her bobbing shoulder.

At last they saw the big curve ahead. Before it there stood a plain wooden post, standing to mark the place of great suffering. Fujiko stopped, and he saw her place the white spiraea on the railway line. But suddenly Fujiko threw herself down on the track. Yoshikawa stood rooted to the spot. In his eyes, blurred with tears, Fujiko's figure and the white spiraea blended together. Her heart-rending cries reached him clearly.

It was noon on a cloudless day at Shiokari Pass.